# Good to the Last Drop

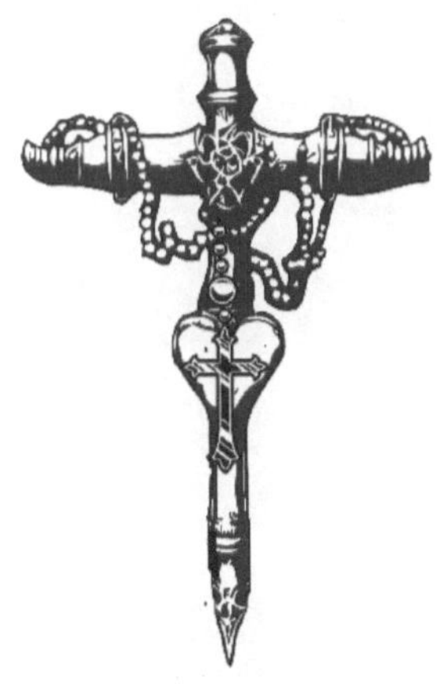

## Love At First Bite

## Book Four

By Declan Finn

Three Ravens Publishing
Chickamauga, GA USA

Good to the Last Drop: Love at First Bite Book Four by: Declan Finn

Published by Three Ravens Publishing

threeravenspublishing@gmail.com

P O Box 851, Chickamauga, Ga 30707

https://www.threeravenspublishing.com

Copyright © 2023 by Declan Finn

Credits:

Good to the Last Drop: Love at First Bite Book Four was written by Declan Finn

Cover art by: Steve Beaulieu


Good to the Last Drop: Love at First Bite Book Four by: Declan Finn /Three Ravens Publishing – 2nd edition, 2023


Good to the Last Drop: Love at First Bite Book Four by: Declan Finn /Silver Empire – 1st edition, 2018


Ebook ISBN: 978-1-951768-78-2
Trade Paperback ISBN: 978-1-951768-79-9
Hardback ISBN: 978-1-951768-80-5

For everyone who came along for this interesting ride.

# Table of Contents

# Prologue

# From The Ashes

December 14<sup>th</sup>

Jennifer Bosley was *pissed.*

The blonde British President of the New York City Vampires Association normally looked well-coiffed, elegant and immaculately dressed.

Now she looked like she had crawled up from the bowels of Hell. Which wasn't that far from the truth.

Back in September, Amanda Colt had survived having an entire hospital wing dropped on her in a massive explosion. She had been dug out in a matter of hours. Multiple factors had been brought to bear. The Mafioso named simply "Enrico" had supplied the construction equipment and the massive tent that blacked out the sun around the dig site. Bosley had been there to pinpoint Amanda's exact location.

After the local hall of the Veterans of Foreign Wars had been blown up, with Bosley still in the building, things were different. The VFW didn't want a known mobster digging out *their* facility. Which meant that there had been no tent, nor any construction crews that knew that the only survivor in the building would immolate in sunlight.

More importantly, there were *no* vampires who volunteered to find President Bosley who were strong enough to sense her in the ground—several vampires who wanted her job in the NYC-VA thought this would be a *great* time to make their move. However, Bosley was politically savvy enough, with enough political capital, that she had countered all of these moves by text message.

Normally, to expedite the process, Bosley would have taken the vampire route: she would have merely turned to mist and gotten herself out. That was stopped by one simple fact—the air ducts had been sealed shut by *tons* of rock that she had no leverage on. She didn't even have the room to punch and claw her way out.

So it was left to normal firemen to come to her aid.

Lucky for her, Police Commissioner Ray Wilson entered the scene. The PC for the NYPD had a lot of things going for him, the first of which being that he looked like a tall Teddy Roosevelt (with the eyebrows of an owl), and the charisma to match.

The police commissioner had explained that his "close friend" had a severe allergy to sunlight, and porphyria, and needed special medication.

Of course, they were close. Wilson and Bosley had known each other since the 70s after he had returned from Vietnam.

She was found near dusk, which is why, after a construction crane carefully moved several tons of stonework, the firemen were surprised by a fist coming through the ground.

As Jennifer Bosley pulled herself from the ground like Dracula risen from the grave—*1968 film, Christopher Lee, God I wanted to do that man*, she thought—everyone on the scene thought that her eyes were glowing red. But, *obviously*, that was just the light from the setting sun. Her clothes were torn, dirty, and she would have suffocated to death days ago if she hadn't been a vampire.

Wilson had kept the fire department back as Enrico approached Bosley and tossed a blanket around her shoulders—which had hidden the thermos of blood and Brandy she downed like a shot of vodka.

Now Jennifer huddled close to Enrico. She didn't like being clingy, but she'd just spent two days buried alive; she'd worry about how it looked later. Though she was worried about dirtying the mobster's trendy coat.

"Where… is Amanda Colt?" she asked, her voice shaky with both nerves *and* rage.

"Right now? San Francisco," Enrico answered. The low colorless tone of her voice worried him. He was a man who did not acknowledge worry.

"Get her back here. She is going to tell me *everything* she knows about this Evil Council of Bastards. Because you and I, love? We're going to find them, and we are going to kill every … last … one of them."

They came up to PC Wilson. Bosley looked at him, smiled brightly, and hurled herself at him. Her arms went around his neck, gripping him like a life preserver.

The Commissioner hugged her back, mostly out of surprise, partially out of self-defense. "Good to see you too, Jen. Want to tell me what's going on? Or are people routinely trying to blow you up, just not while I'm in town?"

"It's a long story, Ray," Bosley answered. "The short version is that we might need some help."

The Commissioner raised one of his dark, bushy eyebrows, and said, "Oh? What did you have in mind?"

"I want to declare war. I just need an army." She looked right at Enrico. "Get me a cell phone. I need Amanda Colt."

# Chapter 1

# A Little B&E Between Friends

December 15th, New York City

**M**erle Kraft's midnight-blue eyes took in the office with a simple glance. The room was neat and orderly. The desk faced the door, and behind it were the large windows that made up the outside wall, giving a perfect view of Turtle Bay and the borough across the water—Brooklyn.

*Ah, the memories... Wait, what am I thinking? I haven't even been on this case a year. Where the hell did the time go? To Hell, almost literally.*

Merle shook his head and turned his thoughts back to the situation at hand. After all, he was standing in the offices of the United Nations Secretary-General. It was quite a view from a flat and uninteresting office, overlooking the East River, and looking at the next borough. The view was better looking than the bare bones office—chairs and desk, but thousand dollar desks and hundred dollar chairs. Who knew you could be so bland, yet spare no expense?

Unfortunately, despite his facility with B&E, Merle didn't even know where to start looking. The files he desired weren't to be left in a file cabinet, or even in plain sight. Assuming, of course, that he *kept* files on that sort of thing. The smart thing would be to just disappear everything.

*And run. I would run. But then, I wouldn't have made deals with demons and vampires in the first place, so who knows what they were thinking.*

Merle moved through the room with his usual efficiency and grace. People often wondered just how he got through locked doors as though they weren't there and find things that no one else knew how to. If anyone else knew the secret, they didn't talk.

Thankfully, Merle also didn't work with anyone. Otherwise they would be making fun of his B&E costume: a blue windbreaker that matched his eyes, and blue jeans. His idea of undercover attire was wearing a windbreaker without FBI emblazoned on it.

"Having fun with your search, brother?"

Merle leaped from the middle of searching the desk and spun to meet the gaze of his half-brother Dalf. The darker Kraft brother was swathed in black, as usual, complete with his wolf's head silver-topped cane. The wolf's head on the cane had eyes of rubies. The cape swirled around Dalf like he was Batman, and

Merle once again examined the Boston Kraft brother for vampire fangs.

Dalf smiled, just to show that his bright white teeth were perfectly normal, blunt *human* teeth. Merle'd never seen them bloodstained, but it didn't hurt to check. *Nope, not a fleck. Check.*

The Eurasian ignored his Black Irish half-brother, turning away with a sigh. "I'm busy, Dalf."

He nodded, taking in the room with a sweep of his eyes. "I see. Having an enjoyable evening of it? Or have you been frustrated in your endeavors?"

Merle gave him an eye-roll. Dalf wouldn't go away until he played along. "What do you *want?*"

Dalf flowed along the room, but not moving closer, most likely just to keep his brother uncomfortable. *Then again, he always did like manipulating me… and everyone else.*

"How have your investigations been going?"

"Circular. Why?"

"I hear that the government has been using wiretaps on the United Nations."

*Blink.* No one was supposed to have heard about that. Not even the New York Times had leaked it yet. "Indeed?"

"Yes, I suspect this case has been *bugging* you, lately."

Good to the Last Drop

Merle didn't even react. *Did my brother just suggest I bug the secretary general's office?* "You're helpful again, Dalf; why?"

The Boston Kraft brother narrowed his eyes and gave Merle a smile that reminded him a little of Marco Catalano. "Because I can't be the one to kill you if a vampire drains you first."

December 17th, New York City

Amanda Colt, vampire, sat on her couch, nose buried in the pages of a book on modern politics. It wasn't so much that she needed the distance to read—in fact, she could read it from the other end of the room. It helped her forget that she was alone, in her apartment … especially when she would rather be in San Francisco, with Marco.

At his bedside, in the hospital.

But *no*, Jennifer Bosley wanted to see her, and had to see her "as soon as possible."

Then she was told to wait.

*Argh.*

She wanted to scream. But screaming would give the neighbors the wrong idea. What a shame.

Amanda and Marco had finally made it. He loved her. She'd told him that she felt the same about him. She'd even told him her real name … assuming the painkillers hadn't totally knocked him out.

"Frustrated" didn't really even begin to encompass it.

So she read. Since she left San Francisco, she had read twenty books. A day. And went to Mass each night. It was good enough for saints and monks, it would have to be good enough for her.

"Have you gotten to the *Queen of the Damned*, yet?"

Amanda started, leaping out of her chair and halfway across the apartment before she realized who had broken into her place—the only person who had ever done so without being eaten.

The red-golden-haired vampire smiled gently. "Hello, Merle. How are you?"

The San Francisco Kraft brother nodded and walked towards her. His hands stayed in his dark blue windbreaker. "I'm well. I'll be damned if I can figure out exactly what's going on over at the UN right now, but I'm working on it."

Amanda reached back and gently put the bookmark back in the book. "Have you considered bugging the UN offices?"

He raised a brow and smiled slightly. "Funny you should say that, someone else just suggested it tonight as well. What do you think about the matter?"

The vampire shrugged. "I have not been thinking about it. It has been…odd lately, that is all." She sighed. "Have you had any success using Marco as bait yet?"

Merle blinked, surprised that she would even need to ask him about it one way or another. "He hasn't told you?"

She sat down and picked up her book again. "We have not talked since I left. Cell phones and hospitals do not mix."

Merle shrugged and moved to the nearest chair, wrapping the toe of his shoe around the chair and pulling it into position so he could sit. "First time I met you two, I figured you were at least dating, if not exchanging bodily fluids… then I discovered you *were*, just not the ones I had in mind. You were inseparable, and not to mention that neither one of you gave a damn about personal space."

She allowed a corner of her mouth to curl into something like a wry smile. "Vampires generally do not acknowledge personal space. It makes it easier to eat their date."

He rolled his eyes and sighed. Deflection was something he didn't have time for, and as far as he was concerned, neither did Amanda. "Give me a break, Amanda, I know you better than that, and so does Marco."

Amanda's eyes snapped up to meet his, and the book slammed shut with what sounded like a rifle shot. "Really? You think so? Do you know how many people I've killed?"

Merle's brows arched. "Do you know how little I care?"

She completely ignored the jibe. "I terrorized half the Red Army during the Revolution. I was used as propaganda against the Whites—a whisper about a demon working against *the progress of Revolution*. I did not even think for months, killing people to feed my hunger, feeding off Lenin's army. I am a predator who had to retrain herself to be a human being."

He scoffed. "Do you know how little *Marco* cares?"

She continued without regard for his comment. "Most vampires are incontinent—sometimes they are merely lesser evils because they are like a lot of humans. They do not think, they just act. Only the thinking ones can be truly evil or good."

Merle nodded slowly, seeing that he would have to give in to the situation and actually address her concerns. "And you're afraid that one of these days, your instincts will take over?"

Amanda could feel her blood pressure go up without her trying to make it do so. The last person who had gotten her this mad was Marco. The little wizard wasn't going to leave her alone on this, was he? "What part of 'I want to kill something' don't you get?" she snapped.

He inclined his head. "You want to tell me that in English this time."

She blinked, not realizing that she had shouted at him in Russian.

Merle continued. "It at least explains a few things about you." He smiled. "I always wondered why you were so much weaker than every major creature we've come up against. Nuala damn near killed all of us without even blinking. We won't even go into Mister Day."

She shrugged. "So what? I am not virtuous. I am, at best, Continent. I know what the good is, want it, and do it. Most of the time. But is it enough? Is it the *right* thing?"

He shook his head. "No, you're not *just* anything. *Rory* is continent, and *he* flinches at crosses if he doesn't brace himself. But you pray, you wear crosses. But I know why you don't have a power level commensurate with your level of virtue. You've been scared out of your mind by the level of power you might access. The nuns called it *fortitude*."

Merle's eyes narrowed, and he leaned forward. "You never asked what more you could do, never tested yourself to see how far you could go. Never tried to see if you could reach beyond what powers you've displayed thus far. You're scared of your instincts, terrified of yourself and what you can do if you actually let yourself go deeper. Maybe you're scared of your power, what you'll become if you tap into it. As C.S. Lewis noted, if you don't want it, it's usually a good sign that you're probably the right person to have it."

Merle stood and smoothed out his windbreaker. He gave her a look that brooked no dissent. "I don't give a good God-damn what your supposed instincts are saying. You've spent decades at least on the side of right. Since you enjoy citing Aristotle so often, remember that thing about habits. It's unlikely that you're going to make a sudden and drastic U-turn and become another Nuala.

"Perhaps you should ask yourself how you were able to so easily turn to mist and use it as a tactical weapon last week. I think you could figure it out if you put your mind to it.

"As far as your boyfriend, not only is Marco a big boy, he can probably kick your undead ass should you step out of line." He sharply tugged at the bottom of his windbreaker. "Like it or not, you're in love with him, and I can only assume that, what I can read from a creature like Marco, is that he may even love you, too. Get over it."

# Chapter 2
# Many Happy Returns

January 1st San Francisco

Marco looked at his phone, reading email. There was yet another email from his… "friend"… Yana, who had the unmistakable handle of CyberWicca and a bunch of numbers afterward that meant nothing to him. Email had become the primary mode of communication with Yana; her cell phone bill wouldn't handle the amount of information she wanted to give him.

*Besides, I get the impression she's distracted half the time as she writes these.*

The source of the presumed distraction wasn't hard to figure out: a woman named "Jackie." All communication with Yana had gone from mournful and depressed over the death of her girlfriend Tara to overly excited over a new woman named Jackie, who was apparently…very fast and overly affectionate.

While Marco was familiar with the old practice of Irish wakes taking people out into the potato fields for a roll in the clover, he didn't think a turnaround of less than a month was included.

Marco frowned to himself. *Eh. I suppose she's happy?*

He saved her email as new, wondering if he should bother replying other than asking about the rest of the San Francisco brigade—the email was overly hormonal for Yana, who he hadn't suspected *had* a sex drive.

*Then again, after Nuala, I guess I should be glad that she's going near sex ever again. I suppose it's healthy?* He sighed, wondering if he would have attempted the redemption of a vampire had he known what the assassin had done with, or to, his witch.

Marco sighed and scrolled down the rest of the email list. The one email account he was looking for wasn't there. Which shouldn't be a problem, because why send an email when you could be doing some…other things.

*And, seriously, what are you worried about, moron? You made out, you both love each other, she told you her real name … maybe, assuming that wasn't the painkiller … She's not a scared teenager in her first relationship, is she? And me, I'm a predator, a self-trained killer, I am…*

*…such an idiot. He who hesitates is roadkill. You're now a smear on the pavement. You let her get away. I don't care if this*

*Bosley person called her away. I should have told that blonde bloodsucker to suck my —*

The PA student growled to himself and closed the phone, a hairsbreadth away from smashing it. He had been in the hospital now for weeks, but no one had even blinked in his general direction. Not a single vampire, good or ill. Not even the one he wanted to see.

He'd even missed Christmas. Freaking vampire assassin.

He closed his eyes and did what he'd been doing every time he got angry for no reason at all. He said an Our Father, and ten Hail Mary's, and a Glory Be to round it off.

Marco looked around the hospital parking lot, cursing the darkness outside. *Why did I have to be kicked out of the hospital after dark? Seriously, San Francisco, what is your damn problem? Or is everyone just out to get me? Honestly, why me? Did I do something to offend You, Lord?*

He picked up his luggage and prayed very hard that his ride would be there, and hadn't been turned into a snack along the way.

"This the bruiser we want?"

Marco flicked his eyes left. He whirled and grabbed the woman approaching him. He lifted her up in the air like she was a leaf, a moment before kissing her.

His broad smile caught the light as he let Yana down on the floor. "Um, hi, Marco."

"How are you, sexy lady?"

Yana, who still didn't know what to do with him, said, "Ah, good. Marco, I'd like to you meet—"

Marco whirled on Yana's companion, an olive-skinned brunette, and smiled, remembering Yana's emails. "You must be Jackie, I could smell the hormones."

She smiled and shook hands. "You must be Marco; I can smell the attitude."

He gave a Gallic shrug. "That may just be my aftershave."

"How are you?"

He glanced the woman up and down. Objectively, he was certain she was attractive. She was a sturdy 5'6", with a frame that was more inverted triangle than hourglass, with wider shoulders and a larger upper body. Her outfit was a standard leather jacket, even leather pants – which he saw as nice, knife resistant clothing. Though her jacket was zipped up part of the way, and he couldn't tell if she wore a shirt underneath. He was a little worried about reading too much into *that*.

*Well, Yana at least went for a woman who could probably hit well enough. Body strength helps. Legs have enough muscle on them for kicks, if one is into that sort of thing.*

"Take a picture," she told him, "it'll last longer."

"You even steal my lines," he muttered. His smile didn't flicker. "You'll do. You've got the right attitude. I presume you're already in the know on the vampire thing?"

"A little. Though Yana tells me there aren't many of those left kicking around."

Marco arched his brows. He knew that San Francisco didn't really have a vampire population until recently—so little that they didn't have a local Vampire Association—but this was ridiculous.

Marco looked at Yana. "Are we thinking that the vampire infestation is over?'

"Um, Merle has a thought on that."

Marco cocked his head. "And that is?"

"That aside from the initial influx we saw, you may have attracted them. And you've dealt with most of the ones who came in before you did."

Marco opened his mouth to object, and then thought it over. He *had* been going through a few busy months. He had gone on several rampages, including one that may have lasted a few months, depending on who you asked. After someone blew up his father's hospital, he had kicked over all the vampire nests in the area. He had proceeded to launch a reign of terrorism that leaned heavy on terror. Then he'd killed a whole club full of vampires by locking them in and set it on fire. Then blew up an assassin with a swarm of ninjas. That had been eventful.

Maybe the general extinction of vampires in town wasn't *that* much of a surprise. Marco had made the town a little off-putting for the locals.

The brunette punched Marco in the arm. "Don't look so depressed, we're doing our jobs."

Marco arched a brow. "Our? How long have you been at it?"

Jackie shrugged. "A few months. Surprised I didn't run into you guys earlier. Especially in September. I guess you were behind all the devastation?"

Yana shook her head and jerked her thumb at Marco. "Him."

Jackie blinked, then nodded. "Oh, he led it."

Yana shook her head. "All him."

Jackie looked Marco up and down, and... *Sheesh, she actually just licked her lips. Wonderful,* Marco thought.

"Niiiiiice," she stated. "Not bad. But you're not that much to look at."

Marco didn't object to that. She was right. He was 5'9", and most people described him as having a body like a dancer—more like *capoeira* than ballet, though. His blond hair and blue eyes went strangely with the last name of "Catalano," and probably better paired off with "Hitler Youth."

"Ah, so charming."

They walked Marco outside to a large black SUV, which looked more like a small truck with armor plating—in fact, if he didn't know any better, Marco would've sworn it was a fully-armored Army Ford F-350—mobile video system, onboard PC, night-vision screen, high-voltage door handles, bomb detection, that sort of thing.

"It's a loan from Merle," Yana explained.

Marco merely raised an amused eyebrow.

The passenger side door opened, and Tiffany sat in the driver's seat. Tiffany was as vapid as her name implied, and she was a walking stereotype—blonde, buxom (silicone, not natural), and would have fit in better with Los Angeles than San Francisco. The only reason Merle kept her on was that she was good with numbers. The only reason Marco didn't kill her was that he was too busy to hide the body.

"Oh, Marco," she huffed. "No one's eaten you yet? Now we have to waste our time on you."

Marco rolled his eyes. "No need. Just get me to the city. I'll be fine."

Yana pouted a little. "You sure? Okay…how's Amanda?"

Marco sat in silence, looking at the scenery go by him. He didn't ignore Yana so much as consider her query. He had barely spoken a word to Amanda since she'd left for the city. It was as if nothing had happened between them.

"She's fine," he answered.

He closed his eyes and started praying again.

# Chapter 3

# Recruitment

January 1st, New York City

Lady Jennifer Bosley, President of the New York City Vampires Association, was not only powerful but very, very rich. "Old world, old money, I can buy and sell China ten times" rich. If anyone had known she existed, or if she had all of her money in the same place under one name, she would have been one of the top ten richest entities on the planet, including nations.

Like many other wealthy vampires, they tended to buy entire apartment complexes, and leave the outside alone, turning the inside into a luxurious palace. On the outside, it looked like a gang-ridden neighborhood had declared war on her building. Inside, it looked like a modern-day palace. Her office was the size of a large living room. The carpet was Persian, the tapestries were European, the paintings were by old masters— some of which Amanda knew as having gone missing during World War II—and the bookcases had nothing but first editions.

Usually, Jennifer Bosley came into her domain very relaxed. The first time Amanda Colt had met her here, Bosley came in wearing a dark green tracksuit—she knew she was rich, and she didn't need to prove it to anyone.

Today, however, Bosley had left Amanda waiting in the center of her office and didn't come into a room like a woman who owned the place, but like a soldier who needed a brawl. Bosley was even wearing dark camouflage pants and deep green top. Her form was curvy, and it still showed in the unflattering outfit, and she no longer moved with the effortless grace of the undead, but with long strides of a woman in a hurry.

Her blonde hair terminated at the base of her neck, with her hair at the sides tucked behind her ears. Her full lips were unadorned, and her brown eyes seemed to just cut through whatever she saw.

She was also smoking.

Bosley threw herself onto the edge of her desk. "Hello, luv," Bosley said, her usually posh British accent reverting to something more "urban London."

"Hello, Madam President."

Bosley smiled around her cigarette and drew on it deeply. She took it out, blowing the smoke off to the side. "Call me Jen. You and I need to talk."

Amanda Colt nodded slowly. She wasn't entirely certain what to do with herself. Even though she had been in Bosley's offices before, she still wasn't used to it. She had only dressed in a long-sleeved sweater and jeans. She was about 5'6," with long red-gold hair that went to the small of her back in a golden fall, eyes that were a warm, liquid Frangelico brown with her Siberia-pale skin.

"What can I help you with?" she said, only slightly accentuating her Russian accent.

"You've got some support on your side, don'cha? I remember 'earing about it before the summer."

Amanda nodded slowly. "*Da*. You have met Enrico, you know we have … resources."

Bosley nodded. "See, what I mean here is, well…" Her eyes locked on Amanda's and started to glow a deep, burning red. Her fangs came out around her lips, and she talked through them as though she'd had millennia of practice. "Those little bastards blew up my professional offices and tried to bury me. Your war is now my war, and I want to kill the little blighters before they even realize that we're at their throats."

Amanda nodded carefully, shocked that Bosley had gotten this riled. She had always been the most controlled, self-possessed vampire Amanda had ever met. Hell, Bosley had once claimed that the source of her power came from being purely pragmatic.

"Are you sure you wish to go there?" Amanda asked. "I would hate for something to happen to you."

The glow in Bosley's eyes faded, and a corner of her lips quirked up. "Concerned fo' the state of my soul, are ya?" She popped the cigarette back into place and rolled over the top of her desk. Reaching into a drawer, she pulled out a cross. She pressed it to her skin and waited.

After ten seconds of silence, Amanda shrugged. "I guess you are good."

"After a fashion, luv." She placed the cross back in the drawer. "We're at war. War isn't *de facto* immoral. And if this isn't a just war, we're probably all quite screwed."

"You seem quite angry."

Bosley smiled, and her eyes narrowed. "Oh, luv, you 'ave no idea." She tossed herself back into the seat, resting combat boots on the desk. "Now, tell me what you know."

Amanda finally relaxed enough to sit down in the chair across from Bosley. "You have noticed the increase in devil worship?"

Bosley smiled. "Where would you want to start? The headlines, or the French Revolution, when the Terror *really* got dark? Dipping bread in the blood of the freshly decapitated." She grimaced. "It was tacky even then. You can talk about the rise of Moloch—America's Cold Spring 'arbor back in the twenties, when they sterilized, euthanized, and murdered…what do they call the retarded now?

"Inconvenient."

Bosley nodded. "Sounds right. You've got your eugenics, your World War II, Soviet Lenin worship, making communism a religion, Hitler's Norse gods, Obama worship… I can go on forever. What are you thinking of? Vampires in the gulags and the camps?"

Amanda shrugged. "All of that. Remember The Council?"

Bosley nodded. "The big boogeyman, *The Council?* The black helicopters of the vampire world?" She sighed. "I know of it."

Amanda nodded. "The demon from September, 'Mister Day'? He was one of them. As was Nuala."

Bosley nodded. "Yes. I had heard of a Mister Day that made political connections."

"He also managed to get into the United Nations."

Bosley's eyes narrowed. "Are you telling me that The Council…is now a *council?* A *UN* council?"

Amanda nodded. "That is what we surmise."

Bosley grimaced. "We're going to need more guns."

Good to the Last Drop

# Chapter 4

# The Trap

January 2nd, San Francisco

Marco Catalano, being unusually stubborn for someone who was both male and only partly Irish, walked through the evening, looking around the crypts of San Francisco to see if there was anything that didn't know well enough to stay dead. In the back of his head, instead of a casual prayer, he had started going through a rock rendition of the Our Father, in German. It was a good tune to have while hunting.

*Because Gregorian chant is not something I want to hunt vampires to.*

"Marco."

He turned and looked at the new girl—Jackie. "Hi there." He looked her over and sighed. "You look quite nice this evening." He glanced at his watch. "Or should I say morning?"

She shrugged. "Just call it 'late.' What are you doing out?"

He looked out at the dark of Grant Street in Chinatown—he was in between cemeteries at the moment. "Hunting or going for a walk. Something like that."

"Oh. Mind if I join you?"

"Sure, I might as well be falling apart."

They continued to walk down the street of the opulent neighborhood until they reached the docks along Fisherman's Wharf. The skyline of the next city glowed in the not too distant horizon, along with a harbor cruise ship that was traveling around the bay with its continuously partying passengers. This view was lost on the two patrollers, mainly because all they saw was two women about to be sucked dry. Two targets were good for the concentration.

"I'll go for the one on the left, you the right. Sound good to you?" Marco looked over at Jackie to see whether she agreed and found the space where she had been standing empty. He looked up to see her going at it with the two vampires.

Marco sighed. "Or we can just charge into the fight without thinking. That's a classic."

Marco pulled out a turpentine-soaked stake and headed after the newbie. One of the melodramatically-dressed Goth vampires saw him coming and charged head-on, letting out a stereotypical horrid hiss. He briefly considered stapling the vamp's hand to his forehead. His angst would send him to dust more quickly.

"Dress normally, would you?" Marco growled, dodging to the right. "This isn't a game." Marco rammed the stake home as though he were clothes-lining the vampire.

Marco plucked the stake out and placed it back in his belt as the vampire turned into dust. "Waste not, want not."

Marco looked over to see Jackie being backed up against the railing by the other equally-overdressed vampire. He was about to go and help her when he took a second look. He knew he didn't need glasses, yet he could swear he saw a look of *enjoyment* on the young woman's face.

Marco rolled his eyes. Yana had spent weeks fretting over how scary he was, and she had managed to hook up with a girl who seemed to enjoy killing the damned as much as he did.

Without hesitation, she leaped on the vampire, grabbed his head, and started making out with him… it seemed. She actually spat water into his mouth.

The vampire pushed her away and dropped to his knees, grabbing his throat as it disappeared under his fingers. Jackie smiled as his neck collapsed in on itself, along with the rest of his body. He then turned into dust, spilling into the breeze and blowing all over her hands, clothes, face, and hair.

"Poor baby, can't handle his drink."

Jackie stood, faced away from the dust and took a deep breath, exhaling a deep sigh of satisfaction. She faced Marco, who still stood at a distance.

*Pity, I get ready to leave, I get someone on the team who might be interesting.*

"Too much?" she asked, sounding surprisingly innocent for someone who had basically poured acid down his throat. But still, she was pretty nonchalant.

Jackie laughed and gave him a smile. Even from where he stood, he could see her eyes dancing in the dim streetlight from the satisfaction of the kill. He found himself staring – he wasn't used to being on the other side of that. "Let's get you home."

"Why?" she protested.

Marco laughed. "I know you seem to be enjoying yourself, but as you can see…" He held up his watch. It was two hours to sunup.

Jackie sighed and replaced the holy water flask on her hip. "Suppose I can't continue hunting when the sun is out."

"Not unless you have a ready answer for why you're walking around with sharp pointy things in San Francisco."

The two exchanged a look of amusement. Marco and Jackie both knew that technically, they could go hunting in the daytime. But neither one of them felt up to the job of explaining why they were kicking open random crypt doors, looking inside for a few seconds and then closing the door as if nothing had happened.

Jackie offered her hand. "It was nice meeting you."

Marco walked up and yet again took her hand. "And where do you think you're going?"

A slight sense of alarm took over Jackie. "I'm going home." She pointed over her shoulder. "I was planning to walk down Grant."

He gave her an incredulous look. "Uh huh. And then what?"

As she gave her answer, she realized how ridiculous it sounded. "Walk halfway across town." She looked up at him and offered an embarrassed grin. He sighed and walked over with her to the curbside edge.

"Where exactly are you taking me?"

"I'm going to put you in a cab and send you home. And if you even think of paying the fare, I'll break your arm off here and now."

This stunned Jackie and allowed Marco to lead her along. She never heard someone *force* chivalry on another and threaten them if they tried otherwise. She quickly realized that this guy Marco was completely, utterly, undeniably *nuts*.

They reached a major street, and Marco waved down a cab. The foreign driver rolled down his window and asked with a surprising lack of accent, "Where to?"

Marco looked over at Jackie, who was still dumbfounded by threatening kindness. "You need me to check your wallet for you?" he asked, a slight tone of impatience coming through.

He shook his head and gave the driver Yana's address. "All right then." She watched Marco as he opened the door for her. "In you go."

Jackie walked around and stepped into the cab, looking back up at him. "You know you don't have to do this. I can handle the—"

He cut her off. "Do you think I was kidding about breaking your arm?" She stopped mid-sentence and just blankly stared at him. "Get in the cab."

Without reaction from her, he placed her hand at her side and closed the door. He looked at the driver. "So how much is the damage?"

The cabby looked back at her, still a bit dumbstruck, and replied, "For her? Twenty." Marco reached into his back pocket, pulled out a relatively small wad of twenties and handed one to him.

Before the driver took off, Marco called his attention again. "By the way? If you try anything, just remember I have your license plate memorized and have no qualms about hunting you down and treating you with the same loving care that a white supremacist would have with you and yours. Am I understood?"

A look of pure horror emerged on the driver's face as he mechanically nodded his agreement. "Good." Marco pounded on the roof of the cab. "Tally-ho then."

"Marco!" a voice snapped at him in the middle of the night. "Get up!"

His eyes snapped open. Yana was at his bedside. *How did that happen?*

"We need to go, now!"

Marco kicked the covers off and rolled off the bed, onto his feet, still fully dressed, with a knife in his hand. "What is it?"

Yana looked over her shoulder. "No time, we have to go, now!"

He stopped, glanced at the door, fully locked and bolted. "Well, whatever you are, you're not omniscient. At least there's that much."

He looked over his shoulder and launched a side kick, his foot going through Yana's chest, like a hologram. He smiled broadly as he pulled his leg back. "I didn't know vampires could have astral projection. Or are you a ghost?"

The projected image of Yana smiled, speaking now with a slight Russian accent. "Glad to meet you, Marco. I've had my eye on you ever since you killed my brother."

Marco winced, taken aback for a moment. A Russian accent meant a Russian vampire, and there was only one other Russian vampire that he knew outside of Amanda. That vampire he had been killed in Brooklyn the year before. Which meant…

Marco smiled drolly. "Yes, your brother Mikhail. I hate to point out that *Nuala* killed him." He raised a brow. "Let me guess, either you're outside, or you have minions waiting? How absolutely cliché. Hell, you're his vengeful brother, should I assume you're a twin?"

The Yana image gave him Yana's puppy-dog eyes and innocently asked, "Why would I have any minions?"

Marco backed up onto his bed. "You couldn't count on me being cooperative enough to leave my room, and you can't get in without an invite. You'd have them because I'm a scary bastard, otherwise, why waste a demon and an assassin on me? I'm honored that the Council still thinks I'm a threat."

"Yana" raised a brow. "Threat? To *me*?"

The New Yorker's eyes narrowed. The vampire didn't contradict Marco's statement about the Council, so that confirmed his supposition. The image didn't say *us*, but *me*—which gave Marco a guess that the Council had only the one vampire left to go. "I know that you can be beaten. Otherwise, you'd just come out and strike. That you're resorting to, well, this means you want to wear us down so you can kill us."

"Let's find out," the fake Yana said. "You've said you are what you're needed to be. Well, I need you dead!"

An ax hit the door.

# Chapter 5
# The Maw

An ax hit the door, only to get a clang as metal struck metal.

Marco grinned. "This is *my* room. I had certain…modifications…made after Nuala. Merle spent time on them while I was in the hospital. I think ahead."

The windows exploded as two people swung into the room. They landed on a rug, which disappeared out from under them as they fell through the floor, onto spikes in the room below.

The fake Yana's eyes narrowed. "But you couldn't have—"

Marco circled around the image, grinning like a death's head. "We were counting on someone coming for me and assumed we'd be spied on. Had you been smarter, you'd have seen that Merlin Kraft had a team of government contractors turn my room into a kill zone."

The door fell in, and it was followed by a dozen men, all of whom were armed with knives. Two of them had axes. They swarmed, taking up positions all around the room as Marco backed against the window, keeping the bed between him and them.

"You have just been suckered."

Marco smiled at them a moment longer, then gave them a wave with his fingers before he leaped back and hit the windowsill. The impact caused him to flip backwards and out the window, grabbing the rappelling rope along the way.

As he controlled his descent with one hand, he pulled out a cell phone with the other and hit autodial 1.

The number was that of a beeper in his room, attached to a detonator… which was connected to large quantities of explosives under the floorboards.

Marco hit the ground before the fire burned away the rappelling cable. *Imagine what would have happened had they tried me in the chem lab.*

"Yana" stood there, where the floor used to be, saying, "I hate him."

The image stood gleaming and translucent in the night air, amid the debris and flaming wreckage where his room used to be.

Marco dove into the bushes, grabbing his gym bag filled with weapons. There wasn't exactly anything he could do besides run very fast. *Someone had to have heard that blast, though.*

Marco heard something and glanced left across the great lawn of the campus. More minions were coming out from behind the building…how many, he couldn't tell.

*Well, this is bad.*

Marco kept running, wondering why no one else had come out of the woodwork—security guards, students, that sort of thing. *Thankfully, these are human minions and not vampires. Otherwise, I'd be food by now.*

Marco slowed as he saw more shapes coming out of the dark ahead of him. They weren't demonic-looking, so they were still killable. He drew two knives from his sleeves. He glanced back over his shoulder at the minions closing behind him.

*This could be bad.*

"You killed my brother, *da?*" asked a deep voice.

Marco glanced over his other shoulder. It was a large vampire, back-lit by the fire of his dying room, easily 6'5", perhaps even taller.

He looked even uglier than Mikhail the Bear.

The first shot slammed into the vampire's head, and Marco expected his skull to explode into a million pieces. Instead, the vampire tottered a little. The bullet passing through the other side as though it cut through the brain and bone without actually punching a hole through it.

*Well, that's not good.*

Marco did the math and knew he was screwed. The sniper in place could wipe out the minions, but not the vampire. As far as his chances of taking out the target…knives couldn't be thrown faster than a vampire could move. He couldn't grab another weapon fast enough without being rushed and crushed. There was only one option left…

Marco dropped the bag of weapons and ran for the woods of Golden Gate Park.

*Our Father, who art in Heaven…*

The vampire's laughter followed him. Marco whirled in mid-step and hurled a knife at his own bag.

The impact set off the nitroglycerin within. The nitroglycerin had been packed around a shell of wooden stakes and knives. The contents exploded into deadly shrapnel that killed minions all around it. The projectiles turned the vampire into a pincushion without turning him to dust, driving him off his feet.

*At least it's winter break. No one else will be horribly murdered.*

He dashed across the empty street, wondering exactly where everyone *else* in the area had gone— *Answer, it's a college area.*

The park was within sight. There were enough trees in there to count simply as woods.

A minion leaped out from behind a tree, and Marco dove under the line of fire, and grabbed the gun with both hands. One hand clamped down around the muzzle, and the other around the back of the gun. He locked his arms straight above his head, and stood, raising the muzzle of the gun, and bending it back against the minion's wrist. In the moment of surprise, he twisted the firearm out of the minion's hands, jammed it under his chin, and pulled the trigger.

Marco took off running before the body fell. He dashed for the tree line.

When he bowled over a pedestrian who came out of nowhere, he was about to apologize when he saw that *she* had a knife. "Damn it."

The woman slashed for his ankles. He hopped over the knife and came down on the woman's arm, shattering it. He shot her in the head, bent down and scooped down to grab her dagger.

"Thanks. Needed this."

As he straightened, a sharp noise cut the air. Marco barely raised his arm in time to block the coming blade. The dagger hit the gun, taking it out of his hand.

A newcomer, a large, wrestler-like attacker stood before him, and slashed again, this time backhanded.

*Someone came prepared.* Marco leaned back, away from the slash, then pushed forward and jabbed his stake into the killer's throat. Marco snatched his attacker's knife away, then nodded at him.

*Two metal daggers. Nice exchange rate.*

He turned as another came for him, gun held high. Marco threw himself to one side, hurling the knife at the minion's face. The knife missed and slammed into his chest, point first. The attacker fell forward as Marco swept up the gun in his right hand.

Marco caught motion out of the corner of his left eye, and he swung the left blade up in a backhand. His blade met the attacker's wrist, opening the fingers holding the knife. At the same time, Marco's right hand came up with the gun and punched the minion in the throat with the muzzle. Then he fired.

Marco slid the blade away in the small of his back. His right hand scooped up the fallen knife as he charged deeper into the woods.

*Come on, pal, you've taken out thousand-year-old vampires, you can take these twerps.*

Marco tripped over a rock in time to avoid being decapitated. He thrust his knife at an ax-wielding minion, going right into his stomach as he fell. Marco landed on his shoulder and rolled, hurling the knife from his back out into the darkness. A figure toppled over, and he hoped he didn't kill a pedestrian. Marco rolled back, grabbed the ax in his free hand, and rolled to his feet.

A knife wielder jumped in front of him, and Marco promptly slammed the butt of the ax into his face like a hammer-fist, then spun to give him the ax blade first. The knifeman crumpled, showering blood on the way down.

Marco gunned down the next three minions who charged him but missed the others. They grabbed his elbows and lifted him off the ground. One pulled away his gun.

Marco struggled a moment, but the lock was too strong on both ends. Unnaturally strong. *Full blooded minions. Crap. I'm screwed.*

Marco dropped the ax and threw his arms out to either side of him; while that wouldn't shake them, it released the squirt guns in his sleeves. He fired into their faces, and they fell back in pain. He drew both squirt guns down upon the next minion charging in front of him, still firing.

The minions howled in pain as the hydrofluoric acid burned away their faces. They melted like they'd seen the business end of Spielberg's Ark of the Covenant.

Marco shook the squirt guns clear of any droplets and tucked the weapons away, grabbing the knives and the gun from the ground.

He straightened…ten more minions were in front of him, and he was certain that he didn't have enough bullets.

*How many losers can one vampire get to volunteer at a time?*

Marco hurled one knife at them as he brought up the gun. The first three fell back as he shot them squarely in the head. The rest dodged with preternatural speed.

*Come on, Merle, save my life.*

Something slammed him, hard. He dropped the gun without resistance. He looked at his shoulder, only to find that he was bleeding. Marco flexed his hand and saw flashlights he knew weren't there. His whole arm wasn't responding properly. There was movement, but it hurt like a bear.

"Ah, damn."

Marco slowly turned, only to have his knees buckle. He fell with his back to the tree, sliding to the ground.

A minion stood over him, gun in hand.

Marco snarled, and threw out his arm, throwing the squirt gun into his hand. "Die."

His hand convulsed around the handle, spraying the minion over and over until it fell back, choking and gasping. He waited until it fell all the way back, and down to the ground before he stopped.

The vampire hunter checked the level of acid. He'd run out. *I'm screwed.*

Marco slowly pushed off the ground, onto his feet.

"You really don't know when to quit, do you?" said the Yana image standing before him. He could see the scenery right through the flat contours of Yana's lookalike image. Where was the vampire sending it from?

He straightened. "That's something we have in common. Don't you ever shut up?"

"Yana" smiled. "I wasn't prepared for your little bomb, but this will do for now. I have nothing but time on my hands."

"You don't have actual hands… not in this form."

"An oversight." It smiled. "On your part," she added as even more men drifted all around "her," converging on Marco. "These are my hands, and they'll do quite well to shred you."

He grimaced as he looked at the others. *Let me think about this. I have one arm, my non-dominant one, outnumbered by ten to one, easily.* "Right. Let's do this."

Marco grabbed a pen from his pocket with his left hand. With one quick move, he broke left and rammed the pen into the nearest minion's eye and into the brain. With a glance over his shoulder, he spotted another one coming for him. His right leg snapped out in a mule-kick, hitting that one in the throat.

With a ferocious growl, two minions had their heads cut off with the single silver swipe of a sword. The sword ended up embedded in the sides of two other minions, pinning them to a tree before something leaped through the projected image and slammed into even more minions, slashing them mercilessly.

The cavalry had arrived.

# Chapter 6

# The Trap Bites Back

In life, Rory the vampire had been a man named Shawn Treacy, Irish Republican Army gunman, who had been quicker on the trigger than John Dillinger. In death, he had become a shorter man, who looked more like the careworn, smile-lined face of the actor Barry Fitzgerald, only with bright red hair that never occurred in nature.

"Catch!" Rory screamed.

Marco caught, with his left hand, a bottle of hairspray. He smiled, flicked a lighter with his right hand, and let the spray catch the flame, turning it into a flamethrower, incinerating any that came near him.

The minions screamed in terror, pulling out their real weapons…

Handguns.

"Crap! That's cheating!"

Marco dove to the left, landing on his side as they started to fire.

Rory smiled at them, his brogue thickening. "Ah, now this is more me speed, ladies."

Rory leaped on one of the men, ripping into him with his fangs. He then tore the gun out of the dead man's hand, bringing it to bear on the others, firing as fast as only a vampire could. It sounded like a machine-gun as he swept the field of fire. More minions piled out of the woodwork, but Rory didn't slow. He ran out of bullets and used full vampire speed to frisk bodies, collect a new magazine, reload, and continue.

"When boyhood's fire was in my blood, I read of ancient freemen," Rory sang loudly, his brogue mangling the lyrics. "For Greece and Rome, who bravely stood, three hundred men and free men." He fired off a three-round burst, then spun, firing off another.

Marco was suddenly reminded of the *Matrix* films, only with someone who could *aim*.

"And then I prayed I yet might see, our fetters rent in twain! And Ireland, long a province be, a Nation once again!"

*Maybe having another gunman on the payroll was a good idea,* Marco thought idly. Bullets flew everywhere, and all he could think to do was to keep his head down. *Why didn't I hold onto that Kevlar from the Nuala incident? Answer: because used body armor is worthless, you idiot.*

Marco hurled the can of hairspray into the middle of the crossfire, and it exploded when a stray bullet caught it in midair. The others were blinded for a moment, and Marco used that reprieve to charge, shouldering aside one with his healthy shoulder, then elbowing him in the throat with the same-side arm. He followed the man down, continuing to crush his throat. He rolled to one side, then swept up the handgun, firing one bullet at a time as the other gunmen were busy trying to keep Rory down with cover fire.

Rory's body wracked with bullets, but he just stood there and kept firing. His bright red hair made him an obvious target in the dark, and each gunmen fired into his chest.

*And, obviously, they're not using wooden bullets.*

Rory laughed aloud as he took another gun from someone who got too close. He changed his tune from "A Nation Once Again" to "Where are the lads, that stood with me when hi-story was made. A ghra, Mo Chroi, I long to-o see, the Boys of the old brigade."

Marco pulled the trigger again, and the hammer came down on an empty chamber. *Nuts.*

Rory fired his last bullet and frowned. The vampire flipped it in one hand and hurled it like a knife into the nearest gunman.

Rory staggered back, an arrow sticking out of his chest. It wasn't in the heart, but he grabbed it as quickly as possible before something knocked it in that direction.

Another two crossbow bolts shot from the darkness, penetrating his chest. Marco's eyes narrowed as he looked out into the darkness. Another second later, three more bolts drove into Rory's body, in a cluster around Rory's chest, at least one of them angled just a degree off his heart.

Rory pulled out one of the two most potentially deadly bolts before one of his attackers jumped him while armed with a wooden stake.

The Irish vampire grabbed the bolt in his hand and drove it backwards, taking out his attacker. That one fell off, while three more minions piled on Rory like he was a victim in a zombie movie.

Each and every one of them tried to slam into a crossbow bolt.

"'Twas long, ago, we face the foe, the old brigade and me, and by my side, they fought and died, that Ireland mi-ight be free."

Rory spun, the force throwing off the first round of attackers—allowing another group to leap out of the woods and on top of him. Ten leaped on him at the same time, and the original group piled on top of that. They only had one goal: to drive the bolts already inside him all the way in.

Rory fell to his hands and knees, wondering why he didn't just go back home to Ireland after he had figured out how to change his face. He could have seen his old friend, Dan Breen, his partner in crime. He could have seen how the Republic had fared without him.

Instead, he was about to die, here, in San bloody Francisco.

He grit his teeth and slowly pushed himself off the ground. He could feel the pressure in his chest. One of the bolt shafts started to press into the ground. He could feel the arrow driving deeper into his body. It had already penetrated his aorta. If he were still alive, he'd have bled to death already.

"Fockmall," he murmured, and locked one arm, reaching for the lighter in his jacket pocket.

He had only one thought in mind: if he was going to go, he was going to take every last one of the bastards with him. If they were going to stay on top of him, and he went up in flames, they'd burn, too.

"Where are the lads, that stood with me, when hi-story wa-as made—"

He grabbed it and didn't even take it out of his pocket to light it. "A ghra, Mo Chroi, I long to see, the Boys of the old brigade."

The flame seared his flesh. He'd catch fire soon.

*I'm coming, Dan. Here's hoping we end up in the same place.*

Rory caught the scent of blood. One of the minions right in front of him was ripped away. Marco Catalano stood in front of him, knife in hand, his entire front covered in blood.

"Come on, damn it! We're getting the Hell out of here."

Rory flipped the lighter shut and shot out from under the dogpile like he had been blasted from a cannon. He nearly stumbled over the half-dozen corpses on the ground, all of them freshly slaughtered.

Rory pulled bolts out of his chest and winced when Marco slapped another pistol into his chest.

"Sorry it took me a while," Marco explained, eyes on the dog pile of minions. "I had to kill all of those guys and find you more bullets."

Rory checked the chamber and nodded. "No hard feelings, lad."

The dog pile of minions scrambled over each other, like ants disembarking from a hill. Rory didn't wait for them to line up in a nice, neat row, but blasted away while they were trying to form ranks.

That still left fifteen of them by the time he ran out of ammunition.

Marco held his knife ahead of him, eyeing his prey. "You take the eight on the left, I have the seven on the right."

The minions circled them, and he winced. He was out of ideas, and options, and even weapons. If the knife broke, he was really screwed.

The minions drew their own knives. He shook his head, wondering why they didn't use handguns again.

*Because handguns have ballistics matches, and you can at least pull out and reuse an arrow after you shoot someone with it. Knives can't be traced. I didn't know vampire minions watched CSI.*

Marco grabbed another pen and hoped he'd get a chance to take at least one more of them down.

Merle appeared behind one gunman, broke his neck, and then swept the legs out from under another one. He chopped into a throat and charged past him to another attacker. The third one stabbed forward as a fourth moved on his right. Kraft deflected the knife by smacking the wrist aside. He locked down on it with both hands as he launched a high kick into the other's throat. Ripping away the knife before the other victim fell to the ground, he slashed the man's windpipe open as he moved past him.

Marco casually hurled the knife into minion number five as Merle charged for minions six and seven.

They broke and ran.

Marco sunk lower to the ground while Merle chased after the others. He wasn't entirely certain what Kraft had hoped to dig up from this experiment, but Merle had offered to pay his expenses. That was good enough for him because tending to a wounded arm would be the first thing on his requisition list.

Looking at his watch, Marco sighed. He blinked as he looked up at the other attackers. Merle and Rory had chased the others, until they joined another, larger group of them. The minions weren't running away, and Marco's watch said that daylight should be here.

For once, San Francisco was *not* covered in fog so thick that it nearly whited out the entire world.

Out of the darkness came one of the minions— Marco knew it had to be one because he didn't recognize this creature. It was tall and heavily armed with an assault rifle, sidearm, and combat knife. There was also an ax on his back, but Marco could only think, *One thing at a time.*

"*Au revoir, mon amis,*" the minion said in a thick Parisian accent. He lowered the muzzle of his rifle.

Marco blinked. "The French? I'm going to get taken out by the *French!*"

The minion smiled. Marco tucked his arms and chin together and rolled away on his good shoulder. He landed on the bad one. A lance of pain drove through his body, and he thought, *Damn, should've remembered that arm.*

A series of gunshots popped off, but none of them hit Marco. He rolled over using his good shoulder and looked up. The Frenchman hovered above him. A final gunshot made the minion's head explode, sending his body perpendicular to Marco.

Marco looked over the source of the blasts, surprised. Merle couldn't fire a gun to save his life…or anyone else's, for that matter.

There stood an attractive, honey-blonde woman he had met a few weeks before, who had lectured him on the uses of being subtle.

"I didn't bring out the assault rifles, Detective Kelly," Marco muttered. "Honest, I didn't."

Kristen Kelly, SFPD, crouched down next to him and smiled like he was an amusing little boy. "But you had to blow up half the dorm and set the park on fire, didn't you?"

Marco blinked. He hadn't used that much firepower. "Huh?" *I couldn't have hit a gas main, we shut those off for the evening in case this happened. So the only real explosive around my room had to have been brought in, but there were only minions, weren't there? Wait…Amanda always compares the power to the dark side of the force, and what did we learn from killing the Emperor in the last film?*

His eyes flickered to the minion. The dead Frenchman had a deep red glow by his open wound. A glow as dark a red as the bloody brain matter Kelly had spread over the ground.

It took Marco a second to realize that the minions were bombs.

# Chapter 7

# Explosive End Result

"Entropy…" was all that Marco said. Kristen followed his eyes to the body and understood. The minions had been soldiers, but the vampire had endowed them with energy, making them faster, stronger, and more deadly.

*And the first law of physics states that matter and energy cannot be created or destroyed. And if the vampire that imparted the active supernatural energies remaining in the soldiers didn't draw the energies back in. The power has nowhere to go…thus boom…*

Kristen grabbed Marco and hauled him to his feet. "Merle, bomb! Get away from the bodies! They're rigged."

*Well, it's true, and it is a lot simpler than trying to run through a lecture on the principles of physics.*

One moment, Marco lay on one side of the park, and the next, he was on the sidewalk outside. Had he blacked out? No, Merle was right there next to them.

*Gotta find out how he does that,* Marco thought.

He looked into the trees, the minions, with weapons raised, charged straight at them—

And then an explosion shook the ground, gouging out a whole section of the grove.

"What was that?" Merle asked Kristen.

She frowned, checking her magazine. "Have you ever heard of charging a human being with energy?"

He rotated his hand back and forth in an "iffy" sign. "Sure, I've heard of minions. But from what I've heard, it usually goes back to the source vampire. It doesn't usually *blow up*. That's according to the Vatican Ninjas I've talked to. Vampires aren't exactly a bottomless well of energy to waste it like that. Even then, the only magic I've ever heard of vampires using is 'soul fire,'" Merle said, making actual air quotes. "It's supposed to be impressive, but you'd think they'd have a better name for it."

Kristen raised a brow and looked around the woods. "Okay, so *something* supercharged the minions, and deliberately let them explode because it had enough energy to just *do* that. Right."

Marco sat up and shook his head. He looked up at the two of them. "I think we caught someone's attention." He stood, clapping Merle on the back. "I told you that something would want my head after taking out Nuala."

The government agent spared him a smile. "True enough. I thought you were tired of being the bait?"

Marco shrugged. "I'm used to it." He tried flexing his wounded arm and winced. "Though, dang it, I'm starting to get tired of being a pincushion. I'm glad I'm getting back to New York." He paused and thought a moment. "I *am* going back, right? That hasn't changed, has it?"

Merle nodded. "We have their attention, and this guy's going to be pissed."

*Thank God. I can go home.*

Kelly shook her head. "You think?" She sighed, looking into the burning woods. "The paperwork on this is going to be a bitch and a half."

"I doubt it," Marco said, suddenly tired. *My adrenaline must be crashing.* "Not without bodies. You may have an arson report or a whole bunch of missing persons in the next week, but that's it."

As they all made their way out of Golden Gate Park, Dalf Kraft lurked in the shadows of the trees. He chuckled to himself.

"You would not find it funny if you had been the one splashed with holy water," came the dark, malevolent voice behind him.

The Kraft brother, dressed like Doctor Strange or Mandrake the Magician, didn't even look over his shoulder at the Russian vampire who had just tried to kill Marco. He gave a little smile beneath his wisp of a mustache.

"Oh, please, Misha," Dalf drolled. "If you had been on your game, the first thing you would have done was level the building."

"I have other plans for him," Misha drawled.

Dalf sighed and shook his head. "You are a disgrace to the forces of evil."

The vampire blinked, taken aback. "You are quoting a Disney movie at me?"

Now Dalf turned to face the vampire, jabbing the silver wolf's head of his cane at Misha, the ruby eyes of the wolf caught the flames of the park, and they matched the glint in Dalf's eyes. "That film had an awesome villain. And Tchaikovsky. *Never* diss Tchaikovsky." Dalf tossed his cane up in the air, caught it just under the head, and scoffed. "Do as you will. It's your funeral."

January 3rd

After living for a hundred years, Amanda Colt had finally, at long last, been stymied.

However, the one who defeated her was already dead and decayed for a few decades.

She hurled the book against the wall in disdain and cursed in Russian. "And *that* for you, Marcel Proust!"

She stood there and fumed at the book but didn't really know who else to be angry at. There were so many options, but the book was harmless. Her first thought was to be angry at Marco, for making her fall in love with him. Or perhaps herself, for allowing herself to be pulled away from Marco just before he was about to be thrown down as vampyre bait.

Father Rodgers had been even less help than she'd expected.

Amanda had told him what had happened, even down to making out with Marco.

As her confessor, he had simply smiled at her. He sat back in his chair, holding a lit cigar in one hand and scotch glass in the other. The priest stared into the scotch, as though it would tell him what to do.

"So, what is the problem with your young man?" he asked in that casually-boisterous voice of his. It always sounded to her like a jovial boom, as though the black priest from Bed-Sty had always wanted to play the role of Santa Claus but gave it up for lack of a beard. "It's Marco."

Amanda smiled to herself. "Yes."

"About time."

The vampire blinked. "Why is it everyone says that?"

The priest merely chewed on his cigar and grinned.

As Amanda looked at the destroyed book, the phone rang. She stared at it for a moment, then sighed.

She answered the phone. "*Da?*"

"Amanda. It's Merle. Can you pick up Marco at JFK airport?"

Amanda blinked, then shifted, uncomfortably. "Can he not get a taxi?"

"I think it might be easier on him if he didn't have to carry his luggage with one arm. Besides, I don't want him alone on the ground."

She flinched, and automatically straightened, her voice as sharp as a whip crack. "What happened?"

"Well," he paused a moment. "We definitely attracted someone's attention."

"When is his plane getting in?"

"It should be there about an hour after sundown. Good enough for you?"

"I will be there five *minutes* after sundown."

Marco awoke on the plane and found Amanda leaning over him, looking deep into his eyes.

He smiled. "You're here."

"Of course I am." She lightly touched his wounded arm. "I did not want you to die on me."

He looked around the plane. It was completely empty. "They let you on board?"

Amanda smiled. "I still have identification from CIA," she answered, dropping a few articles as her light accent thickened a little. "It says FBI, and no one looks at expiration dates unless they are police."

Marco nodded slightly and said nothing. His ever-present smile was stuck on his face. He couldn't say anything because, well, his brain was frozen on one, inescapable thought.

Amanda looked *gorgeous*. Her hair flowed over one shoulder and past her left arm. Her bright amber eyes drew him in like nothing else he could describe. He caught her scent–it wasn't perfume or shampoo, but her skin. She always smelled like vanilla to him. Her proximity was such, he could feel the heat coming off her body.

If he didn't think of something, he was going to grab her, kiss her, and be thrown off the plane for inappropriate conduct.

Amanda smiled. "Your heart has spiked," she said teasingly.

"Can't imagine why."

"Perhaps you are allergic to me."

Marco gripped the arms of the chair so he wouldn't grab her. "If so, I'll live," he said lightly. "Let's get out of here, shall we?"

Amanda slowly slinked into the aisle. Her boneless, flowing movements made his blood boil. When she stepped towards the front of the plane, he said, "Wrong way. I'll go ahead of you. I'd hate to accidentally hit you with the luggage."

Amanda furrowed her brow prettily, then shrugged, and moved back, taking his suitcase down from the overhead bin. Marco got up and out, grabbing his carry-on briefcase from under the chair in front of him. He awkwardly sidestepped his way down the aisle, with the vampire behind him the entire time.

Marco kept moving, focusing on the space in front of him. He had insisted that Amanda stayed behind him for one simple reason: if her movements just stepping into the aisle could set his blood burning, he didn't want to imagine what his reaction would be if she walked in front of him the whole way.

Marco's hold on the luggage turned into a death grip by the time he got to the ramp. The temptation to turn and embrace her was so intense, his chest tightened with his level of restraint.

*Get off the ramp. Then get out of the way of the people going to board. Get out of the way of general traffic. Recalculate molestation of Amanda when you see conditions on the ground.*

By the time he wheeled out the suitcase, Marco thought about something he hadn't really taken into consideration. Amanda had been showing signs of telepathic abilities.

A hand touched his back, and Marco had to restrain himself from reacting.

Amanda gently guided him through the airport, and whispered, "Yes, Marco. I can hear you."

Her fingers curved, and she gently raked them down his spine—she didn't break the skin or rip the fabric of his shirt, but he had to restrain himself from flinching or shuddering at the sensations pulsing through him.

Amanda's hand slid around Marco's waist, and she brought them hip to hip. She brought him to a stop, went tiptoe for a moment, placing her lips next to his ear, and whispered, "We'll get to that later. I promise."

"Trust me," he replied, moving forward with her. "We're going to want to stay in public as long as possible. I don't want to have to go to confession the day after I get back. I already went before I got on the plane."

"Hmm?" Amanda … mewed. He couldn't think of a better word to describe it.

"I'm trying to avoid explicitness even in my thoughts," he explained.

"…Oh. Then it is a good thing that we are not going to be anywhere private for some time."

"How do you figure?"

Amanda gave him a gentle squeeze. "I got a ride from a friend."

The black Hummer wasn't as ostentatious as the standard stretch model that looked like a limo and a Humvee had had a baby. A man came out of the passenger side and picked up Marco's checked luggage like it was nothing.

"Friend of yours?" Marco asked.

"Not quite."

The door of the black Hummer opened. The back had two seats, facing each other. In it sat a blonde that Marco had never seen before. She was prim and proper in a crisp black business suit. Her legs were crossed neatly, her hands clasped around her knees. She smiled with thick blood-red lips, her wide mouth baring plenty of teeth. If Marco had never met Amanda, she would have been attractive. She had large broad eyes that shined brightly.

"You must be Marco," she said in a refined British accent. "I am Jennifer Bosley, The President of the New York City Vampires Association."

Marco smiled and gave a slight nod, being polite but not too polite. On the one hand, she was objectively beautiful; on the other, she was a vampire he didn't know directly. "I am. I've heard of you."

Bosley grinned. "Good things, I hope."

He shrugged. "I know you're on our side and considered pragmatic. Should I know more?"

She arched a brow. "Really? Good for you, Amanda, you haven't even shared anything with your pet here. Though I think he really would make a good minion."

Marco chuckled. "Only half-right."

Bosley cocked her head and waved them both in to take the seat across from her. Marco shrugged and moved in ahead of Amanda. He reached back and offered Amanda his hand.

Bosley's man closed the Hummer door, and the car pulled away smoothly.

President Bosley looked at Marco. "What do you mean 'only half-right'?"

"I'm already her minion," he said casually. He put an arm around Amanda and drew her close. "I would do anything for her. No fluid transfer required."

Bosley laughed. "Oh, dearie, just wait a little."

Marco blinked and wondered what the heck Madam President meant but decided to move on. "I find it interesting that you're giving us a lift. I thought you couldn't help us, or even, be seen with us in public. Something about your pragmatic nature saying it was a bad idea?"

Bosley nodded, still smiling. Her big round eyes sparkled as she studied him. "True enough." Her face and smile hardened. "But that was before the buggers tried to blow me up." She looked from Marco to Amanda. "As you can attest, I've done nothing for you except suggest that you go and look a little deeper here and there. Aside from that, what have I done?"

Amanda thought it over for a moment. "Mostly? You sent me out digging for what was behind Mister Day."

Marco nodded. "Which brought Amanda to San Francisco in time to save my hide last week."

Bosley nodded. "Indeed. Your assassin, that Nuala, must have suspected someone tipped you off. Since you went on a tear after leaving my place, it wouldn't have been too hard to conclude that I had something to do with it."

Amanda frowned. "You were being watched?"

President Bosley shrugged. "It's not too much of a leap. They also could have been watching you. Either way, I'm not concerned about hiding my intentions anymore. They made one move against me. They won't get another try. I haven't gotten where I am by being stupid."

Marco nodded slowly and carefully, trying to think three moves ahead in this conversation. "In which case, how many of your people can we rely on in the near future?"

A corner of Bosley's mouth quirked in a smile. "How near are you thinking?"

Marco and Amanda exchanged a look and then shrugged. "Days? A few weeks?" He looked back to Bosley. "They know I'm alive, and I can only imagine that these people will want to step up their plans. They were in such a rush to kill me they just took a swipe twelve hours ago."

Amanda poked him. "About that. Do you know who was behind it?"

Marco sighed. "Believe it or not, Mikhail's brother. Well, that's what he called himself. I didn't get a good look at him, but he was about the size and build of Mikhail. Though even uglier … except …" He closed his eyes and tried to picture the vampire's visage. "Someone had taken a bite out of his face."

Amanda froze. "Really?"

He nodded. "In any event, he's seriously bad news. He has magic. He projected an image of Yana in my room. His minions were supercharged enough to blow up when they died."

Amanda and Bosley quietly exchanged a glance.

The silence went on for more than ten seconds. At which point, Marco raised a brow. "What am I missing?"

Amanda: "Vampires who use that level of magic are … rare."

Bosley scoffed. "More like unheard of. To be that level of evil, the sins involved go beyond killing someone for food or because you want something from their death. You'd have to be complicit in …something much worse."

Marco cocked his head to one side. "Really? Joy." He looked at Amanda. "Remember that rumor we were talking about when Mikhail showed up the first time? There was a rumor of him at Tunguska?"

Amanda and Bosley winced. The Tunguska event was the equivalent of a thirty-megaton explosion—and the atom bomb that hit Hiroshima was around fifteen *kilo*tons.

Amanda saw where Marco was going. "Perhaps they met this brother instead."

Marco nodded. "Exactly. In which case, I'm fortunate to be alive. If this guy had used his *total* power…?"

Bosley held up a hand. "*If* this is the same bloke behind Tunguska, he couldn't do the same trick today without massive repercussions. If a satellite sees him in the act, it's an excuse to nuke wherever he is. He'd be classified, rightly, as a Weapon of Mass Destruction. Anyone who could field the forces to do it would destroy him. He's evil, not stupid. You're not important enough to risk being wiped out in nuclear fire."

Marco laughed. "I wish to high Heaven I knew why I'm as important as they think I am. The enemy has blown two massive resources on me, Day and Nuala."

"And," Amanda added, "all of Day's political contacts. *As well as* Nuala's minions.

Bosley arched a brow. "Indeed. *Someone* thinks you're important."

Marco rolled his eyes. "Lucky me."

Amanda ignored his response. "Did he say anything in particular?"

"We didn't have an intimate discussion. He did make a reference that I'm surprised he knew."

Bosley arched her brows quizzically.

Marco explained, "I once told Yana that I am whatever I needed to be. This new vampire? He echoed it back to me. I'm a little concerned that he knew that much about me in the first place."

Bosley raised a finger, as though raising a point of order. "Would you like to explain your initial statement to … whoever this Yana person is?"

Marco shrugged. "When I focus on a problem, I try to adapt myself to it. I become the solution. I'm not saying I'm a changeling, but I can mold myself—my thoughts, my posture, my actions—to what can solve the problem. In some cases, it's glorified acting, but just ask some actors about how their biochemistry looks when they fall too deep into a part."

Amanda said nothing and merely sat back as though she was hearing about this for the first time. Months ago, during the initial recruitment of the gangster known only as Enrico, Enrico had held Marco's father hostage. Marco became a pure thug. Even his scent had changed. It was like he had become a different person right in front of her, only wearing the same fiery blue eyes. But instead of burning hot, they burned cold. Certainly, that sort of thing could happen with emotional shifts, but she had never smelled someone change their biochemistry before.

Bosley mulled that over a moment. "Interesting. I'd like to see you do that trick sometime."

Marco's smile became sly. "No. I don't think you would." He leaned forward and looked her straight in the eye.

Bosley grinned. She met his gaze without hesitation. Very few humans wanted to meet her eye once they knew what she was. Because, really, who wanted to meet the eye of a vampire? But Bosley had no problems humoring Marco if he wanted to play chicken like this…

Suddenly, without any warning, more noise than she'd heard outside of a rock concert bombarded Bosley. Behind Marco's eyes existed a solid scream—three different Gilbert and Sullivan patter songs at the same time, a selection of death metal, and what she thought was Fermat's last theorem.

She pulled back. Was it Amanda's imagination, or did Bosley look… paler than before? She gave a sidelong look to Amanda. "You have a very useful pet here, love. You should hold onto him."

Amanda nodded. "I intend to."

# Chapter 8

# Home

Marco Catalano watched Bosley's man unload the last of the luggage on the top of the brownstone's stoop. He looked back to the NYC-VA President, and she gave him a wide grin. "Don't worry, friend. In a few days, you and I are going to have a conversation regarding our plan of attack. You have allies you don't know yet."

Marco arched a brow and looked to Amanda, who shrugged. "No idea," she told him. She looked to Bosley. "Who did you have in mind?"

"An old friend. You'll meet him soon enough. But I'm not going to try and pull everyone together tonight."

He threw her a casual salute. "Have a good evening, Madam Bosley."

She nodded, leaned back in the car, and her man closed the door for her.

The car drove off, leaving Marco and Amanda alone.

Marco looked to Amanda, his omnipresent smile of amusement growing just a little. "Oh, look. We have no one else around."

Amanda smiled, showing just the slightest hint of tooth.

Marco took a step forward and—

The front door of the brownstone burst open, Doctor Robert Catalano in the doorway, arms outstretched to welcome home his son. "Marco! You're home!"

Marco's head snapped around, shooting daggers at his father. "Hi, Dad. Hold on a second."

He turned back to Amanda, and they launched themselves into each other's arms, coming together in a clash of lips and tongues. They held each other close, kissing for all they were worth. Despite the cold night air, and that he still wore a light windbreaker for San Francisco weather, all he could feel was Amanda's warmth. He breathed her in, and he swore that warmed him even further.

Marco held her in his arms, tasting her, loving her, and was, at long last, home.

After the first minute, Doctor Catalano merely sighed, grabbed the nearest piece of luggage, and dragged it inside, muttering, "About time."

Amanda and Marco pried themselves away from each other about five minutes later, and entered the house, holding hands. They walked past the front sitting room and went straight to the living room. As usual, it looked like one part living room and one part office. Bookcases lined most of the walls, with a few exceptions of artwork and a television. Doctor Catalano had a desk against one corner, keeping it for himself.

A couch sat in one corner of the room, and Marco headed straight for it, Amanda beside him.

Doctor Robert Catalano was slender, stopping a few pounds before "thin" could settle in. His short hair had once been a solid black but was now heavily salted. His features were sharp, and the only hint of the Italian in him was his generally dark coloring— coloring which had skipped Marco entirely. He looked up from the book on his desk, gave them a little smile, and said, "Decided to come in out of the cold?"

Marco shrugged. "Didn't really feel that cold."

"Indeed." Robert closed the book and folded his hands on top of it. "Should I ask how long this has been going on?"

Marco looked at the ceiling, doing some math. "Total? Maybe an hour. If you want the starting point, about two weeks?"

Robert smiled. "I can appreciate the difference. What happened? You finally figured it out, and something immediately came up?"

Amanda nodded. "That is correct, sir."

Robert rolled his eyes. "It's still me, kids." He paused, then frowned, realizing that he had called a woman twice his age a "kid." He shook his head, moving on. "Usually, my first question would be to ask if you two have thought this through. On the other hand, your mother and I—and Father Rodgers, and Bram, and Merle Kraft, and even Enrico—have been waiting for you two to get together for nearly a year now." He looked off to one side. "Come to think of it, Enrico thought that you two were an item since day one. I can't really blame him for that."

Marco and Amanda both chuckled at that. When they had first met Enrico, Marco had played the tough guy, and Amanda the "Russian sex kitten"—both were lucky that they had kept a straight face.

On the other hand, Marco was a little thrown that his father was casually referring to a spy, a mobster, and a SpecOps agent like that.

"Though I should ask," Robert continued, "did Madam Bosley pick you both up, or did you take a taxi here?"

At that, Marco's eyebrows shot up. "I'm sorry, did you say—"

"Jennifer Bosley?" Robert prompted. "President of the local Vampires Association?"

Marco leaned forward. "I'm sorry, but how—?"

"She and Enrico have been helping with the reconstruction of the hospital," Robert said as if this was perfectly normal. "I'm not sure which is stranger, the vampire or the mobster, but Enrico has shown himself to be competent, and she's been quite generous."

Marco furrowed his brows and looked at Amanda quizzically. She didn't say anything. He knew that Enrico had proven himself useful—when his father had come under attack last week, Enrico had been right alongside him. It had been around the same time as the attack on Bosley…

"Bosley left out some details," Marco concluded.

Robert and Amanda looked at him strangely.

Marco leaned forward, onto the edge of the couch. "How long have you been meeting with Bosley?'"

Robert shrugged. "Once a month since the original hospital bombing. Maybe a little more."

"Ever since she showed up after the bombing," Amanda concluded. She looked at Marco. "She and Enrico collaborated to get me out of the rubble, remember?"

He nodded. "Exactly. We wondered how the Council knew that Bosley was helping us. I guess she thought she could pass off the hospital as community support."

"I can believe that," Robert said, "Perhaps they had spotters when they attacked us all at Enrico's house."

Amanda and Marco both looked at him. Robert shrugged. "What?"

"You were attacked *twice* last month?" Amanda asked.

Robert nodded. "Yes. Though the RPG attack on the hospital was far more dramatic. Heck, Kraft and Bosley dealt with most of them at Enrico's. I don't think I even saw those attackers alive."

Amanda frowned. "But they knew you were there. They saw you go in. The attackers were minions, and their master saw what they saw. That's how they knew that Bosley was working with you and Enrico."

"And Merle Kraft," Marco added darkly. "That's why all three of you were attacked later on. We should have seen this coming. The first attack was to wipeout Enrico, maybe Merle. The attack at the hospital was definitely to kill you, Dad, to get at me. And getting Bosley was a priority because they didn't know exactly what she was doing." He smacked himself in the forehead. "Idiot. I should have known what was happening."

Amanda patted his head. "Do not do that, I like your head the way it is."

"And you didn't know," Robert added. "Things were a little busy."

Marco scoffed. "That's one way to put it."

Robert nodded. "But we can talk about all of that tomorrow. In case you want to settle in."

Marco looked at his watch. It was only six o'clock. "I have a few hours before I go down. Right now, I want to head out into the city, walk around, see if I can feel like a normal person."

Robert gave an aborted chuckle. Amanda coquettishly cleared her throat.

Marco blinked, frowned, and looked from his father to his love and back. "What?"

Amanda leaned in close to his ear, and slightly emphasizing her Russian accent, said "A normal purr-son?"

A shiver went down Marco's spine, and he suppressed the sudden urge to kiss her in front of his father. "Normal for me, in civilization." He looked to his father. "San Francisco. Ugh. I can't imagine how any sane person can live there."

Robert leaned forward over his desk, hands together, and said, "Marco, I have raised you to be a chauvinist about New York."

"No. I've just seen San Francisco. There's a difference."

Robert rolled his eyes. "Indeed." He looked at the two of them. They cuddled on the couch, touching at the hip, knee, and shoulder. Marco's hand was on Amanda's, the tips of his fingers sliding between her fingers. "If you two are going to head out, should I be expecting you back tonight?"

Both of them stopped, looked at Robert, and cocked their heads in opposite directions. They narrowed their eyes, and said, at the same time, "Why wouldn't you?"

Robert smiled. "Never mind."

# Chapter 9

# Drink And The Devil

Jennifer Bosley stepped out of her SUV, and onto the walkway in front of the Bensonhurst mansion. She smoothed her suit as she took inventory of the armed guards. There had been six on the front gate, and another ten in the front of the main house.

She thought they might be a good start in the event of a minion attack. In case of vampires, they were probably screwed. Unless they were all far more religious than she thought they were.

Before she got to the front door, it opened to reveal the Mafia wiseguy known only as "Enrico." He was tall but quite elegant. He had first been introduced to the world of vampires at a hospital desk, holding Doctor Catalano hostage in his own hospital. Once he was entirely on board, he had become most useful— not quite invaluable, but enough for government work. The man was less DeNiro and Pacino, more Michael Rennie of the original *Day the Earth Stood Still.* He had a medium build, with thick cheekbones, and an easy, conman smile… when he wasn't threatening to kill someone.

"Jen, I'm so glad you could make it," he called in his smooth baritone. "How do you like the modifications?"

Bosley grinned. "They're okay. But only sixteen people?"

Now he really smiled. "Good. You only saw the ones I wanted you to see."

Bosley's eyebrows shot up. She had been part of British intelligence in World War II; that, on top of her vampire senses, usually meant she could find any and all human security, and most tech-based security. She thought that hiding people from her was impossible. "Really? Very impressive."

He shrugged. "I hired people from the deeper end of the gene pool. Mostly former soldiers. The ones you see are bait. You could even say they're dispensable."

She nodded. It was time for her to sharpen her skills again. "Understood."

Enrico held the door for her as she entered and closed it behind her. He said nothing, but walked ahead of her, moving through the living room. The massive hole she had made in the floor last month had been repaired—one of the benefits of being in the construction business.

They ended up in a stylish room decorated in the 1970's, Marlon-Brando-as-Godfather fashion: dark gray carpet, dark wood paneling, comfortable furniture, with a wall of bookcases.

Bosley looked around and nodded in approval. "I've definitely seen worse."

Enrico laughed. "You'd be surprised."

He closed the door and moved behind the desk. The gangster reached out and slid up the blinds. The windows weren't filled with glass, but metal. "I brought in someone who designs SCIFs. And had him make it a safe room on top of that." He gave a wry smile. "I didn't want to be dropped in on like the last time."

Bosley blinked. She closed her eyes and tried listening for the guards she'd seen outside in the hallway. She couldn't even hear them. The room was actually soundproof. Even for a vampire.

She opened her eyes and nodded. "Most impressive."

"I thought you'd appreciate it." He waved her towards the couch behind the coffee table off to the side. She took the couch, and he took the chair next to it. "Tea?"

She nodded. After all, she was still English. "Yes, thank you."

He grabbed the teapot and poured. "How have your preparations been?"

"Quite well, thank you." She took the cup and added a lump of sugar. She stirred and sipped. "I've brought everybody on board that I believe I could trust, and quietly growing the ranks as we move along. Our numbers are already beyond my projections."

Enrico nodded as he poured his own cup—espresso in a large coffee mug that read *I'm having coffee: talk to me at your own risk.* "And what about your friend the Commissioner?" he asked before he took a sip.

"Ray is doing well." Jennifer smiled slightly. "Jealous that I have friends in high *and* low places?"

"Not at all. Why would you ask?"

Bosley gave him a knowing look. "Ray and I go way back, to when he first ran into people like me. He's been very thoughtful and smart about everything to do with the association. He's also been married for forty years."

Enrico chuckled. "The idea that it would stop a vampire would be more amusing if I didn't know you already."

Bosley rolled her eyes. "I haven't read a novel about vampires since Bram Stoker." She paused before she took another sip. "Okay, I have read Jim Butcher and Larry Correia, but vampires are only a part of what they work with. So please don't talk to me about Ann Rice or that Hamilton woman. Ask me less about that Meyer creature." She scoffed. "Sparkles, indeed. As though we're animated ponies." She put down her tea. "Have you had any more problems with incursions?"

He shook his head. "Not by vampires. Though there are a few police officers who give us funny looks every time they drive by. I don't know if they're in on the vampire secret, or if they want to keep an eye on me."

She shrugged. "It amounts to the same level of protection, doesn't it?"

"Not if cops try to stop vampires attacking the front gate and get eaten."

Jennifer nodded once. "That *would* be a problem. Though my conversation with Ray has given me the impression that we have about ten percent of the department in on the secret."

Enrico's eyes widened briefly at that. "Really? That's about four thousand cops."

She nodded. "Give or take. I hadn't known that many people could keep a secret, but apparently, a lot of them have had run-ins with the wrong side of my people." She took her tea and thought a moment before sipping. She looked deeply into the cup. "Then again, one percent of seven million people is still seventy thousand."

The wiseguy tried not to choke on his coffee. "That many?"

Bosley smiled. "Don't you mean that *few*? That's just a guess, mind you. It could be as high as three percent." She shrugged. "For perspective, keep in mind, homosexuals are approximately that much of the planetary population, and they have their own lobby. Just be grateful that we haven't come out of the casket and decided to purchase some politicians—we have more savings than anyone can imagine."

"Understood. Though how many of them are on our side?"

Her smile turned into a front. "Good question. Many of them aren't on either side. Remember, most of the association is about money, power, and status. If our members don't track them, then we can't. I won't say they're outside our sphere of influence, but much like there are limits to your reach, there are limits to ours. Any vampires who aren't in the Association can stay under our radar with relative ease if they're smart about it. It's not as though we try to take over the entire vampire community."

Enrico nodded and thought it over. She had a point. In the beginning, the Sicilian mafia used to be the law in places where the law wouldn't or couldn't dare go. But, like other extra-legal organizations, the mafia became a criminal organization. Protection became less about protection from the criminal or the corrupt and became about protection *from* the mafia. As cities grew, the mafia could only apply pressure to a limited range. Over-extension was easy if they weren't careful. The mafia itself was limited to geographic areas. What Bosley was dealing with was something similar, only vampires could be anywhere, go anywhere, and it wasn't as though they were wired with GPS upon being turned.

Then he frowned. "But can't vampires sense other vampires?"

"To some extent. The more powerful the vampire, the more they can sense people and things in general. The only limit is with vampires on the demonic side— they can't detect anything protected in or by the divine."

Enrico nodded, then emptied his espresso. "I got the impression that the assassin who went after Marco and Amanda could sense them fairly easily."

"Correct. They escaped her with a combination of prayer and dirty laundry."

"And how many more minions do you think there could be?"

Bosley winced. "I can't imagine. Tracking minions is even harder than tracking non-member vampires.

From what we could tell, the assassin sucked the life out of all of her minions to survive being staked with a crucifix and being blown up."

Enrico smiled. "Well, that'll do it." He finished his cup. "Do you have time for more tea?"

"I have an appointment at nine or so, but we have time."

# Chapter 10

## Sergeants In The Army Of Light

January 4th

Marco looked up at one of the lions in front of the New York City Public Library, perhaps best known as being in the opening shot of the classic film Ghostbusters. He pressed his hand against the massive stone base, as though testing the truth of its existence.

"Good God, it's so nice to be back home." He hammered the pedestal with his fist lightly. "A city where the construction is sturdy, and—mostly—not pretentious." He smirked and looked at Amanda. "You know these things are supposed to roar when a virgin walks by?"

His friend smiled. "*Da*, and they've never roared."

He shrugged. "Just means they don't work. I've walked by multiple times."

Amanda's face lit up with a grin. "How sweet."

"Sweet?" He chuckled. "That's new."

She punched his left shoulder, and he flinched, smarting. "Stop it."

Marco rolled his shoulder. "Ow?"

Amanda furrowed her brows, confused. "Is that a statement or a question?"

"Yes." Marco slid his jacket off at the shoulder and rolled up his shirt sleeve. There was a bruise already forming on his arm, in the perfect impression of her knuckles.

Amanda gasped in shock. "Marco, I—"

He held up his other hand, staring at the mark. It was almost as though she had forgotten her own strength or had gotten stronger since they'd last talked.

*On the one hand, pain meds might be nice. On the other hand, they didn't work that well last time.*

*Perhaps it's time to have that talk.*

"I'll live. I'm tougher than I look, after all." He frowned at the red mark, then slid his jacket back on. "Could be worse. I could be attacked by a dozen feminists who think I'm a proto-fascist because I carry a rosary. Heh. I can see our next battle against the forces of darkness…the National Organization of Women."

She narrowed her eyes. "What have you against feminists?"

"Nothing, sort of am one—the traditional ones you remember. The equal pay for equal work crowd."

Amanda raised an eyebrow and smiled slightly. "You realize that many of them would get into fist-fights with anyone who would disagree with them? A few even considered blowing things up?"

"Sigh. Yeah. But nowadays, the ones who used to throw bombs have become the 'abortion on demand' lobby." He grimaced, remembering her lecture on the rise of demonic activity over the course of the last few centuries. She'd explained everything from the French Revolution using blood from decapitations with bread in a mockery of the Eucharist, to the Russian Revolution becoming a religion, and finally about the current practice of human sacrifice endorsed by every leftist with an agenda and a lawyer.

She sighed. She had heard this lecture before—she had *given* this lecture—and she wasn't in the mood for that.

And they hadn't had a practice session for a while.

"En garde!"

Marco back pivoted as she shot forward with a right cross. He grabbed her wrist and pulled her toward him, shooting out his foot to trip her. She leaped over it and landed on her feet, and then flipped him over her hip. He fell flat on his back and rolled off his shoulders, going heels over head onto his feet.

He smiled. "Where did you get the leg hopping trick?"

"It just came naturally, I guess."

"Not bad. I like it. Again?"

She came at him. He blocked her punch, and she grabbed him and flipped him over her shoulder. He landed on his feet and spun, chopping down on her from above. She twisted and blocked it, as well as his chop at her hip. He stepped forward with a left jab for her face. She grabbed him and pulled him towards her.

Neither one of them was quite sure what happened next, least of all who had kissed whom first. No one knew whose idea it was, but they knew it was mutual.

After five minutes, they broke apart. They looked at each other, Marco a little bit dazed. "Well, that was fun."

Amanda's eyes glittered. "*Da*, it was."

Marco smiled, deliriously happy now. "We should have done this sooner."

"Oh? How much sooner?"

Marco's face sported that strange little smile that always reminded Amanda of the one memorable line from *Scaramouche*: "He was born with the gift of laughter and a sense that the world was mad."

He gazed deep into her eyes. "Day one would have been good."

She frowned playfully and took a swing at him. Luckily, he anticipated the swing because when her fist touched the stone pedestal of the library lions, the stone cracked.

Marco raised an eyebrow. "Did you mean to do that?"

Amanda blinked. "*Nyet*… I can't imagine how I do that, period. I was not trying."

Marco quickly scanned the area to see if anyone else had noticed that she cracked the stone with her bare hands. Thankfully, no pedestrian gave a damn. He jerked his head towards the upper level of the stairs, and they stopped at the first landing of the library, which was more like a patio that extended the length of the block. He went off to one side, where the patio went off behind some trees on the property. She caught up to him, and he leaned up against a park table, bolted into the concrete.

"Amanda, how much have you been up to lately?"

"Nothing, I swear."

"You've been doing your church attendance?"

She nodded slowly. "*Da.*"

"Praying a lot?"

She nodded absently. Considering the last few weeks away from Marco, all the time she typically spent with him had turned her thoughts inwards and upwards, toward Heaven. Msgr. Rodgers had "joked" that if she became any more spiritual, she would become a mystic. Rodgers had jokingly asked her if she could hold off getting stigmata or other phenomena until the parish's annual charity appeal.

Amanda hadn't even considered taking the priest seriously until now.

"You've become a better person," Marco said, smiling, moving closer to her. "I'm just sorry that I couldn't take the credit."

She smiled softly, thinking back since she had first met Marco.

"Are we so sure about that?" she whispered.

Marco cocked his head and arched his brows. "Huh. That's… an interesting idea." He cupped her chin in his fingers and met her eyes. "Show me what you mean."

They stared deep into each other's eyes, and she brought him into her mind.

When a vampire had kidnapped Marco's ex-"friend who was a girl," Amanda had considered how Marco would feel, since the vampire got away. Suddenly she had become faster, nearly catching up with the bastard, until she was almost hit by a train.

When they had first made out in the cemetery, she had confessed her love for him, pretending that it was part of the act—it was one of the first times her eyes had glowed without bloodlust. They burned again during their first, genuine make out last month.

When Amanda fought the demon Asmodeus, or "Mister Day" as he called himself, she thought of Marco during the fight, and became faster.

After the bombing of the hospital, knowing that Day was after Marco, she ran all the way. Amanda became a blur, passing all traffic, and kept up that speed until she arrived at Marco's side.

When they had their second genuine makeout session, where Marco wanted to show how little he cared about her eating requirements, she'd read his mind without meeting his eyes—a trick she had never pulled before.

When Marco's life was on the line and they had been separated by a wall of fire in a burning house, she had effortlessly turned into mist. She'd circled around the fire, picked up Marco, and they both got away. Amanda moved more quickly than ever before and had kept her clothes through the transition as well. These were tricks that she had only seen powerful vampires pull off.

Perhaps her love for Marco *added* to her power. There were plenty of paths to God…and if romantic love weren't one of them, then what was marriage a sacrament for, anyway?

When they were done with their mind-meld, Marco blinked. His little Scaramouche smile widened just a hint. "Perhaps we should test the theory."

Amanda smiled seductively. "Sure it's safe?"

Marco's eyes became hooded, almost lazy. "Of course. How crazy do you think I am?"

"Marco… has that yet to stop me?"

"Um…"

She kissed him again.

Marco held onto her, kissing her for all he was worth plus a little interest. He broke the lip lock only a moment, kissing her cheek, her jaw…

"Why didn't we do this earlier?" he murmured between kissing her ear and her neck.

"I was scared…" she murmured between kisses of her own.

"I want you so much, I don't want to let you go."

She whispered in his ear. "You have to, eventually. If only to take our clothes off." She bit his earlobe lightly, maybe even using her fangs.

A third party stated, "I'd tell you to get a room, but you won't live that long."

Amanda and Marco whirled as one, turning to see a vampire the size of a professional wrestler, with a face that resembled a victim of smallpox. The deformation was a clear sign that this vampire was more than one of the usual rank and vile—more like a high ranking member of the army of darkness.

*And me without a chainsaw,* Marco thought.

"He is not bad," Amanda commented. "I did not even smell this one coming."

Marco grinned. "You were busy."

Marco flicked his wrist, and his hand shot out, throwing a wooden knife at the newcomer's chest. The vampire didn't even move, merely swept his hand to one side, knocking the stake into the air. Marco didn't even bother trying again. Even Amanda sidestepped away.

"Even your whore knows better," the vampire growled.

Marco's eyes became as cold as arctic seas and as menacing as a mushroom cloud. This was what he had previously hidden from her, from everyone—a part of his very self, the part that could kill mercilessly if anyone hurt his people.

The vampire leaped, punching out at Marco. He used all of his advanced strength, and Marco pushed the blow aside with a left palm strike. Marco then caught and held the vampire's fist with his other hand. Three seconds later, the hand started to smoke and smolder, causing the newly arrived vampire to jerk away in agony.

The vampire growled and leaped at Marco again. Marco did the unexpected, and jumped *at* him, wrapping his arms and legs around him, gripping him like a starfish onto a rock. The vampire became suddenly weak as pain burned all over his body. Unable to support his body weight and Marco's, he sunk to the ground. He no longer felt physical pain, because all his nerve endings had been burned away.

The human dismounted him and stood, reaching behind his back. With a little rip of Velcro, he pulled down a wooden sword—the crossbeam had been at the small of his back, under the shoulder blades.

"Wooden swords… loser," the vampire coughed.

Marco smiled and flipped the sword upside down. He grabbed the blade by the hilt.

The vampire suddenly realized it was a wooden crucifix with sharpened edges. And that wasn't all Marco had done to him. The human had rosaries around his wrists, neck, ankles, and waist.

The massive vampire thought, *It was a trap*, right before Amanda ripped his head off.

Marco slid the crucifix away. "I think he got the point."

Amanda nodded. "I hated sitting back while you killed him by yourself."

"I just wanted to test the rosary plan, see if it would work. He didn't notice a thing until it was too late."

She smiled. "I need to walk off the adrenaline a little."

Marco blinked. "Oh. Um. Okay. How about we try patrolling a little? Eh?"

"Worried about being alone with me?" she teased. She leaned forward to whisper into his ear. "I only bite when you ask me to."

He smiled again. "I'm not worried about you; I'm worried about me." He touched her face with two fingers and pushed a strand of hair over her ear. "That was always the problem." He shrugged. "Come on, let's kill something."

Good to the Last Drop

# Chapter 11

# Bankrupt

Officer Donald "Duck" Tolbert, of the New York City Police Department, stood in his pristine uniform in front of yet another dump.

He was a tall, light-skinned officer of Jamaican heritage, two generations back, who not only worked in Greenpoint, Brooklyn, but lived there. This proved a problem at times because he started to get a knock on the door from his fellow parishioners every time they wanted police action. They often decided coming directly to him was quicker and easier than calling 911. Yet another reason to take the night shift.

Tolbert decided that if anything went bump in the night, he would bump back.

Most vampires generally stayed low key. It was a tossup between what would be worse—to have dozens of centuries-old vampires coming down on them, or if the standard human population decided that they were going to hunt them all down and kill them. In the daylight, with crucifixes, torches, and pitchforks. Of course.

Tolbert looked around the dimly lit street without fear—there was no one else around. It was an area of Brooklyn where the property values could have improved drastically if they just invested in upkeep. It was just off of Manhattan Avenue, but it looked nothing like Manhattan. Interlinked residences lined the darkened streets, and the local idea of a doorway must have come from designers who forgot to plan for a door. Rather than a real stoop, the builders just pounded a slab of steel into the wall. The flexi-mesh and steel bars gave the area an unearned industrial feel with a side order of heightened paranoia. He quickly found the anonymous toughened barrier he wanted.

Tolbert knocked, then kicked the door with a loud metallic gong.

To his surprise, it popped open.

*Wow. I didn't expect Marco's trick to actually work.*

Tolbert cautiously entered and wasn't surprised at the interior. The place looked unfinished, with raw wood floors and exposed brick face. However, it was devoid of human detritus—no one had added to the mess by leaving their belongings lying around.

*Around here, you don't know what critter is going to drag away your possessions if they're not nailed down.*

The furniture was obviously secondhand, but serviceable. The only complaint the officer had was the sporadic lighting. Occasional lights plus a few blinking strings from last Christmas did not cut well into the nest of confusing hallways. Tolbert liked to see what might be coming for him. In this case, he suspected rats the size of dogs.

Tolbert moved in while ignoring filthy surroundings. He'd had to clean worse crap off his uniform than what was lying around here.

A short and sturdy bald fellow walked into the living room. A green Chinese water dragon tattoo adorned his scalp. He'd expanded it with an incongruous breath of flame from the dragon's mouth.

Tolbert was so, so close to explaining why that was inaccurate, but decided not to waste his time. The leader of "the Dragons" street gang probably thought it looked cool. It even matched the logo on the back of his leather jacket.

Zeng Nyugen raised his hand in a brief wave. "How you doing, Don?"

Tolbert nodded at him. "I'm good, Zeng." He looked over Zeng's shoulder, looking for the current leader of "*Los Tigres.*" "Where's your lesser half?"

Zeng shook his head. "Sleeping. He hasn't been right since he lost Vega back in September."

Tolbert frowned and looked at the shorter gang leader. When the hospital that Robert Catalano ran had been blown up by the demonic suicide bomber, he didn't recall Hector Vega being among the deceased. "Really? Was Hector lost in the hospital bombing? I hadn't heard."

Zeng shook his head. "We lost *Vega* in an attack in the sewers before the hospital thing happened. He was on spears and got too close to the Molotov cocktails when the vampires were lit up. He got cooked."

"Like I said, you lost Hector."

Zeng sighed. "No. We lost *Vega*, Hector's *cousin*. *Hector* is still running the gang. Such as it is."

Tolbert arched his brows. "Wait, you guys called him Vega, even though they have the same last name? Wouldn't that get confusing?"

"Nah. Everyone calls Hector … Hector, and his cousin was always Vega. Ever since he played *Street Fighter*." Zeng shrugged. "Though I guess it was a good thing for Hector that he lost his cousin."

Tolbert frowned. "Why?"

"Right before the attack, Hector was hitting on Amanda. Since his loss, no one has brought it up again."

The cop cringed. He had seen what was left of some of the human beings who had offended Marco. There was one particular YouTube video that left *him* cringing, mostly because Marco *didn't* kill him. It would have been better for everybody if he had. The PA student had crippled a large, healthy college athlete. And all because of a random stranger that Marco had decided to protect. Tolbert didn't want to see what would have happened to Hector if Marco chose to come to *Amanda's* defense.

"You know that Marco is actually back in town, don't you?" Tolbert asked.

Zeng cringed and took a step back. "Does he know I helped you guys in the whole hospital attack last month?"

Tolbert nearly laughed. The *next* attack on the hospital had taken place with a collection of vampire minions, armed to the teeth with full-on military gear, including rocket-propelled grenades. The NYPD had to call out its own heavy weaponry to finally finish the attackers. Zeng had been vital to the defense by throwing his own Molotovs from the top of the building across the street. "I don't think I even told him that *I* was involved. He's spent the last few weeks since in his own hospital bed, and only got released in the past day or two."

Zeng gave a weak smile. "Is he still scary, you think?"

"You want to bet against it?" Tolbert took off his hat and put it in the crook of his arm. "But now that he's back, I figure trouble will be hot on his heels. And from what I've heard, we're going to need to be prepared."

# Chapter 12
# Love In The Ruins

Amanda smiled as she walked through the night air, almost skipping along the street outside of Central Park. Marco said he was going to scout ahead and be back in a few minutes. But she didn't care. She liked knowing that life would get so much more interesting with him. As she unclipped her cell phone from her belt, the damn thing slipped out of her grip and slammed on the pavement.

She sighed at the Nokia. "Stupid Japanese crap." She muttered to herself as she bent down to pick up the phone from the sidewalk.

As she bent over, she felt a blazing heat streak across her back. The mailbox ahead of her spontaneously exploded and vaporized.

"*Blyad!*" she swore, feeling the fire on her back. She dropped her legs and allowed herself to fall flat on her back, putting out the small line of flames.

Amanda rolled to her feet, scanning the area. She almost instantly found the source.

A vampire built like Mikhail the Bear.

Unlike the now-totally dead vampire, this was … something else. He looked handsome and suave, almost as if he were a dark angel. He had black hair, matching eyes, and a chin so strong he could use it to break blocks. The man exuded sensuality. Except for one distinct scar marring his face— an old crescent-shaped wound, like a bite mark in his cheek.

He wore black pants, boots and a top that looked like a Tsarist cloak meets *GQ* magazine. The devil had stumbled into Armani and gotten a makeover— apparently, the Devil had given up Prada. Normally, Amanda's first thought would have been that she was in trouble—if this thing could cast fireballs that vaporized mailboxes, taking her out wouldn't be all that much harder.

But it was much worse when he spoke her birth name.

"Hello, Alina," he said in a deep, melodic voice…and in Russian.

He cocked his head and smiled. No amusement touched his cold black eyes. Amanda had seen eyes like that in the bottom of her Christmas stocking one year when she had been a bad girl. There were still whites to his eyes, but little else offset the darkness.

"So," he said, in a voice as cold as the ninth circle of Hell, "we meet again. Funny, considering how long it's been since we last met, I'd think you would have become a little more…intimidating."

Amanda smiled, trying to look casual as she leaned against a wall with one hand. She grabbed a vile of holy water with her other hand. "Only because you have not seen me in formal wear."

*I hope his reflexes are not very good…besides, if those fireballs were so easy to make, why didn't he try again after the first one missed? The question, of course, becomes: how did he make that one?* "It is good to see you are still alive, Misha. I wanted to kill you myself."

He smiled broadly. "You remember me!"

"You are hard to forget. However, last time we met, you did not look anywhere near this handsome, *mudak.*"

Misha smiled at the insult. "You may call me *god.*"

Amanda didn't remember the delusions of grandeur. *Wow, and some call Marco a narcissist.*

He grinned, and slowly spread his hands wide, obviously ready for another attack. Amanda's cell phone buzzed again, and he flinched. A very large hole appeared where the cell phone used to be.

The instant he flinched, Amanda grabbed her phial of holy water and flung it at his head. The "god" didn't even blink as he looked at the sidewalk, and a pebble went up and intercepted the tube in midair, and crushed it.

"Oh, crap." Amanda flung herself to the side as Misha sent the next pebble at her. The impact against the wall where her head had been turned a portion of the brick to powder

Amanda rolled to her knee in a crouch, twisted, flung a stake at Misha, and then pushed off her feet into a run.

The stake flew past her ear, as she expected, and she also expected to hear the rush of a fireball coming for her. Instead, bricks from the buildings on either side of her exploded out from their moorings and came at her. The crossfire of bricks looked like Indiana Jones trying to escape from the poison darts at the opening of *Raiders of the Lost Ark*.

*Well, it could be worse.*

As she charged for Central Park, several trees exploded into thousands of tiny razor-sharp toothpicks and headed straight at her. *Nuts.*

She instinctively jumped, knowing that there was no way in hell she could dodge any of those needles. She closed her eyes, hoping that she would at least make for a very pretty pincushion....

Then she landed on the ground.

On her feet.

She blinked. *I do not think I could have done that a day or two ago…Wow, as Marco would say, now I can leap over tall buildings in a single bound. And now, for faster than a speeding bullet…*

She tested that theory as the street exploded behind her in a rain of dust and concrete. *May the road rise up to meet you… What do Irish think with that blessing?*

Pieces of curb rose up to meet her. She dropped and rolled as they crashed into one another, turning into concrete dust.

She needed time. A machine gun might have helped too.

*I have to change tactics; this is going nowhere. He can make trees explode, but can't make me explode… could it be because I'm wearing a cross? Or could he do anything else to me directly? Or does he need to throw things at me, like fireballs? And do I want to get close enough to find out?*

*Maybe I can force the issue.*

Amanda's eyes fell on a nearby building in the park, and she banked left, narrowly missing a telephone pole that had been harpooned at her. She leaped up— narrowly avoiding a manhole cover that would have cut her legs off— and flipped over the rail iron fence. She promptly ripped off one of the iron rails.

*How to force close-quarters combat…move into closer quarters.*

She ran for the Central Park Zoo.

And almost into Marco.

Marco spun around and caught Amanda before she fell. "Where's the fire? I was just about to call you. I think I have two potential bloodsuckers for us to kill. I mean, geez. Don't these people ever *learn*? I know Giuliani left town, but it's not like the rest of us have."

He looked at the iron rail in her hands. "Something wrong, darling?"

Amanda smiled wryly. "Someone wants to kill me. You?"

The blond smiled an annoying little smile. "Not yet. But the evening is young."

The ground vibrated where Misha hit the concrete behind them. The huge vampire smiled. "A human, how nice. They are so amusing, aren't they, Amanda?" he boomed.

Marco narrowed his eyes at him. "Oh really? I try to oblige."

Misha stepped forward. "Then be good little boy and run. I need to kill this." He smiled. "I'll catch up with you later, Marco Catalano."

Marco nodded, wondering exactly how that this creature knew who and what he was. The voice wasn't familiar though. He sighed and reached into the back of his belt. He pulled out a flask and unscrewed the top.

Both Misha and Amanda looked at Marco askance.

"You don't drink," she said.

Marco's smile became a smirk. "For this, I'll make an exception." He took a sip. He offered to Amanda. "Drink?"

She smiled. "I generally do not drink … wine."

Marco turned to Misha. "You?"

"Vodka."

Marco shrugged.

Misha jabbed at Amanda. She lifted the rail to intercept it, and the fist struck it like a gong going off, leaving knuckle imprints in the bar. Amanda spun, slamming the blunt end of the rail into Misha's face. Misha barely blinked, instead grabbing the bar and ripping it out of her grasp. He turned back to her and lashed out with a fist. Instead of dodging, Amanda closed inside the swing and braced for the impact—she swore it broke something when it landed. She unleashed an uppercut into his nose that would have driven it out the back of a normal person's head. Misha's nose didn't crack, but his head snapped back. Amanda followed with a headbutt and a hammer blow into his ribs.

Misha grabbed her by the throat and lifted her off the ground. He smiled. "You at least have style."

The entire battle was over in an eye blink.

Marco threw the contents of the flask at Misha.

The vampire only realized he was in trouble when he barely had enough time to lean back. The water splashed on his chest.

The left side of Misha's chest burst into flames.

Misha screamed in agony, the roar coming through like an avalanche of pain as his body went up in a blaze. He reached behind with his right hand and pulled out a knife that looked like a short sword. He jammed the edge of the blade down into his collarbone and down to his hip.

He literally cut off the areas splashed with holy water. They fell to the ground, going up in flames.

Misha staggered back, dissolving into mist.

By the time he had reformed into a whole person, Marco and Amanda were gone.

"And that's why I carry holy water in a flask," Marco said with a smile as he settled back into the seat on the subway car.

Amanda gave him a slight smile as she cuddled against him.

"Did you hear me? I think we should call Merle."

The redhead nodded slowly, thoughtfully, looking out the window of the train as the lights in the subway raced past. Amanda sighed deeply, so much so that she emptied all the air in her lungs and forgot to refill them.

Marco raised a brow, then put an arm around her shoulders, hugging her against him. "There a problem?"

Amanda looked at him with tired eyes. "Yes. There is. I do not think… not now, Marco."

He nodded slowly, wary about what his love was capable of. He had also noticed the bite mark on the vampire's cheek, remembering something that Amanda had once mentioned to him. The only scar a vampire ever took on from a non-holy object was the wound they had used to turn a human being into a vampire.

*Amanda became a vampire by biting the one who'd tried to kill her.*

They had just come face to face with the vampire who had made Amanda what she was.

Amanda's eyes went dead as she looked out of the windows. Her hands clenched and unclenched slowly. Each time she squeezed them so hard, her knuckles turned dead white.

Marco watched the fingers flex on his shirt and arched his brows. He had noted similar behavior right before he was ready to go ballistic on people.

He stroked her hair and went over the subway map in his head. "Can you wait a few stops," he whispered. "We'll stop off at a place in Brooklyn that should have some targets."

Amanda pressed her hand flat against his chest and whispered harshly, "I haven't felt like this in so long. I'm just so … angry."

Marco gave a short laugh. "I know, love. I know. I feel that way all the time. I'm sure we can find something dreadful and…"

Marco's voice petered out as the train came to a stop. The doors slid open, and a group of nine men came onto the otherwise empty train car, spotting both Marco and Amanda. The one on front smiled, revealing fang.

"Oh look," Marco drawled, "something dreadful."

"Look at what we have here," said a Brooklynite turned vampire. "You twoz need some help getting home? Cuz if youse knew— Wha da fuck?"

Amanda turned on them and growled. Marco looked over at her and grinned. She leaped at them, slicing off one of their heads with one hand and hurling some holy water with another. The vial she threw down a vamp's throat. A spin kick slapped the second vamp's head off its body, and an underhanded stake throw took out a third.

Amanda went through them like a buzzsaw.

She elbowed the last one in the eyes, driving him against one side of the car. "Bu—bu—chu're just a kid."

Amanda's eye twitched. "You think I wanted this? Wanted to be a monster who drinks blood? You know how long I had to hunt down criminal scum so I could feed on them?" She grabbed his head in both hands and proceeded to bash his skull in against the window of the moving train. "You think I want to be hunted my entire fucking life, you *sukynsin? Mudak!*"

Marco watched as Amanda pounded the vamp's skull into the window until it cracked, and then his head went through the window. A passing metal girder caught his skull, ripping his head off.

As the body disintegrated, Amanda braced herself against the window frame, nearly falling against it.

Marco's gentle touch against her arm almost made her flinch. He lightly pulled at her arm, coaxing her away from the window. She slid into his embrace, wrapping her arms around him and holding him tight against her. Burying her face into his chest, she cried. He held onto her and said nothing.

He merely braced himself against the rocking of the train and kept her close.

# Chapter 13
# Call To Arms

The Church of Saint Anthony—Saint Alphonsus was a Catholic church in the midst of Greenpoint. Built in the 1850's, it looked like it could be the pinnacle of construction back then. It had a tall, 240-foot spire as black as iron that shot straight up to the sky, with a red brick face trimmed in white limestone. The inside was cavernous and Gothic, like the architect attempted to construct a small Saint Patrick's Cathedral in a space not half as large.

The pastor of this particular church was a slightly pudgy, older black man. His hair had not yet started to gray, but he was already mildly wrinkled. He had thick plastic frames for his glasses, even though the lenses were thin.

Monsignor Bill Rodgers sat back in his chair in the rectory, smoking a cheap cigar as he listened carefully to the Vatican Ninja across from him. The ninja was Captain Robert Hendershot, a generally colorless man, obviously Germanic in background. He talked with a light German-like accent; he was Swiss, and one of *the Guards*. Blond and blue-eyed, he kept his expression so neutral that Marco often muttered that Hendershot might as well have been a block of cheese. He also had quick muscle, not gym muscle… though he usually had enough heavy weapons on him that it must have added a hundred pounds to his frame.

"We are," Rodgers said in his booming voice, "of course expecting something else to come after Marco and Amanda, aren't we?"

Hendershot nodded. "We've transferred all of our people here. And as much equipment as we can. We've been building it up since we vanquished Nuala and Marco told us that we were going to be finishing this fight in New York."

"So, is he finally growing on you?"

Hendershot rolled his pale blue eyes and drank deeply of his coffee mug. "I do not like him. Or dislike him. He is useful. *Bram* likes him."

Ibrahim "Bram" Javaherian was the sniper for the Vatican Ninjas, and possibly the only one that Marco had ever gotten along with. Amanda got along well with most of them.

Hendershot set down the coffee and continued. "We have the silver ball hollow-points, the wooden bullets some use for practice rounds, the flamethrower, a few barrels of holy water. We've been in talks with Merlin Kraft's own SpecOps team about getting a few other toys."

Rodgers nodded. "Good. I want to be prepared for anything to go wrong. We've been lucky so far."

Hendershot scoffed. "We were prepared."

Rodgers shook his head. "No. We won solely through the grace of God. And luck. If the demon had been a little smarter in September, the angel wouldn't have come in, and we would never have survived."

Hendershot grunted, but said nothing, preferring to drink from his coffee mug. The demon who had called itself "Mister Day," really Asmodeus, had been forced out of its human host—by destroying the host—and manifesting as a physical being. Once the demon had tried to kill Marco, demon-to-person, Marco's guardian angel could step in, and he had trashed the demon like Superman punching a Thanksgiving parade balloon. Rodgers was right: had it thought a little more, it would have jumped hosts, and continued the battle until it was exorcised. Or had it not been so arrogant as to punch a tank filled with liquid nitrogen and destroying the host.

"But at least we were prepared for Nuala," the captain replied.

Rodgers scoffed down. "Really, Captain? Nuala escaped our trap. Had Marco not expected her to show up in his hospital room, he'd be dead, and she'd be in the wind by now."

Hendershot grimaced. The assassin Nuala had been problematic. But she'd been in a house sprayed down with holy water, riddled with wood, blown up, *and* staked in the heart, and somehow managed to survive by draining the life out of all of her minions.

That was cheating.

Hendershot and Rodgers heard their phones vibrate. It was a new text message, from Marco.

*New bad guy followed me home. Can we kill him?*

*Keep your heads on a swivel. The fun's about to start.*

New York City's One Police Plaza looked like an office building, even though it was home to the Police Commissioner of the NYPD.

On the top floor of 1PP, Police Commissioner Ray Wilson sat behind his desk. He sipped his Diet Pepsi, careful not to drench his bushy black mustache as he glanced at paperwork. A large, tall fellow, with a full head of dark hair, he was in his sixties, but he looked more mid-fifties. The average New Yorker took it for granted—from the vague hints in the bio on the NYPD website—that his conditioning probably had something to do with being Naval Intelligence in Vietnam.

Which most people read as: "I used to be a SEAL."

"Hello, Raymond," came an eloquent, silken-voiced woman from the door.

Wilson smiled and looked up from his desk. "Hi, Jen."

Jennifer Bosley primly walked into his office and took a seat.

Wilson actually grinned, despite his staff claiming he could not do so. The two of them had met during a murder investigation in the '70s. That was after he had returned from Vietnam, and had already had his own run-ins with the supernatural. As a police officer, there had been more than a few murder cases deliberately lost in a drawer because the killer had been reliably dealt with, off the books, by Jennifer.

He had taken it as a compliment when she compared him to a young, taller Teddy Roosevelt.

"Can I get you anything to drink? Or eat?"

Bosley shook her head. "Maybe later. I'm good for right now."

Wilson's smile grew broader and tighter. It was still genuine, as it reached his eyes. "Jen, how long have we known each other?"

She smiled "Forty years. Why?"

"Why do you insist on putting on the high-class accent? Or did you not think I'd noticed by now?"

Bosley gave a self-deprecating chuckle. "Because I like impressing you, love," she told him, letting her London accent slip through a little.

Wilson looked at her a moment, considering, thinking, and gave a little shrug. "I understand."

She smiled sadly. "No. I don't believe you do."

Commissioner Wilson rose from behind the desk, walked around, and turned the second desk chair facing her. He sat and took her delicate little hand in his massive paw. He looked her in the eye. "Yes. I do."

Bosley's usual mask slipped, and her face became a landscape of conflicting emotions. A grin, a grimace, tears, laughter, joy, and frustration. She settled on passive and looked to the hand that held hers. It was his right hand. She glanced to the left. The silver band that was still on his ring finger. "You're still wearing her ring. It's been ten years."

Wilson nodded slowly. "I know. Habit."

Without looking away from her, or taking his hand from hers, he used his thumb to slide his wedding ring off his finger. He slipped it into his jacket pocket. It was the first time Bosley had ever seen him without it on.

Bosley leaned forward for Wilson…

Her cell phone buzzed at the same time his did.

Bosley growled. Wilson sighed.

"Our jobs are both like that," he said.

"Yes. Only I don't like having to wait any longer than I have to." She pulled her phone out as he did the same.

Wilson frowned at his phone. "There's trouble in Central Park."

Bosley actually laughed. "And I know the cause."

Merle Kraft was leaning back in his recliner when his cell phone buzzed. With one hand, he kept reading his PC Gamer magazine, and with the other he absently pulled out his phone. His midnight blue eyes flicked to the text header: Marco.

*Aw crap.*

Merle sat up, and the recliner helped him up. He unlocked his phone and read the message.

*Any spare forces you may have would be appreciated. I think the vampire followed me home.*

Merle frowned. He started dialing immediately. "Yell-low."

"Marco, Kraft speaking."

Merle could almost hear the eye-roll from Marco. "You sound so formal, Merle. Why so serious?"

"Marco. What. Is. Happening?"

Marco sighed. "I think that the creature who was hunting me in San Francisco has *already* caught up to me. I guess he might have been on the next plane after mine."

There was a resounding discordance in the background, as well as what bore a great resemblance to an explosion.

Merle furrowed his brow. There had been no shout of pain or discomfort from Marco, so he had not been injured. If he was not the target but was having a discussion with Merle, then who was the source of the noise? "What's going on over there?"

"Oh," Marco said casually, "nothing of any import. Just a local problem. Listen, this vampire really doesn't seem to like us. He *definitely* doesn't like Amanda. If you have any assets on hand, locally, that would be nice. Is there any problem with that?"

Merle frowned and rose from the recliner, walking over to the window of the apartment. He stood behind George Berkeley, who kneeled on a pad with a set of binoculars. "I suppose not. Listen, Marco, about what we've come up with—" Merle broke off at the sound of a crash. "What the—"

"Oh, just a usual night in Brooklyn. Pay it no mind. How soon can you be here?"

"I'll see what I can do."

Merle hesitated. Marco had been a great help since the whole mess had begun. He had probably wiped out 90% of the vampires in San Francisco over the course of a few months, allowing Merle to continue in his role as "government agent for the strange." There hadn't been that many to start with, but the depopulation had been thorough, cutting off an impending boom at the knees.

Merle sighed. "Listen, Marco, there's a problem. Events are coming to a head. If this guy is related to our mutual problem, then it's possible he may act without warning."

"They usually don't send a memo in advance. Quite rude, I know, but what can you do with vampires?"

Merle frowned as he heard more screaming in the background. "Are you watching a horror movie back there?"

"No, my idea of horror is watching medical students on thirty-six-hour shift, realizing that they take three times as long as I do to do the same job. Are you making any arrangements as far as our mutual problem?"

Merle smiled. He knew that they were discussing the United Nations. "They're being put into place as we speak. I'll be certain to send some your way, all right?"

"Excellent. Now that that is attended to, Merlin, I must go. I shall see either you or your representative shortly. Night."

Merle Kraft turned off his cell phone. He stared out the window of the top floor of Tudor City apartments, directly across the street from the United Nations.

*If I took a private jet to come out here, and Marco flew commercial, what did the vampire take? Magic carpet? Flew? Maybe he took whatever Dalf uses for transportation? "The Speed of shadows," indeed.*

*But what was happening back there?*

When they got off the train, Marco had first placed a call to Jennifer Bosley, explaining the circumstances of the attack. Then he asked for any nearby problem spots of evil vampires that could be cleared out for the general good of humans and the New York City Vampires Association.

Bosley had one on hand.

To save the very long details, imagine a graveyard. Any graveyard, really. Then imagine a straight path of destruction. A literal straight line where crypt doors were ripped off hinges, then used to decapitate vampires. Headstones were used as projectile weapons, crosses had been pulled off graves and thrust into a vampire's chest. After nailing him to the ground, holy water had been poured into his open wound. Trees were felled so they could be used as clubs. Vampires still wailed in pain as they had all been impaled on the same gigantic cross. They slowly disintegrate while large portions of fence were ripped out and used pin six or seven vampires to the cement.

Or, to make this a shorter tale, Amanda had started killing at 10 pm, EST. Marco had simply sat back on a headstone, slipped a book from his back pocket, occasionally looking up to check on her progress.

Around 1 am, Marco was on his second book.

At about two in the morning, Amanda ran out of vampires and started to flail at headstones, infuriated and angry.

Marco slipped in a bookmark, closed the book, and came to her. He wrapped his arm around her waist and drew her to him. In the end, sooty, rumpled, blood smeared and slightly singed, she collapsed, crying in his arms.

Marco held her close, being as gentle as possible. "Come on. Let's get you home, shall we?"

"Damn it," she muttered. "I look like an idiot." She wiped her hands on her spattered white shirt. It was a good thing he really didn't mind the smell of blood.

He held onto her a little longer, and brushed some of her long, dark red golden hair into place "No, you look really sexy when you go all homicidal." He smiled, then kissed her temple. "What's wrong, darling?"

She looked at him, staring deep into his eyes. "I knew him."

Marco was about to joke and ask which vampire, but he knew, the vampire from central park. "Where from?" He suspected the answer, but even Marco thought that impressing her with his logic would not be wise right now.

"You know him, too."

He blinked. He had figured that there was a connection to the creature in San Francisco, but that one was ugly as Hell. "I do? I can't say that we've met.

He looked pretty darned normal to me. And for vampires of that power level, I'd have expected him to be as ugly as sin. That was a male model on acid."

She smiled sadly. "Marco, remember how vampires become closer to their souls after death?"

He nodded. "Yeah, that's why evil vampires look so damn ugly. It's the Dorian Gray effect, only the stains on the soul appear on the body. So?"

"It also allows better control over physical appearance." Amanda paused, looking over the area, just to be sure. "He is so powerful that he has that control. He can look however he wants."

Twenty seconds of silence. "The one who said he was Mikhail's brother. The guy I turned into a pincushion back in San Francisco. It's the same guy."

"*Da*, but he is also something else…he is the one who created me."

Marco nodded slowly. He had figured that much from the bite on his face. Marco kissed her on the head, then on both cheeks, then lightly on the lips. "God made you—quite well, I might add—and you made yourself into an agent in the army of God. All this idiot did was pick a fight he couldn't win. He supplied you with the blood that let you mold yourself into the woman that I love." He dipped her back and kissed her again.

"I guess I should thank him…otherwise, I would never have met you." He smiled weakly, then gave her waist a squeeze. "Just for that, I'll be certain to kill him as quickly as possible."

They boarded the train and sat together. Marco had one hand on Amanda's waist, the other on his book. As Marco read, he felt something on his side. Amanda leaned over, letting her breast rest on Marco's arm as she pressed her lips against his cheek, then on the lips, and held for what seemed like an extraordinary amount of time. After pulling away, she rested her head on his shoulder and fell asleep.

He looked at the sleeping vampire and finally took the time to examine her features in detail. Her face was relaxed in her state of deep sleep, her whiskey-dark eyes hidden behind her eyelids and red lashes. Her dark golden hair playfully swayed to and fro about her face in time with the motions of the train.

He allowed his searching gaze to fall on her lips, two pieces of pinkish-red silk sitting on her naturally pale skin. With her eyes hidden from view, her lips were easily her most becoming feature. She seemed too young, but he wasn't about to say she looked too innocent. After seeing what she was capable of, "innocent" did not come to mind. No matter how angelic she looked while she slept…or when she was awake.

But then again, it wasn't like he cared about the ripped sleeve, or the blood stains. Marco loved her, and he hadn't joked about how cute she looked while completely homicidal.

They had never had an in-depth, detailed conversation about her being a vampire. Not about what was it like, or if she even enjoyed her afterlife as it was. He had never before suspected that she was unhappy with her undead status since she had done so much with her time on Earth. She smiled constantly, laughed like the lightest of Mozart's music, went to the movies with him. Amanda was the liveliest woman he had ever met and didn't know anyone who loved life more.

Basically, as far as he knew she was always happy and optimistic for as long as *he* had known her…

…For as long as *he* had known *her*…

…or as long as *she* had known *him*.

Marco blinked. *How long has she been in love with me?*

# Chapter 14
# Thou Shalt Not Pass

January 5th

Marco and Amanda walked onto his street; his good left arm hooked in her right elbow.

As they turned the corner onto the street, something large and fast fell off a roof and dropped right on to Marco, slamming him to the concrete. Marco's arm went up defensively. Sharp jaws, like a vise with sharp teeth, bit into his forearm. The creature pulled back on his arm, tearing into the skin and meat of his arm. Claws raked his chest and stomach.

Marco thrust down his arm so he could get a better look at what attacked him.

A wolf clamped its jaws over his arm. Bits of his skin and jacket fluff were trapped between its teeth. Marco winced. The thing's breath bothered him more than the carnage. Strangely detached, it felt like watching a monster movie focused on his left arm.

He blinked.

Amanda was on the wolf in that instant. She grabbed its snout in one hand and the lower jaw in the other. It took more than a few seconds to pry the jaws open—ripping it off of Marco would have ruined his already savaged arm.

When Amanda got a good grip, she pulled the wolf's jaws open with a crack, hyperextending and dislocating the lower jaw so its mouth hung open like a ruptured mail box. She hauled it up off Marco and twisted its neck hard and fast. It wasn't a simple break, but a full *Exorcist* twist, shattering the spine. She lifted it up by the jaws, and whipped it around, slamming it, lengthwise, onto an iron fence, topped with iron spikes, deliberately puncturing the spine at several points.

"Bad dog," she said. "Stay."

The wolf continued to thrash and buck and growl, even though it should have been dead three times over already.

Amanda reached down, took Marco by the arm, and lifted him to his feet.

And he was a mess. The front of his heavy, winter jacket had been ripped into a mass of bloody shredded nylon and cotton batting. Through the jagged remains of the jacket, she could see claw marks down his chest and stomach.

She gingerly grabbed an undamaged section of his hand on the injured arm and lifted it, peeling off the sleeve of the winter jacket. "Let me see."

The sleeve lay in tatters, and the forearm was a bloody mess, covered in blood from fingertip to elbow. Tufts of lint from the jacket stuck to the gore.

"Inside, now."

Marco nodded and said nothing. He stumbled as Amanda pulled him along. Looking back at the still thrashing wolf, impaled on the spikes of the fence, and said, "Well, that's something you don't see every day."

"Vampires can command animals to do virtually anything," Amanda muttered as she led him up the front steps to his door. "Even Stoker knew this. I'm surprised no one has tried it sooner."

Marco's omnipresent smile flickered back to life through the daze. "Probably because wolves can't carry machine guns. Though I'm surprised Igor only sent one wolf."

Amanda reached into Marco's pocket for the front door key. She got the door open, led him through the front door, and up the stairs straight to his room. The front hall light was on, but if anyone else was there, Amanda couldn't tell right now. All of her focus was on Marco.

She looked around the spartan accommodations of his room. Book cases lined the walls, each one jammed so tightly with books that the shelves had warped. Marco was big on function, as were his parents.

She took him by the shoulders and put his back to the bed. Carefully sliding the coat off of him, she made sure he didn't drip any blood on the floor. She ripped the ruined sleeve off and tossed it in the garbage can at the foot of his bed. Then she folded the relatively clean part, blood-side in. She tore off his shirt—which was a bright orange shirt that had read "I have to think to myself: It's not worth the jail time"—and threw that away as well. The only thing covering Marco's upper body was a chain with a gold cross and a Miraculous Medal.

Amanda took a step back and gasped as she saw the full extent of Marco's chest wounds. She could see muscle in some spots, bone in others, and others were just lines of blood.

There was an awkward silence as she looked at his bloody body. It was surprisingly more toned than she remembered. His muscles were so well defined, the rivulets of blood had flowed down and dried in the lines between them.

"Have you been working out?" she asked.

Marco looked at her and nearly laughed. "Nice timing. No. Not any more than usual. I've spent the last few weeks in a hospital bed, remember?"

"Lay back," she ordered. "I will wrap your wounds, and we can work on the rest later."

Marco nodded and didn't say anything for a moment. He merely looked at his arm and his chest, covered in blood. "Well, this isn't great."

"I know. It is bad. I am sorry, I should have gotten to it faster."

Marco shook his head. He reached for his nightstand, grabbing an old, partially empty water bottle. "That's not the problem. My arms feel fine. *Both* arms. It's almost as if…"

With both hands, he carefully opened the water bottle, then moved to the garbage can. He poured the water on his forearm, making sure it ran into the can.

He raised his arm and displayed it so she could see. The bite marks were no longer bleeding but clotted. They both stayed there, watching, over the next five minutes, as they scabbed over, then scarred over, then faded.

Marco winced, as though he was only *now* in pain, and reached for the chain around his neck with both hands, carefully moving it from around his neck, and dropped it on the bed. The silver chain with the

Miraculous Medal on it had left a burn mark all the way around his neck, down to his chest.

He looked down at his check, then at the points on his fingers where he touched the silver chain. His blinked slowly, sadly.

"I'm allergic to silver," he flatly stated. "My muscle tone has improved since I put the shirt on this morning. I heal supernaturally fast. And I was just bitten by a wolf not more than ten minutes ago."

He looked at Amanda and met her eye. "But I don't *want* to be a furry."

Amanda rushed to his side and took him by the shoulders. She stared into his eyes and shook him a little, keeping his focus on her. "It does not need to be a bad thing. George Berkeley is a lycanthrope. *He* does not turn into a monster."

Marco raised one eyebrow, and his smile became wry. "Really? Lycanthropes don't turn into the thing that bit them; they turn into the predator that best reflects their dark side, right?"

Her hopeful expression fell. "Yes."

"And George Berkeley … the big, laid-back fellow who never gets angry … He turns into an Irish wolfhound." He nodded slowly. "Do either one of us want to guess what *I'm* going to turn into when the moon rises?"

Amanda flinched, thinking over the moments when Marco had let her see the darker sides of his nature. The side of his nature which was sadistic and homicidal. "Oh. Yes. That… No. No, not really."

"Yeah. Exactly." He sighed slowly and shook his head. He clapped her on the bicep. "Oh, well. Step one, we find out how bad this can get. Step two, we consider a cure. Although that should probably be step two and three, right after finding the current vampire and offing the son of a bitch."

Marco slid his arms around Amanda, and hugged her close, ignoring the water and drying blood covering his chest and arm. As he buried his nose in her hair, breathing her in, he muttered, "Well, one good thing: We know that you've grown more powerful in multiple ways. At the cemetery, you were faster than almost every vampire we've met. I guess loving me might actually make you better."

Amanda lingered in Marco's embrace for another minute and then pulled back just enough to look at him. She studied him a moment, her eyes flicking back and forth in his gaze as though trying to find something. "Merle came to meet me a while ago."

He furrowed his brow, confused. "Oh?"

"He said something similar to what you did." She gave a short laugh. "I also think he wanted someone to talk vampyres with while *not* blowing up their hangouts."

Marco rolled his eyes. He scrunched up his face in thought and scanned the room, looking around Amanda.

Amanda tried to follow his gaze and figure out what he was doing. "What is it?"

"Hmm." He ran his fingers through her hair, and gently placed her cheek against his chest. "Marriage is basically consecrated love," he began, half to himself. "JPII made a point out of canonizing married couples. After all, marriage is on par with Holy Orders as a sacrament. Right?"

Amanda didn't bother to correct him. With her arms around his naked, supernaturally toned chest, and with the threat of him turning into a furry, four-legged killing machine the next time the moon was full, she wasn't up for a theological discussion. Terror, concern, love and passion burned in her, conflicting with one another.

Marco kept looking, and stepped around her, barely letting go of her until he stepped past her. He went to the nightstand, pulling out the drawers and sliding them back almost immediately.

She stared at his naked back as though he was insane. Which wouldn't be new for her. "What are you doing?"

"I do my Christmas shopping all year round," he told her, still searching. "And last year, before I knew I was leaving for San Francisco, I bought something that will do some double duty. I purchased it in the name of friendship, but it'll do."

Marco pulled out something in his fist and walked towards her. He stood ramrod straight, as though on the parade ground. But he moved in flowing, almost dance-like movements. "I wasn't joking earlier about your powers being connected to how close you are to someone. And, I wasn't joking last month either, in the hospital bed."

Amanda wrinkled her nose in a manner that Marco found adorable. "I do not recall you making many jokes. You were also under heavy sedation."

"Let me remind you of this one then." Marco dropped to one knee, and in one smooth motion, flipped over a ring box. He presented her with a Claddagh ring, gold with a green marble heart… made from Irish marble, just like his rosary.

Amanda took a step back, as though she'd been struck. Her eyes widened, her jaw dropped, and her hands came up in a "slow down" gesture.

Marco merely continued, "Alina Savinkova … do I need to even fill in the blanks on this one? The knee and the ring should give it away, I'd think."

Amanda squeezed her eyes shut and shook her head forcefully. "No—what? No. Marriage? Why? How can you ask that? We haven't yet—we should start—we should consider—"

Marco let her ramble on for another minute before he held up his empty hand. "Amanda, love, stop. You've been speaking in Russian since I got down on one knee. Do you want me to make it official? In which case, Alina Savinkova, will you—"

"Stop," she said clearly, in English this time. She stepped forward and grabbed both of Marco's hands. Closing them around the ring box, she pulled him to his feet. "Marco, we've only just started … us, and you want to propose?"

Marco chuckled. "Actually, I was going to wait so we settled in and no longer had all the impulse control of rabbits in heat. Igor's threat only encouraged me to move up my timetable."

Amanda stared at him, incredulous. His deep blue eyes were calm and clear, and strangely sane. "Are you hoping this is a power upgrade, like a video game?"

Marco blinked. "Um. No. I'm saying that I want to get the proposal in before we're under mortal danger yet *again*." He frowned and looked down at the remaining blood stains on his healed body. "Also, I'd like to propose sometime before I become really hairy."

Amanda followed his eyes down to his naked chest and swallowed. She blushed. "I am going to throw some water on my face. I believe I am covered in vampire remains."

He shrugged. "Gotcha," he said absentmindedly. "I should probably check the load-out. I had some of the ninjas assemble a package for me."

She closed the door behind her.

Marco shrugged, and went to work, his laser-like focus turned to the room. He took his gym bag out of the closet, removing wooden throwing knives, sheaths, and his dress sword from the Xavier High School Junior ROTC. He double-checked the tape on his stakes, to make sure the firecrackers were still attached. Carefully, he strapped sheaths to his forearms, calves, ankles, and assembled the full body sheath. It had slots for knives at the neck and shoulders.

He looped the neck piece over his head and slipped on a fresh shirt on over it so he could attend to the shoulders. He removed a large Snapple bottle of holy water, checked the load on the squirt guns, and slipped them into the small of his back. Then he removed a box, carefully padded on the inside, and checked his load of nitroglycerin in vials.

Marco moved through his weapon assortment thoughtfully, thoroughly, efficiently, and elegantly.

A female voice spoke from the ether, heavy with a Russian accent. "So you do this every day?" Yana's voiced asked.

Marco rolled his eyes and didn't even turn around this time. He started loading the next weapon. "Has anyone ever told you that you're annoying, Igor?"

The projected image of Yana, the vampire Misha, leaped onto his bed as though sitting on the edge. "One, you know that is not my name. Two, no, I never cared enough."

Marco frowned. "But you care about me?" he inquired, loading some more.

"The thing is, I'm not sure what you are. Trust me. I've known everything, seen everything, but not you."

He chuckled. "You've got to get out more. They call me a man."

Misha / Yana leaned forward. "Don't you want to know why I tried so hard to kill you? Why we've *all* been trying so hard to kill you?"

Marco didn't visibly react, but that had been nagging on him for some time. The amount of disproportionate force sent after him in San Francisco had been staggering. "You're part of the Council. Come to think of it, you're probably all that's left of the Council. Though I'm certain that revenge is part of it."

"Her" eyes lit up. "Oh, more than that. I intend to use you." The image of the young, redheaded "witch" bounded off the bed and bounced over to Marco's side. "Her" voice was low and conspiratorial. "You don't believe in your own limits, so they don't apply. You make your own pathetic reality. Then you *enforce* this reality on the rest of us."

Marco rolled his eyes. Bosley and Amanda had talked about him doing something similar. "It's called adapting."

"Oh no," the image said, "that's where you're wrong. You had it right the first time, when you said you are whatever you need to be. You are. That's been our problem. And soon, it will be everyone else's problem."

Before it could say another word, Marco charged out of his room, rammed the door with his shoulder and swept down the stairs, gym bag in hand. He drew the weapon and leveled it at the door of the brownstone seconds before it broke open.

Marco stood at the top of the stairs and fired.

The first bullet went through the minion's shoulder and slammed into the chest of the one behind him. That impact knocked the second minion into the third.

Marco readjusted and fired again, the bullet passing through the shoulder of the second minion, obliterating the collarbone of one, and crushing the one behind him.

The fourth minion shoved them all aside, coming up with an Uzi. He wheeled around the door to the brownstone, pressing himself up against the wall just between the door and the stairs.

Marco fired through that as well, punching through the walls and slamming into the minion's body armor. It knocked him back, spilling out onto the stoop outside.

Marco leaped over the railing, landing on one knee on the floor of the hall. He fired again, dropping the final minion.

Marco lowered the gun. At his side dangled a fifty-caliber Desert Eagle semi-automatic with a sound suppressor attached.

# Chapter 15

# Dark Knight Of The Soul

Amanda flew down the stairs and stopped halfway down. She stared at the love of her afterlife and gaped. He stood in the doorway, gun pointed straight down.

Instead of being horrified at the bodies on the floor, or anything clichéd, she stared at the hand cannon and said, "Where did you get that!"

Marco looked up. "Oh, this?"

Before he could say anything more, several figures burst from the living room entrance down the hall.

Marco nearly whirled on them and started blasting but paused. "Damn it, where the hell have *you* people been?"

The three men rolled their eyes and put away their guns. One wore a police uniform, another a three-piece pinstripe suit, and the third the dark blue and green of the Vatican Ninjas.

Enrico, the mafia enforcer, thrust his suit jacket over his shoulder holster. "Next time, can we shoot *him?*"

The Vatican Ninja, Captain Hendershot, with his blond hair, blue eyes, and face like it was chiseled from rock, gave a simple nod. "*Ja.*"

The police officer, a tall black man named Donald Tolbert, shook his head. "Don't even joke, fellas."

Hendershot looked at the cop. "Who was joking?"

Marco scoffed. "He's Swiss. He has no sense of humor." He looked down at the minions again and holstered his gun. "Come on, we have a problem."

He kicked the guns away from the minions before he grabbed the first minion by a wrist and an ankle. He dragged him outside, and, with strength born of adrenaline and his werewolf bite, hurled him into the middle of the street.

Even Amanda furrowed her brows, confused at what he was doing. Marco came back inside and grabbed another minion. "The minions in San Francisco were so overcharged by their vampire that they literally exploded when they died."

Amanda was immediately by his side. She hurled two of the bodies into the middle of the street like they were flowers.

Officer Tolbert looked over Marco's head, looking out into the street. "Should I even ask why—" Tolbert was cut off as two of the bodies started to glow internally and erupted into a white-hot ball of fire that consumed the middle of the street.

Marco turned back. "And I'm serious, where were you people? Whenever the ninjas are here, this house is like a fortress. I was attacked outside."

Hendershot gave him a look like a dead fish. "There was a disturbance in a nearby graveyard. I sent my men to recon."

Marco and Amanda shared a look that quite clearly said, "Oops."

Enrico nodded. "And when you said there was a problem I came over immediately. So did Officer Tolbert. We've been here for hours."

Marco winced. He had sent those texts around 10 o'clock. If they had shown up immediately, they really had been waiting for hours. "Why didn't you guys text me back?"

"We texted Amanda," Tolbert answered. "She can hear the texts arrive even when the phone is on mute. Didn't you get any of them?"

"My phone is now slag," she answered. "Destroyed after Misha showed up."

"Who?" Enrico asked.

"Long story," she answered. She looked back to the gun in Marco's hand. "Again, when did you get that? How did you get it here?"

Doctor Robert Catalano walked out of the living room, polishing his glasses. "I would like to know that as well."

Marco gave a happy little finger wave. "Hi, Dad."

Robert slid his glasses back on, and narrowed his gaze at Marco, pointedly ignoring the bullet holes in the wall. "Don't 'Hi, Dad' me, young man. You were attacked hours ago, you called in the cavalry, and then you disappeared. I thought you were dead."

Marco winced. "Sorry."

Robert sighed and shook his head. "The gun?"

Marco shrugged. "I asked the ninjas and George send me some supplies. I was hoping to keep it a surprise. Mikhail's brother was chatting with me. I figured he would strike before anyone could react." He shuffled uncomfortably and moved his holstered weapon to the small of his back. "He's obviously got more minions."

"Uh huh." Marco's father looked down at fire consuming the middle of the street. "Can we close the door before we let all the heat out?"

Marco moved to close the door when two more men in combat gear jogged up to the front door. The first one was tall and redheaded, and the other was Persian.

Marco grinned. "Hey, Bram, Tim."

Ibrahim "Bram" Javaherian nodded at Marco as he came up the stairs and stopped when he saw the bullet holes. "Huh. You guys start the party without us?"

Timothy Dougherty frowned, and said in a lyrical brogue "Well, that wasn't very nice, now was it?" He jerked his thumb down the street. "Though it explains the werewolf we found impaled on a fence. Is there a reason no one finished it off?"

"No silver," Marco answered. "Also—"

"A werewolf?" came a new voice behind Marco.

The PA student didn't even look over his shoulder. "Yes, Father Rodgers, a werewolf."

The old priest laid a hand on Marco's shoulder and tugged gently so that Marco would face him. "You were bitten by a werewolf?"

Dougherty and Bram stopped halfway up the stairs, and everyone else became still. Even Enrico winced.

Marco looked around at them as though they were all crazy. "Guys, it's not like I just got a terminal diagnosis. George is a lycanthrope. He seems to be doing okay. And unless I turned into Godzilla, locking me up three nights a month shouldn't be that bad."

"But that's him," Rodgers said by way of an explanation. "Maybe we should take this in another room."

Rodgers guided Marco into the front room, and Marco took a seat at the coffee table. He leaned back in the chair and watched the priest move into the room. Rodgers closed the door behind him, taking the couch.

Marco could only ponder the dire news that would be coming his way if the priest felt he had to separate them from the rest of the household.

"So, tell me how bad you think this is?" Marco asked.

The ninjas and the vampire moved the corpse outside, into the backyard, so that no one could see the human side of the dead werewolf.

As they wandered into the primary living room, the mafia enforcer just hung up his phone. He looked to them with his calm brown eyes and said, "I've got some people coming over who specialize in body disposal. The werewolf will be fertilizer shortly."

Bram nodded. "Thanks."

The ninja-sniper took a seat in one of the cloth-covered chairs. "It's nice to not have to bury more of those guys. Nuala's minions were tough enough as it is."

Enrico scoffed. "No kidding." He settled onto the couch off to the side of the room. "How did he get bit by a werewolf?"

"It jumped from off the roof," Amanda explained. "And landed right on him."

Robert Catalano, seated behind his desk, leaned forward, fingers interlinked, elbows on the table. He looked at Amanda with dark, piercing eyes. "Now, before anyone goes any further, I want someone to tell me exactly how bad this werewolf thing can get. I only know what I read about and see in the movies."

Enrico held up both hands as though surrendering to the police. "Don't look at me, I have no idea what's going on with that. Closest I've ever gotten to a werewolf is the movie theater. Or, as Miss Bosley would say, *the cinema.*"

The doctor looked around the room, and not even the ninjas wanted to volunteer information. Dougherty hadn't entered the room yet. He deliberately hung back in the hallway so he wouldn't have to answer. Even Bram, who had the best relationship with everyone, inched away. Hendershot, strangely enough, started looking at the walls, floor, and ceiling, deliberately avoiding the doctor's gaze.

After another beat, Robert leaped to his feet, slammed his fist on the desk, and bellowed, "*What is going to happen to my son?*"

Everyone in the room jumped, and Enrico's hand instinctively went to the butt of his gun.

Amanda looked at Robert, seeing only a tiny glimmer of Marco's temper. She sighed and took a deep breath. This was going to be a difficult conversation no matter how she spun it. Even the best case scenario was fairly hairy, and she didn't even think of it as a pun.

"He may not turn into a wolf," she began.

Robert's eyes locked on her. "Explain."

"This isn't a specific medical condition. It's mystical, magical, metaphysical. The infected host modifies the disease."

Robert settled down, slowly lowering himself into his seat. "Much like the virus that makes you a vampire."

Amanda raised her hand parallel to the floor and waggled it. "A little. My actions form who I am, and makes my powers grow or lessen depending on how I act. Lycanthropy manifests differently.'"

Robert's eyes narrowed. "Obviously. You don't uncontrollably turn into a four-legged beast."

Amanda braced herself. She was obviously obfuscating. "The point is that lycanthropy doesn't turn you into the type of creature that bit you. I believe George Berkeley—one of Merle's people—was bitten by a feline were of some sort. He changes into an Irish wolfhound. From what I have seen, a very well-behaved one."

Robert's mouth tightened. "So what *does* matter?"

"The creature the infected changes into is the one that best reflects the person's dark side."

Robert's eyes widened for a moment, then he grimaced. "Oh. I can see where that might be a problem when it comes to Marco. Are we sure we can't just lock him in a silver cage every full moon?"

She flinched. "It is not that simple."

Father Rodgers lit a cigar and patiently drew on it. He let it out slowly, blowing the smoke away from Marco. This was going to be delicate, no matter what Marco thought he knew.

"You know you're not going to turn into something soft and cuddly like George," Rodgers began.

Marco's little Scaramouche smile lengthened a bit. "No? You think?" he drawled sarcastically. "Again, lock me up three nights a month. I'll live."

Rodgers sighed and shook his head. He had to stop being delicate about this. "You only think this is easy because it is for George. I presume he hadn't told you about his own experience."

Marco shrugged. "Never asked. I figured it was his personal issue, and I wouldn't pry unless invited."

Rodgers nodded. "Do you know how long he had been infected by the time you met him?"

"Months."

"He had the time to get this under control."

Marco gritted his teeth together, and his fists clenched. "Get *what* under control?"

"To start with, it's not just the full moon. This is going to affect your behavior all the time." His eyes narrowed, looking at Marco's tense posture. "Starting with limited to no impulse control."

Marco winced. He forced himself to relax, and his smile finally faded. It stayed gone, and he frowned, thinking it over. "This," he said thoughtfully, "could be a problem."

"It gets worse."

The little smile returned. "But of course it does," he snarked. "Now what? I get this uncontrollable urge to bite people?"

"No. But you're subject to control by other lycanthropes."

Marco's eyebrows arched, and he gave an amused scoff. "Seriously? It's hard to imagine that I'm *not* going to be an alpha."

Rodgers shook his head. He was going to actually have to penetrate Marco's ego. Marco didn't usually express one so much that it was actually a problem. "You don't understand. This has nothing to do with what animal you are, or how strong the animal is. It takes *months* for new lycanthropes to gain enough control over themselves to resist the slightest impulse or resist commands given by older, more experienced lycanthropes. You may be an alpha wolf, but even a beta with experience could give you commands."

Marco steepled his fingers and frowned. "I'm in trouble."

Robert Catalano held up a hand as he looked at Bram and Amanda, who had both finished telling him about the various and sundry problems of lycanthropy.

At this point, Enrico was the first person to speak up: "Your boyfriend's got an attitude that makes my hitmen look calm and relaxed, and he's going to turn into a creature that *reflects* that? And until he gets everything under control—something that takes *months*—he's going to be *more* impulsive, and subject to taking orders from other furries? And, oh, *our bad guy has his own furries*? Is there any *other* way this can get worse? Because I'm thinking there's nothing much worse than a powerful, supernatural monster with poor impulse control, who can be subverted by the other team at any point."

The entire room went quiet.

"That's not going to happen."

The room turned to look at Marco, standing in the doorway, Father Rodgers right behind him. He stepped into the room, his smile back in place. He stepped over to the couch, bent down, kissed Amanda on the cheek.

He breathed deeply, inhaling her scent … then cupped her chin in his hand, and kissed her deeply, right on the lips, in front of everyone.

Enrico shrugged and looked to Bram. "At least *that's* finally out of the way."

Marco slid in next to Amanda on the love seat. "That wasn't the lycanthropy talking, that was my announcement that we're together."

Robert smiled, despite himself. "Yes, we're all happy for you, but what about your new problem?"

Marco nodded. He was clearly happy that his father had asked the question. "Before we have that discussion, let's begin with a blessing. Monsignor?"

Rodgers nodded and reached into his pocket, pulling out a book.

Tolbert blinked, confused. "Wait, is that a thing now?"

Marco calmly explained, "Twice, this vampire has manifested an illusion in my room, once in San Francisco, once here. It was a full audio-visual interactive hologram and could *listen* as well as see. Which means that this guy could be eavesdropping on us right now. I figure a blessing is an easy jamming device. Call me paranoid."

Rodgers said a quick benediction. Then did another one, just to be safe. He slid the book away. "That should do it."

Marco nodded. "Step one, if I can be jerked around by an Alpha, it should be one of *our* alphas. I've sent

Merle Kraft a text message, and we'll see how fast George Berkeley can get here."

"That's one solution," Bram agreed, nodded. "And the impulse control?"

Marco opened his mouth to speak, then looked at Amanda, closed his mouth, and looked embarrassed. Amanda furrowed her brows, looking at him. Embarrassment wasn't one of Marco's typical traits.

"Everyone here has seen me survive a lot of things that I shouldn't have?" he asked.

Some nodded, some didn't. Enrico shrugged. "Not that I recall. Why?"

Marco sighed. He hated having to explain a concept that was so familiar to everyone else. "You had a run in with the minions last month, right?"

Enrico gave a humorless laugh. "They shot up my living room."

Marco nodded. "Exactly. Minions take more punishment, they survive more, they're stronger, faster, almost like fighting a vampire, only without the problems. Part of this involves a human being ingesting the vampire virus without actually being close to death—or without ingesting enough of the virus to turn them."

The mafia knee-breaker frowned. "What's that to do with you?"

"The virus is present in vampire saliva. Every time a vampire bites someone, the victim gets a fraction of the virus. It's why more people aren't killed when bitten by vampires—the more of the virus the victim absorbs, the more the victim can survive. Most of the time, I've had Amanda sample my blood before combat. It's probably the only reason I've survived half the stuff I have."

Enrico smiled. "Can we have some of that? I can think of some guys who would really like being that strong. Blood or saliva. Either way."

Bram cringed. "Normally, the saliva thing isn't usually recommended like some sort of performance-enhancing drug. It's not a steroid. It's a supernatural force. And the blood to make minions … there are a lot of side effects you don't want."

Robert cleared his throat, loudly. "Marco, what does this have to do with your problem?"

Marco smiled. "We treat the vampire virus as the methadone to my shapeshifter virus' heroin."

Robert laughed. "I hadn't seen that coming."

Captain Hendershot looked around the room, as even Enrico nodded. "What am I missing?"

The doctor laughed at him. "Methadone is used to treat heroin addiction because it competes with the same sites in the brain that heroin uses. If the vampire virus is in Marco's system at the same time as the lycanthropy virus, the two should fight each other. At the very least, the vampire virus should look at the competing virus and see it as something that doesn't belong in the new host."

Enrico snickered. "So that means she has to—"

Tolbert gave him a dirty look.

Marco looked at him and growled.

The mafia knee-breaker fell silent.

Amanda slapped Marco lightly on the arm. "Behave, Marco."

He chuckled. "Come on, I don't get to have *any* fun around here?"

Robert raised his hand, and waved it, drawing everyone's attention to him. "Pardon me for interrupting, but I think this is a little more urgent. First, the werewolf that bit him is still outside?"

Dougherty nodded. "Aye, sir, he is. At least his body is, we put a bullet in his head on general principles."

Amanda shook her head. "We could have interrogated him."

Marco took her hand in his and squeezed it. "Unlikely. We're talking about a lone wolf attack—" He winced at his own pun. "Pardon the expression. I can't imagine he was sent in with a goal of surviving.

If he said *Allahu Akbar* on his way to dusty death, I wouldn't be at all surprised."

Bram raised a brow. "How did you know that he had the ISIS logo tattooed on his shoulder?"

The doctor cleared his throat. "The *second* problem is simple: the next full moon is *tomorrow night*."

# Chapter 16

# Once Bitten

ithout a word, Marco took Amanda's hand and rose from the love seat, walking straight out the living room and upstairs. She didn't even hesitate to follow him, because she knew what he had on his mind. It was business, but it would be pleasurable enough.

Marco opened the door for her with his free hand and drew her into his bedroom before him. He closed the door, and they pulled each other closer, coming together in an embrace that would have appeared to an outsider that they were tackling each other. They kissed each other with an out of control passion that was less about his soon-to-be-furry medical condition, and more about unbridled impulse. Her arms wrapped around his neck, holding him to her lest he escape.

Marco's hands slid down her back, untucked her shirt, running both of his hands along her lower back. Amanda combed her fingers through his hair as her tongue penetrated his mouth and deepened the kiss.

Unlike the last time they had molested each other with this much fervor, their fronts were pressed against each other. Amanda had hardly noticed until they both started moving to the bed and found herself poked in the stomach.

Amanda gasped at the sensation. Marco growled, as though he was a car that had just revved its engine. But neither one pulled away as they fell onto the bed.

His mouth went to her neck as though he was going to devour her.

She started to pant. "I'm supposed to bite you. I *have* to bite you."

Marco growled. It was only slightly playful and mostly feral. "And I want to do more than that with you."

Amanda's fingers curled on his back, her nails just barely digging into his skin. He growled even more fiercely and pressed the length of his body against her. She groaned.

Amanda flipped Marco over, pinning him at the wrists as she straddled him. Her mouth shot to his neck and kissed and licked at his skin.

It was his turn to gasp. And then groan.

Then he felt the pinch.

Her fangs had slid into his carotid artery. She gave a contented little purr as her lips closed around the skin.

She didn't drink, but continuously ran her tongue over the punctures. This drove her saliva into his blood, and with it, the vampire "virus." She allowed herself to simply taste his skin.

He was hers. All hers.

As she felt Marco pressed against her, Amanda could only imagine being all his.

At the thought, her heart stopped, dead, for five seconds, and then sped up. It both thrilled her, and terrified her, like a roller coaster with a deliberately rickety feel to it.

Amanda pushed it out of her mind—all of the excitement at the prospect of marrying him, and all of the terrors it brought with it. She focused on his taste, on his touch, and most importantly, his smell.

It was certainly the smell of home.

Police Commissioner Ray Wilson hung up the phone, then looked at Jennifer Bosley. He sighed. "You know, your friend Marco is quite a handful. Did he come back to New York to start a war on his first night home?"

Jennifer rolled her deep brown eyes and shook her head. "I only just met him a few hours ago." She grinned at him. "You can't blame this one on me, dearie."

Wilson shook his head. "There's got to be something within the vampire community to ride herd on this sort of thing, isn't there?"

She tilted her head forward and looked at him, as though over glasses she didn't wear. "You have a problem with him ridding your fair city of troublesome vampires?"

Wilson deflated and leaned back in his chair. "No, I guess not. But it would be nice if he didn't go on a rampage and leave a mess for other people—namely my men—to clean up."

"The last thing I would do is tell you how to do your job—or how your men should do it—but fighting people like me isn't neat or orderly."

Wilson scoffed. He had encountered more of his fair share of the fang-and-fur set in Vietnam than he could ever tell anyone, so he understood her statement as well as anyone. "Right now, I have to clean up a large part of Fifth Avenue because it looks like a row of buildings had bombs planted in them. Then I have several reports of wolves roaming the streets. Can you believe it? Wolves? What's next, dragons?"

Bosley winced. Wilson cocked his head at that. She tended to be unflappable, so that was telling. "What am I missing here?"

"If all of this is connected … dragons would be the least of your problems."

Marco finished duct taping the curtains of his room so no sunlight would penetrate and sat back next to Amanda.

"Are you sure you do not want to come to my place?"

"That's about ten miles from here," Marco answered, "and in the dark. I don't want you to be a walking target." He shrugged. "No offense, but we don't know how Igor located you so easily last night. For all we know, we could have some kind of vampire-offspring connection we don't know about. Besides, I don't want someone to take a shot at you."

She smiled. "How sweet." She glanced around the room, crucifixes dangling from the ceiling and rosaries hanging on the walls. "And the shrine chic?"

"I don't want Igor eavesdropping on us."

"He's Misha," she corrected.

"Whatever." Marco smiled. "Besides, there are some things I want to try, now that I'm in control, and not a furry." He raised both hands before him in what looked like a modified boxing stance, but what was actually a Krav Maga pose. She was a little surprised that he bothered with that level of formality. Most of the time, he would say that it gave away precisely what to expect from him.

But then again, Marco would expect someone to anticipate him and plan to use that against anyone who presumed to know his skills

So, Amanda decided to act accordingly—and assumed that he would do something other than use Krav Maga. She tried to think of any fighting style Krav didn't steal from and failed.

Amanda sighed, then leaped for the ceiling, pushing off with her hands. She came down on Marco, pinning him to the floor without a problem.

She smiled. "Was that what you wanted to try?"

He grinned slyly. "You have me right where I want me."

She raised a brow at this. "Oh?"

"Yeah," Marco muttered. He shifted beneath her, uncomfortable with just how much he enjoyed his predicament. He didn't want to move, he did not want to stop, and he didn't want to jab her with his growing arousal. "By the way, do you know why I went to San Francisco?"

She stared into his deep blue eyes a moment. The little microscopic motions of her eyes made it look like she tried to look inside his head. Amanda finally nodded. "Because you were in love with me."

"Ah…" was the best he could come up with. Now he gazed straight into her eyes. Lord, he just wanted to… "So, when did you figure it out?"

"When you told me you were in love with me. After that, it did not take a genius to reason backwards from there. You were afraid to let me get near. Why?"

Marco smiled, an expression absent of any real mirth. "There are times I scare myself. Being a killer by instinct isn't exactly relaxing. Personally, I don't give a damn that I had it, but around you…"

"So you applied for the farthest away college you could find."

He nodded. "I was afraid of hurting you…I'm quite effective at hurting things. Though in your case, I was afraid of hurting you emotionally."

"And now you know better, right?"

Marco laughed. "You're kidding, right? Now, you're the one who'd better be careful of hurting *me*." He sighed, content.

Amanda's lip turned up slightly at the comment but decided to go back onto the subject. "Why didn't you tell me how scared you were?"

He knew what she meant—his predatory nature. "Because I didn't want to be reduced to Ajax."

"The cleaning solvent?"

"Ajax, perhaps the second greatest fighter of the Trojan war. He wasn't Achilles or wily Ulysses; he won through brute force. But when the war was over, there was no place for him in the peaceful society he'd helped create. He was a warrior who had nothing to fight. In the end, he killed himself, rejected by all that was left, because he gained nothing from the war, though he helped win it. For the modern set, think of the first Dirty Harry movie—he's the opposite end of the coin from the serial sniper of the film, brutal, cold-blooded, and the only thing that stands between the monsters and society, but at the end of the day, he's left alone, and society doesn't want old soldiers around. They're 'too brutal,' 'too violent.' It happened to Sherman, Ariel Sharon, Ajax, Patton, all because they had to go into the hell of war, play by the rules of death, and were demoted in the eyes of all because 'that's not how civilized people behave.' Well, I don't want to be just a counter-predator."

She raised an eyebrow. "What do you mean?"

"Anti-terrorism is blowing a hole in an ISIS leader's brain from a mile away with a sniper rifle. Counter-terrorism is bombing Arafat's compound and half of the West Bank, fighting terror with terror. A counter-predator is like having a serial killer that preys on other serials."

Marco's eyes went dark and nearly black, letting his rage, his intense violent streak burning through. "This is me." He blinked back to normal. "And this is me." He looked into Amanda's eyes and smiled, letting all of his love and passion burn through differently. "And this is me."

He leaned up and kissed her deeply.

Marco paused and almost jerked when he felt Amanda's hand grip him. She smiled herself and whispered, "And this is you, too."

They stopped for a moment and stared at one another for a shocked moment, unsure of what do to next. Both of them had been terrified of what they would do to each other. But they still wanted each other with a passion that neither one had felt before.

Marco's hands roamed over Amanda's stomach, dipped down under her shirt, and came up, sliding along her skin. His hands didn't go anywhere wrong, just around her waist, and up her back. And Marco went in for the kiss.

Amanda turned her head, and Marco didn't stop, going for her shoulder, and slowly kissing up her neck. She gasped at the sudden contact.

"Marco," she said tensely, "I think I need to bite you again."

"Hmmmmm," he growled. "I think it's my turn to bite you," he said as he took her earlobe between his teeth and tugged slightly. "And you taste good." He pressed against her. Amanda's breathing speed up. His lips touched her ear, and he said, "I want to eat you up. And I don't mean in a bad way."

That was enough out of character for Amanda to slide her hands from his back and place them on his chest. She didn't want to push too hard since she didn't want to send him into the wall. "Marco, this isn't you. This is the animal talking."

Marco paused, his lips still on her neck. He pulled back, studying her face, confused. "You're kidding, right? You know what I thought when I first saw you?"

"Take a picture, it will last longer?"

He shook his head. "That's what I *said*. I thought you were the most beautiful woman I've ever seen." He leaned in, going almost nose-to-nose with her, his eyes boring into hers. "I want you."

She pressed on him a little more. "No, you can't. You don't believe in —"

Marco blinked, his eyes going straight to blue. "Wolves are monogamous. They mate for life. Like Catholics." His left hand stayed on her lower back, and his right touched her face. "I'm proposing…again. I don't want your body, I want you… *and* your body."

Father Rodgers sat in the recently vacated love seat. He took a drag on what was left of his cigar and relaxed, looking up at the ceiling. "Well, we have a temporary fix to a long-term problem."

"I'm worried about the next three nights," Robert answered. "Everything else can wait, as far as I'm concerned."

Bram looked back and forth from the priest to Marco's father and back again. "Neither one of you is worried about what's happening upstairs right now?"

Robert smiled as he rose from the bed. "He's turning into a were-something, and she's a vampire. They went up…" He looked to the priest. "What? Three minutes ago?"

Rodgers bobbled his head in a semi-nod. "About."

"If something untoward were going to happen, we would have heard the bed collapse by now. I'm interested in turning in if no one else minds."

Hendershot nodded, then looked to Bram and Dougherty. "Take up positions. We need to secure this house, and perhaps this block. We've seen some of the weapons that the assassin's minions have used before. I don't want an RPG coming in through the front window. Monsignor, do you wish me to take you home?"

Rodgers shrugged. "I can sleep on the couch, if that's okay with you, Doctor?"

Robert nodded. "Sure. Not a problem."

Enrico shrugged. "I'm going to wait for the cleanup crew, get a ride with them."

Tolbert nodded. "I'll be around for a few. My patrols have been stranger and stranger lately."

The ninjas all pulled out of the room. The doctor went straight up to bed. Enrico moved into the hall, looking through the glass of the new front door for his clean-up people.

The only two people left in the living room were Rodgers and Tolbert.

The cop looked at the priest for a moment, studying him as he slowly, thoughtfully processed the cigar. "What's on your mind, Monsignor?"

Rodgers blinked behind his coke-bottle glasses and looked at Tolbert. "What do you mean?"

Tolbert crossed his long legs and folded his hands on his knee. "You have the look of my L.T. when he starts thinking over problems."

Rodgers nodded slowly. He focused his eyes on a spot over Tolbert's head for a long moment. "Marco told me about his run-in with Misha—the latest threat."

"And?"

Rodgers' eyes were still off somewhere else. "Back in September, the threat was invulnerable: it healed so fast, cutting his head off was like cutting through water – the wound was healing before the blade came out the other end."

Tolbert cocked his head and narrowed his eyes. "That Mister Day thing, right? I understood that he was some sort of demon."

Rodgers nodded. "He was Asmodeus, one of the princes of Hell itself. Which makes me wonder what *greater* threat this vampire might be."

The cop winced. "I'm going to need a bigger gun."

"Oh, if that were the case, guns wouldn't help much." The priest shook his head leaned back, considering the next problem. "In addition to that, after a certain level, vampires begin to manifest other powers. Stronger powers. The one I'm worried about is Soul Fire."

Tolbert laughed for a moment, thinking over just how ridiculous it sounded. "Soul fire? Sounds like a crappy *Game of Thrones* title."

Rodgers chuckled. "After a fashion. In this case, it's a weapon. I would even call it one of the most powerful weapons in the arsenal of vampire powers and abilities."

The cop shook his head. "So what? They throw fireballs? Big deal. That hasn't been impressive since the flamethrower."

Rodgers' eyes narrowed behind his glasses, and his mouth went into a straight line. He pulled the cigar out of his mouth. "Has anyone explained to you why crosses burn one type of vampire, and not Amanda?"

"One's good. One's evil?"

"After a fashion." The priest sighed. "You see, vampires have free will. They're not automatically evil. After one becomes a vampire, the soul and the body of the vampires become so close together, *any* actions taken on their part literally become part of them. The more good or evil actions they commit, the stronger they are. And if they're evil, everything in Bram Stoker applies."

Tolbert nodded. "So, the farther along one of them is in power, the harder they are to kill. I figured that much."

"*White* Soul Fire," Rodgers continued, "are for those who are so good and almost saintly, and their souls are almost perfectly aligned with their bodies. They cannot do more than that since perfection is God's alone. White Soul Fire requires not only talent but incredible strength of will. It can heal, and it can destroy evil, at will. Sometimes both at once.

"*Black* Soul Fire," he added, "is evil. It burns with cold, and it kills any who get in the way. This is fire that consumes everything. It either sets it on fire or disintegrates it to ashes. It is as supernatural a tool as their ability to shapeshift. It can set pieces of *reality* on fire. I wouldn't dismiss it if I were you."

Tolbert cleared his throat nervously. "Understood. You think this new guy might have it?"

"Misha? A vampire who wields it would have to be almost literally demonic. Evil would have to be an art form to him. If Misha uses it, and he will burn through us if we can't contain him. If he is, in fact, the brother of Mikhail the Bear—the leader of the vampires we dispatched last Spring—then it would explain Tunguska."

"Tongue-who-ska?"

The priest sighed, and dragged on his cigar. "Mikhail was sighted at Tunguska, a place in Siberia. The so-called Tunguska event is usually written off as the air burst of a meteoroid."

Tolbert shrugged. "So? How bad can that be?"

"It was as powerful as a nuclear explosion."

"Oh."

Rodgers nodded. "Mikhail had been there before the event, but he wasn't powerful enough to cause *or* survive such a disaster."

"You figure that means that his brother Misha was behind it? Or helped him survive it?"

Rodgers nodded. "If that's the level of power involved here, then this isn't about Marco, or even New York. This threatens the *world*."

# Chapter 17

# Time Suck

Marco Catalano woke up energized and alert. This was even though his room was still dark. His new duct tape and curtain fix was holding up well.

But the best part was Amanda in his bed, one arm draped over him, his face next to hers. His nostrils were filled with the scent of her hair (strawberry), and her skin (vanilla). Her body was warm, her entire right side pressed up against his. His arm was around her waist, and he was sorely tempted to move his hand up, or down—the only reason he didn't shift it away from temptation was that he didn't want to wake her.

Then he furrowed his brow, confused for a long moment. His bed was a twin. It wasn't made for two people.

Marco lay there, closed his eyes, and concentrated on Amanda's presence, absorbing her just being there. At that moment, he suddenly realized he had everything he had ever wanted, right there in his arms.

Marco smiled, and hugged her closer, lightly brushing his lips against her cheek. *If this were a romance novel, we'd be done already. We can call it a day.*

*Freaking vampires. They should have read the script.*

"Can I help you?" Amanda asked lightly.

"Yes," he whispered. "Marry me."

Amanda's musical laugh preceded her pushing up from the bed. Her hair came down in a golden-red curtain around them.

*Good God,* he thought. *She looks beautiful in the morning.*

"No," she answered him, kissing him lightly on the lips. "We have barely begun the relationship. You want to get married already?"

Marco took her by the shoulder and sat up, kissing her, hard and deeply. After he pulled back so he could catch his breath, he looked her dead in the eyes. "Yes. Is there anything about me you don't like?" He paused, frowned, thought it over, and added, "Aside from everything about me that I'm not particularly happy about, that is?"

Amanda laughed lightly. "I love you. I even like some parts of you that you don't like."

He spread his hands in a shrug. "Then what's the problem? Given the usual length of wedding preparations, it'll take at least a year. Worst thing that happens is that, if we're still alive, we won't stand each other, and we call it off." He leaned forward, and kissed her again, this time on the cheek. "In any case, think it over some more."

Amanda blinked as he bounded off the bed, wondering when she had last seen him this energized. "You seem happy this morning."

Marco stripped off his shirt and reached into his closet for the next available one. He pulled out a dark blue t-shirt with the logo of the Fighting 59th Army Unit.

The door to Marco's room swung open, even though the door had been locked a moment ago. Merle Kraft stood in the doorway, wearing his midnight blue windbreaker, despite the blistering January cold. Behind him waited George Berkeley, dressed in straight up black tactical gear.

Marco arched his brows. "You could have just knocked, you—"

"Sit!" George barked.

Marco turned for the bed, taking two steps before he stopped. His eyes narrowed, and he looked over his shoulder at the lycanthrope and Merle. "Oh, I see. Cute. Sorry, doesn't quite work. We found a workaround."

George arched his bushy black brows, looked at Merle, and shrugged. He flipped Marco a thumbs up, turned and walked away.

Marco chuckled. "One day, I'm going to figure out just how George manages to get through life by saying so little."

Merle cocked an eyebrow. "I can't imagine why you'd find that hard to process," he said dryly. He stepped into the room and hooked the door with his heel, kicking the door closed. "I'm happy you both managed to at least wait until you got to New York before finding yourself in deeper trouble than when I left you."

"Missed you, too, Merle," Marco drawled.

Amanda rolled her eyes at the interplay between them. "I am so happy you could get to New York so fast, Merle." Her eyes narrowed and studied him up and down. "Except you were already here, weren't you?"

Merle gave her a little smile and a nod. "Caught me. We're still here on the whole United Nations case."

Marco sighed, almost deflating. He sat next to Amanda, putting his arm around her. "Suddenly, I'm tired all over again."

Merle didn't roll his eyes but started for the curtains. "It's a little dark in—"

"No!" Marco and Amanda shouted at once.

Merle stopped dead in his tracks, frowned, looked at Amanda, and his expression dropped. "Sorry about that. Wasn't thinking."

Marco stared at him for a moment, as though he were stark-raving mad. He focused on his breathing for a bit to calm himself down. "No kidding. Did you forget that she's a vampire? Really?"

Merle smiled sheepishly. "Kinda. Sorry, you pass for human quite well."

The two lovebirds exchanged a glance. Merle was so strange, every time they thought they were used to him, he did something new.

"Do you have anything on the UN?" Amanda asked.

"Anything?" Marco added.

Merle sighed. "Little that's new. Something about the UN getting new troops, or training. The bugs were a little vague – yes, Amanda, we took your advice. And someone else's." He looked around the room for a chair, and shrugged, leaning up against a bookcase. "We all suspect that your big boogeyman of 'The Council' is a UN Council. Right. Got it. Big deal. Now what? If we wanted to go through the history of corruption at the UN, we'd have to start at day one with Alger Hiss in Lake Success and move on one corrupt year at a time, until current events."

Amanda frowned. The United Nations were just a small sample of what was going on in the world. Merle was correct: pinning down the corruption to precise activities was—

"Easy," Marco stated. "They're evil, right?" His little Scaramouche smile returned as he looked deep into Amanda's eyes. "What's the nature of evil?"

"Aside from overreaching?" she asked him.

He nodded. "It's a world-wide political organization. Day played geopolitics. I know what I would do if I had all the time in the world and played politicians like a chess game. I'd take over the world."

At that point, Merle laughed out loud. "You're joking, right? Vampires take over the world? That would require greater freedom of movement than vampires can manage without five pounds of sunblock and large, wide-brimmed hats."

Marco shook his head. "Vampires were on both sides of Europe in World War II. Technically, being on either side meant that they won. I mean–"

Amanda suddenly grabbed Marco's shoulder. "They won."

Marco looked at Amanda. "I'm sorry, what?"

Amanda looked him right in the eyes. "The Soviets. They won. They kept vampires on the payroll. There were several attempts to roll back their influence after

Stalin, but if we assume they went everywhere that the Soviets went…"

Merle and Marco winced this time. Soviet influence during the 20th century was everywhere, including the entire Middle East, Asia, Latin America, and America.

"This explains a few things," Marco muttered. "They're everywhere. Merle, your wiretap picked up something about new soldiers. Just imagine, if you had guys like al-Qaeda using vampires for terrorists—"

"They do," Merle said.

Amanda and Marco looked at the government agent. "What?"

Merle sighed. "That's what I've been doing when I'm not looking into the UN," he informed them. "I've been in the Sandbox hunting vampires. They've been spreading throughout the area."

Marco and Amanda winced.

"Vampires are like cockroaches," she stated.

"For every one you see, there are at least ten you don't," Marco added. "This is bad,"

Merle shook his head. "I don't get it. When we had this conversation before, we started with a conspiracy that—we think—goes back to the French Revolution, with perversions, demonic rites, and the Soviets repeating a lot of the same crap, leading up to a resurgence of Moloch once abortion went into high gear. But how does all of this lead to them taking over the world?"

"Depends," Marco said. "Of all the dictators of the world, name one that *wouldn't* think that vampires make great super soldiers."

Amanda and Merle looked at Marco. "Where did you get that idea?"

Marco shrugged. "It's not my idea." He poked Amanda in the side. "You told me that Stalin and Hitler used vampires in Gulags and concentration camps." He looked at Merle. "*You* just said that terrorists are using vampires. How much of a stretch is it to field vampires as enforcers in a banana republic? Or any two-bit dictator who has delusions of his own adequacy. And if the Council is a *UN* Council, they have the connections to make that happen."

Merle spread his hands and held them up as though he were attempting to halt traffic. "Wait. No. Stop. What do you two expect me to do with all of this? Nuke the United Nations?"

Marco scoffed at the idea, then laughed. "While I'm all for burning the UN to the ground like the buggers deserve, we have a much easier solution than that. Even if the Council is more than just Misha — and really, I'd bet that he's the only one left — he needs support staff. Hit the UN vampires during work hours, you'll probably cripple them."

Merle arched a brow. "Oh? Really? And what did you have in mind?"

He looked to his love beside him. "The sprinklers?"

Amanda nodded. "The sprinklers."

Merle sighed. He was being left out of the conversation. Again. He raised his hand like an annoyed student who just didn't get it. "What now?"

Marco rolled his eyes. "Look, do you remember the fire hose trick when you first came here? It was part of the cemetery trap?"

"Yeah. You ran a tube from a fire hydrant through a 500-gallon drum of holy water. Adding regular water to holy water makes it holy water. It made a nice water cannon. Why? You intend to hit the UN with a squirt gun?"

Marco shook his head. He smiled evilly. "Not with a squirt gun."

Marco closed the door behind Merle, and whirled around, energized. Amanda simply watched him from the stairs, a small, amused smile playing on her lips. He bounded up a few steps, quickly kissed her on the lips, and turned, ready to head down. When Marco stopped and turned back, his usual smile had grown predatory. His eyelids had become hooded. He gave a little "hmm" sound which came out more like a purr.

Reaching out, he took her by the waist, and lifted her off the stairs onto the level with him. Drawing her in, Marco kissed her deeply.

Amanda laughed a little before he pressed her to him, his hand coming up along her spine and burying in her hair. He effortlessly held her as he dipped her back, pushing her against the wall of the staircase as the purr became more like a growl.

After so much time had passed that Amanda lost track of time, Robert Catalano cleared his throat at the base of the stairs. "Are you two done yet? There's food."

Marco stopped kissing Amanda, leaving her gasping.

The gasp was less because of the kiss, and more because Marco's eyes had gone from their deep blue color to a bright, startling gold.

"I think you need to take a breath."

Marco gave a grin that Amanda could only describe as wolfish. "You don't want me to do that," he whispered gently. "The more I breathe, the more of your scent I catch. It will only spiral from there."

Something poked Marco in the leg. He spun, swiping at it so fast, he cut through it.

Robert lifted what was left of the pointer stick, eyeing the smooth, even break, then his son. "Anyway," he drawled, "there's food. I suspect I should be making the steaks rare?"

Amanda's hand clamped down on Marco's shoulder. She nodded. "Good idea. I have to work with Marco a moment."

The doctor rolled his eyes as he walked off towards the kitchen. Amanda pulled Marco back towards her and kissed his neck. He relaxed back into her, and she held him against her chest as her lips locked onto his skin. Her fangs slipped easily into his neck. She sucked on his neck, getting a small taste of his blood, and started licking the punctures.

"We need to get married," he muttered. "We really do. I'm not sure we can keep our mitts off of each other for years. I'm kinda hoping we can manage for one. Just one. That's not too out there, is it?"

After three minutes of Amanda's bite, Marco's breath slowed enough for him to relax even further. She released him, and he turned to face her. His eyes were back to the calm, deep blue she knew so well. "I was that bad, huh?"

Amanda nodded. "Come. Let's feed you before you bite someone."

# Chapter 18

# Flushing The UN

The assault on the United Nations began at noon, as soon as the sun came out. Since it was only a few days into January, the clear sky meant that it was freaking cold. Welcome to New York City—if it was cloudy, it was warmer. If it was a sunny day, it was cold. Because not even the rules of God or man made sense in New York.

In either event, the assault on the United Nations had to be a three-tiered operation. It was a plan that Merle had started thinking about since he had learned that "vampires" were an option.

Merle had to worry about any access points coming from the UN to Turtle Bay—after all, these vampires didn't seem to have any problem with running water. It wasn't like they could drown. The UN was built on Turtle Bay itself, which was originally a cove of the East River, and called Deutal Cove by the Dutch— "deutal" meant "knife," but sounded enough like the English "turtle" that the name stuck when the area shifted ownership from the Dutch to British colonists.

Thankfully, the water was easy enough to keep it covered as an access point after a few simple sweeps with a mini-submersible Merle had hired locally. There was no way in or out of the United Nations by water unless a vampire wanted to create a tunnel with his bare hands.

There was a route for anyone who wanted to escape by East River Drive—best known to locals as "the FDR." But that would also require punching through metal and concrete.

Alternately, there was also an easier way out through the underground. The nearest subway access was just over three blocks away.

The biggest problem was the sewers. There was, technically, easy access from the UN to the sewers around the building. A strong enough vampire could quickly move from the UN to the residence complex across the street, or even the massive building dedicated solely to the ventilation of the Queens-Midtown Tunnel. It would be a leisurely break from there to the rest of Manhattan.

The last thing Merle wanted to do was play tunnel rat through thousands of miles of New York City sewers and subways.

Thankfully, he'd recently added someone to his speed dial who could make the necessary arrangements. He got the appointment he needed earlier that day.

When Merle walked into One Police Plaza, Police Commissioner Ray Wilson was already standing, waiting for him. Despite looking like he hadn't slept the night before, he was immaculately dressed in a three-piece navy suit, reaching out to shake Merle's hand.

"What can the New York City Police Department do for you, Mister Kraft?" Wilson asked as he led Merle to the couch in his office. Wilson took the armchair and settled in with a coffee mug big enough to hold 24 ounces of coffee.

Merle just sat. He didn't take off his windbreaker or help himself to the coffee tray arrayed on the table. He sat on the edge of the couch, leaning toward the Commissioner, his midnight-blue eyes locked on the city's chief police officer. "I'm going to need to shut down a few blocks of the city. By noon."

The PC's face didn't move for a moment. His lips pursed a little, but that was about it. His eyes locked onto a point of the floor next to Merle. Merle could see the wheels turn in the man's mind. He could almost smell the wood burning.

"Which?" he asked.

"Well, it might be more than a few."

"Of course it is. Which streets?"

"First Avenue from East Forty-Second to East Forty-Eighth, and from First Avenue to the River down both of those streets."

The PC leaned back in the chair. "The UN."

"Correct. We have reason to believe that there is a nest of malevolent vampires working there. We want to flush the building. In more ways than one."

Wilson frowned. He folded his hands together and placed them on his chest. Then he stared straight down his body to the floor again. Merle could see him doing the math.

"Are you going to shut down the FDR as well?" Wilson asked after a few seconds.

Merle shook his head. "I can't see any reason for it. Even the UN tunnel is unlikely. Especially with the way we have the operation set up."

Wilson raised a brow. "Define 'operation.' Are you going to hit them with ordnance? Because if you intend to have a pitched battle in the middle of my city in broad daylight, there's only so much I can do."

Merle shook his head. "I'm going to need some action with the DWP. Shutting down the streets is just a precaution. We're just going to, well, flood them a little."

Both of Wilson's eyebrows went up this time. "Really? Explain."

Merle smiled.

By the time the conversation was over, Merle had full authorization to launch his cleaning operation on the United Nations.

The first wave of the attack was an "accident," mostly with explosives under the Secretariat building, the concrete and glass domino that stood up and out from the rest of the UN compound. The explosion wasn't designed to do any more than break some tall sheets of tinted glass that shrouded the building. A good collection of the windows cracked and shattered, letting in plenty of glorious purifying daylight.

From the images on the thermal scopes, three dozen vampires went up like flash paper within a few seconds of being hit with full sunlight.

That was only part one.

The explosion and the vampires going up in smoke was more than enough to set off the fire system. The entire sprinkler system went off, saluted by fire sirens and red flashing lights. Before it went through any of the pumps, the water had first gone through a 500-gallon barrel drum of holy water.

Most of the vampires didn't even have the chance to say "I'm melting! What a world! What a world!" The screams of the vampires flooded the building, merging with the cries of panic from the humans who worked there, too.

Other vampires tried to escape. Not only were there sewer tunnels, but there was also a specifically-designed escape tunnel that was meant to take vampires out of the building and to safety. Just in case of a daylight attack.

However, that was another part of the plan that Merle needed to clear with the commissioner. An hour before the explosion shook the building, Merle had his people find every fire hydrant around the UN building, run them through the drums of holy water, and flood the street, and straight into the sewers. The explosion cracked the escape tunnels, engulfing them in water.

The vampires who rushed into the tunnels ran right into the ankle-deep tides of blessed water. Thanks to the nature of the damage, blessings dripped on them from above.

No one was around to hear their screams.

The entire process took very few hours.

# Chapter 19

## Lost In A Good Bite

By the time Merle Kraft and his commandos had polished off the vampire population of the United Nations, Marco had finished four steaks and mugs of beef barley soup.

"Merle and George said you'd be hungry," Robert explained as he sat at the table with a sandwich. He smiled sardonically at Marco tearing through the food. "I'm glad I listened. I would hate for you to eat the pattern off of the plate."

Marco swallowed the last mouthful and shrugged. "Sorry about that. No idea where that came from."

"Unlike my virus," Amanda explained, "the shapeshifter virus uses what resources your body has. It takes away from you, as well as adds. You're going to lose what little body fat you have."

Marco frowned. Looking back, it would explain why he had never seen George Berkeley eat anything. He had probably done all of his eating in private. And his body fat had already been used to heal his arms last night.

He narrowed his eyes at the blood on the plate, thinking over the effects. "Your virus enhances my stamina because it wants to keep the food stock alive. The shapeshifter virus uses what I have to mess with my physiology." He shook his head and found it hard to concentrate.

Robert frowned and looked at Amanda. "So every time that you bite Marco, your virus is actually doing double duty—it has to boost his stamina, *and* fight off the shapeshifter virus?"

Amanda nodded. "Exactly."

Marco looked from Amanda to his father and tried to track the conversation. It was stupid because he *knew* something about what they were talking about, but it was like trying to think through a fog.

There was a chime of Darth Vader breathing, then another. Marco blinked, trying to figure out what it was. Robert and Amanda looked at him.

"Are you going to get that?" Robert asked.

Marco blinked again and shook his head firmly. He felt his pockets, pulling out his phone. He squinted at it, suddenly tired. He stared at the screen that had the text alert. "Huh. How did I forget my own alert sound? Who would I program for… oh, it's Hendershot." He clicked open the text message. His eyes widened. "This could be bad."

Marco stood so fast he knocked the chair over. He charged for the front hallway. He grabbed the door and ripped it open.

There, standing in the clear light of day, was a tall, dark and menacing figure.

Misha.

He stood in the middle of the street, in front of the hole made by the exploding minions the night before.

Marco leaned over to one side, hoping that this was yet another illusion, like the Yana image he'd had a conversation with. Frowning, he picked up a rock from the stoop and tossed it underhanded. It bounced off of Misha's chest.

The vampire raised an eyebrow. "Really? You couldn't tell?"

Marco shrugged. "It's been a tough day or two."

Misha grinned. Though it was broad daylight, the vampire's eyes had become deeper and darker. His eyes were even losing the whites.

A loud *boom* broke the silence, and Misha's head snapped to the side. He staggered a little before he straightened. Misha looked up over his right shoulder, at the third-floor apartment window. There was a fifty-caliber rifle at the window.

Marco looked from the rifle muzzle to Misha. The bullet had gone right through the vampire's head, without a trace of damage, though Misha's head should have blown clear off his shoulders.

The vampire pointed right at the window. "You get one shot."

The ninja in the window fired again. Misha looked away, and the bullet simply bounced off the air near Misha's head. "Where were we?" Misha asked.

Four windows opened at four different apartments around the area, and suddenly the air exploded with the sound of fully automatic gunfire. Bullets pinged off of what looked like a shield around Misha's head and shoulders. Every projectile just suddenly stopped for no reason.

Misha paid them no attention and merely smiled at Marco. "I can smell the stink of lycanthropy running through your veins." He stepped forward, and the trail of bullets followed him.

The rear doors opened on a van down the street revealing a Dillon minigun, which fired thirty-caliber rounds at 3,000 rounds a minute. The sort of thing that could cut down a tree while setting it on fire.

The minigun opened up with a roar. The stream of bullets punched through Misha, cutting through the air and Misha like he wasn't there. The bullets continued through, striking a big black car on the other side of the street. In a shower of sparks, the bullets punched through the massive jeep, ripping it crosswise from the grill to the tailpipe. The resulting wreckage looked as though it had been split with a can opener.

Misha's coat split in half in the hailstorm of bullets. The hem of his long coat fell off, and his shirt was neatly shorn in two.

Misha sighed as though bored. The air solidified from the crown of his head and down his sides, all the way to his feet. The rounds from the minigun stopped dead only a few inches from Misha's coat.

"I prefer my clothing to be neat. Do you know how hard it is to find Armani in my size?"

Marco stared at the vampire. The casual sartorial comment jarred him, striking a very distant bell of memory. Only it felt like an alarm bell.

Amanda stood at Marco's side and growled. Marco did as well, but slammed his hand against the door frame, keeping himself from stepping past the threshold, and keeping Amanda there as well.

Misha smiled. He stepped forward, and the bullets stopped. Either the ninjas had decided that he was a waste of ammo, or they were coming up with a new plan. Or both. "Very good. I want you both dead, but I'd hate for it to be *too* easy. Amanda forgetting herself and coming out into the daylight with me?"

"What are you doing?" Amanda spat. "If you were really so powerful, you would be destroying us right now."

Misha narrowed his eyes and smiled at her. "No. If I were truly powerful, I would be down at the United Nations, slaughtering Merle Kraft and his men. But they're throwing too much holy water around for my taste." He grinned, revealing his fangs.

Marco reached into his pocket and pulled out a vial and stopper. He looked at the clear liquid, and studied it, as though it was a surprise that it was in there.

Marco looked at Amanda. "Holy water."

Amanda did a double take. "Of course."

"Oh. Good," he said casually. He pulled back and threw it for Misha's body. The vampire didn't look too nervous. His eyes flicked to the sidewalk. The concrete of the curb broke away from the street, shot into the air, and intercepted the vial.

Misha held up a finger and slowly waggled it back and forth.

Amanda clapped her hand on his shoulder. "Marco, he can stand out in broad daylight and block any incoming ordnance that isn't holy. Why is he just standing there?"

"Crap."

The sounds of windows shattering came from all over the house—upstairs, the side windows, the back of the house. Marco turned, ready to engage all comers.

Amanda kept her eyes on Misha. He grinned and raised his hands. Rectangular slabs of concrete ripped up from the sidewalk, dripping gravel and debris. They hovered like flying saucers, spinning in place.

The concrete then flew straight for the both of them.

Amanda tackled Marco, throwing him off to the side. The concrete sliced through the doors the stairs, and the wall of the front hall embedding in the wall. It crumbled in place, taking parts of the house with it.

"This isn't good."

The dining room of the Catalano residence was straightforward. It was a long room, designed for a long table. Off to the side, there were some pieces of furniture—a sideboard for drinks, a china cabinet for the good plates, and, atop the china cabinet, a wooden box for the good flatware.

When Marco and Amanda rushed outside, Doctor Robert Catalano went immediately for the box of flatware. He took it down from the top of the cabinet and moved his back up against the wall, so he could see both entrances to the dining room. He opened it up, and immediately took out the good carving knives, as well as the several serving forks, and five steak knives.

When all of the windows broke in, Robert knew he would have a use for all of the sharp objects.

The first freak to come through the door from the kitchen by way of the back door. Big and bulky, enough hair covered it that Robert couldn't tell if it was a were-something or a hippie with low grooming standards. It snarled like an animal—or like a meth head on a bender—and leaped for him.

Robert knew that he didn't want to get scratched by this creature, if only to avoid supernatural *or* regular infections. He ducked as it swiped for him. With the precision that came with training, Robert lashed out with the carving knives. Jamming the blade in the space between its legs, he slashed the inside of the thigh.

The were-something flew past him and whirled, snarling, ready to take him on again. It took one step forward on the slashed leg and crumpled. The creature looked down its snout and saw that the leg was a mass of blood.

Robert had slashed open its femoral artery with the carving knife.

There was a reason that Robert had insisted on keeping the good silver close at hand.

A growl echoed from behind him.

In a matter of seconds, his attacker seized Robert by the arms, and lifted him into the air. On the way back down, he slammed against the dining room table, breaking the table top and the legs.

Robert looked up at his attacker, and this wasn't a thing. It was a six-foot fall, well-built, bipedal wolf.

And it smiled at him down a muzzle filled with razor-sharp teeth.

Misha laughed as the havoc broke loose around him. The Vatican ninjas opened fire once more. The only thing that made the ninjas a problem for Misha was their prayerful mediation *during* combat. This practice created a bubble, making them almost invisible to vampire senses. They were impossible to detect by an average vampire who made a passive scan. A vampire of Misha's ability, actively scanning every inch of the space, found the ninjas' locations from voids in his search. He could find their presence because they created a gap in what should be there.

In Misha's case, these bubbles made Vatican ninjas untouchable to his supernatural abilities—he couldn't strangle them with his mind, nor could he otherwise manipulate them like any person or object unblessed.

However, that didn't stop him from throwing building faces and concrete *at* them.

He reached out *under* the rubble generated by the sniper who first shot him with the fifty-caliber. He grabbed the nearest load-bearing wall, and pulled with his mind. A solid slab of stonework that was over ten feet long, eight feet wide, and a foot thick ripped out of the rubble, shaking debris off and raising through the building. Then he let it drop, collapsing several supports in the building with a shudder and a symphony of crashes. The structure creaked loudly but still held. A cloud of dust rose, clouding the sniper's view and swirled around Misha like a cloak.

But he wasn't done.

His eyes narrowed slightly in concentration, and the slab rose from the wreckage of the lower floor, then rotated so that it was horizontal.

Misha's eyes flicked to the building across from the sniper. That ninja brought out a crossbow to nail him through the heart.

Misha sent the massive stone wall straight for that ninja's perch. It sped across the street like a stealth bomber, leaving an ominous, wide shadow as it traveled. Then the wall smashed into the building, slicing the top floor in half, from the window sill to the roof.

The other building creaked and trembled. Misha heard the sniper gasp as the walls and floor started to buckle and sag around and underneath him.

Misha grinned.

Time to deal with the others.

The window to the front room imploded, showering glass in a wide scatter. An anonymous body armored man in all black burst through the opening, wiping away glass with a well-protected arm. He was built like a bear, wearing a helmet, and carrying an AK-107 automatic rifle. With another sweep of his arm, he took the curtains with him, ripping the curtain pole from the window, and flooding the front room with sunlight. As he came to his feet, he knew he was protected from Amanda Colt.

However, that didn't help defend him from Marco. He charged straight at the shooter, hands outstretched. He slammed into the automatic rifle, grabbing it. Marco spun, but the minion held on with all of his preternatural strength.

This was fine with Marco because he was swinging with all of *his* new supernatural strength that came with being a shapeshifter.

Marco's pull lifted the minion off his feet and slammed him headfirst against the brick of the fireplace. The helmet probably saved whatever life he had. Marco grinned as he reached up behind the helmet, then over and around. He grabbed the helmet's visor and pulled it down, snapping the minion's head back. The minion's throat was exposed.

Marco's throat strike broke bone.

Before the minion could explode like the others had, Marco twisted, throwing the minion out the window into the street.

As Misha turned his attention to the remaining ninjas, one of his minions came flying out through the first-floor window of the Catalano brownstone. It hit the street and rolled, landing at Misha's feet like a spurned offering. The body already glowed with the energies that had been dumped into it.

"Oh darn."

Misha leaped to one side a split second before the corpse exploded in a white-hot fireball that pocked the pavement. Not even the vampire wanted to test himself against it, nor did he have the time to drain off the minion's energy before exploding.

Glass bottles of holy water sailed down from the windows above him. Misha waved a hand, and two parts of the street ripped and folded like sheet metal. The strips of asphalt bent and twisted up in front of Misha like a shield, taking the holy water for him.

The one manning the minigun in the van opened up with the weapon again. Misha spared it a glance, and with a flip of his wrist, flipped the van nose over tail with his mind, simply knocking it onto its roof, facing the other direction. He could kill the operator of the minigun later.

The next bottles came over the asphalt barriers, and Misha jumped away, landing down the street. He wheeled around, skidded to a stop on one knee, and with a roar, he held up both hands. Mentally he *pushed* on the base of the two homes where the ninjas had taken up positions.

He was going to bring down the buildings with the ninjas inside.

# Chapter 20

# Fallen Knight

Amanda had barely gotten off of the floor when she heard Marco scream "Catch!"

Amanda's hands were up and waiting when an AK landed in them. She was about to ask what she needed a gun for when she heard footsteps on the floor above her.

A minion swung around the staircase, gun at the ready.

Amanda wasn't going to just wait to see if his bullets were effective against vampires.

She raised the rifle and put three in the man's stomach. The minion fell back, confused that he was still alive. Amanda leaped onto the stairs, then jumped from one landing to the next. She grabbed the minion by the body armor and drove her teeth right into his neck. This time, there was no hesitation, no slowness.

This man was simply lunch.

The minion screamed in horror and tried to thrash against Amanda as she drained the life out of him. She held fast and continued to suck his blood.

Most importantly, she continued to drain the power out of him. This was less a matter of sating her hunger, and more about diffusing a bomb … But every little bit helped.

There was the sound of a shotgun being racked on the floor above her.

Amanda twisted, hurling the minion into his colleague. She launched off her right leg, landed on her left, and kicked with the right, delivering a low roundhouse kick that struck through both of the minion's knees. Joints bent sideways. She came back with a hammer fist, shattering his sternum, and dropping him.

Amanda stripped his weapons, then broke the man's elbows so he couldn't suicide and self-destruct.

She frowned to herself. "That was easy."

Then she felt the crash downstairs.

Marco burst from the front room, kicked off of the wall of the front hallway and bounded into the dining room.

The dining room table was half collapsed, with his father slammed against the surface. A six foot, bipedal monster stood over Robert, claws raised, and fangs dripping with drool.

The wolf looked at Marco with gray eyes. "Don't–"

Before the wolf could issue a single order to Marco, Robert stabbed the wolf in the leg with one of the silver steak knives. The tip of the knife went in behind the Achilles tendon. Robert punched out, ripping through it with the silver blade.

The wolf screamed and whimpered.

Marco lunged for the wolf, tackling it around the waist, and bringing it down to the ground. He straddled its bulk, his knees in the wolf's armpits, and his left hand pressing all of his weight down on the side of the wolf's muzzle. He pressed the wolf's face flat against the floor.

Marco let out his own deep, animal growl as he punched the werewolf in the throat, over and over again.

He ended with a punch so hard it broke the wolf's windpipe, its cervical spine, and the floor beneath it. The wolf's thrashing and kicking grew weaker. Marco reared back, his fingers open and splayed like claws— his fingernails a bit longer than they had been a minute ago. He lashed forward and ripped open the wolf's throat. He wrapped his nails around the exposed part of its spine and pulled out a fistful of vertebrae from the wolf's body.

As the dead werewolf began to twist and shrink beneath him, turning back into a human being – that was three inches shorter and fifty pounds lighter than the wolf it had been, Marco threw his head back and laughed.

It nearly sounded like the gleeful yips of a wolf.

Captain Hendershot of the Vatican Ninjas squinted through the dust at the wall that Misha had so casually thrown at his head. It had sliced neatly through the wall where he had been standing, and the walls on either side of him, and even into the roof.

But it was the angle of attack that had saved his life. Slanting down from where he stood to the window where it broke through, it even protected him like a shield against further attacks. *I'm always grateful for the save, but I don't need proof that prayer works.*

He frowned as he looked around the area; he had work to do. He had enough room to crawl out, and even make it to the door.

Then Hendershot saw that the door was also sliced off at the top by the projectile wall. He scanned around for his bag. Crawling over to it, he shook off debris and dragged it over to the door. He pulled out the shotgun inside and blasted the hinges and the doorknob, taking the door right off the frame. Using the butt of his shotgun, he slammed it out of the way and pulled himself forward. He stood as soon as he was able, straightened, and charged down the stairs.

Hendershot stopped before the front door. He already had a solution the moment he saw that Misha could stop bullets with his mind but had to stop a container of holy water with a rock.

*Misha couldn't affect holy objects with his telekinesis.*

Despite the sounds of warfare going out on the street, he didn't hurry. He took out the belt-fed machine-gun and calmly loaded it. He then took out an atomizer and sprayed down the tips of the bullets with holy water.

Hendershot took a deep breath, said a prayer, and pulled the door open.

There stood Misha, in the middle of the street, trying to bring down the sniper perches on his men.

He swung out into the street and opened fire with the blessed machine gun of Our Lady of Sorrows.

The first three bullets stitched along Misha's back. He roared in pain. It was a deep, bellowing sound like it had come from a towering dragon the size of a skyscraper. It echoed from the depths of Hell. He fell forward, twitching as it burned. He rolled between the two blocks of asphalt he had ripped up from the street.

Misha wheeled around the concrete shields, holding back a scream. His eyes watered, he grimaced again, and detected the whiff of a struck match. His skin sizzled. He grew weaker as the bullets penetrated his hide, buried in his body, and drained his power. Raising a trembling hand, he blocked the sun from his eyes as it became suddenly harsh. Everything he had done with swagger and aplomb before would now be the death of him if this went on much longer.

*The bullets must be holy. But how could they be holy bullets?*

Misha extended his fingernails into claws and reached into his wounded flesh. Digging into his own skin, he grabbed the back end of the bullet. He roared again as he ripped it out. He raised the bullet to his eye.

It was a wooden bullet.

It had been sprayed down with holy water.

"Monster!" came a voice from the direction of the wooden bullets. "If you want my men, you will have to kill me first."

Misha growled and reached for the small of his back. "I can oblige you that." He whirled to face his new adversary.

Commander Robert Hendershot didn't even blink as Misha came into his sights. He opened fire on full automatic, hosing down the creature before him. He didn't care that the bullets weren't striking the heart. It was clear that the monster was already growing weaker—if he hadn't been, Hendershot knew that he would have been dead already.

The bullets streamed down the street, pelting the vampire. And Misha stood and took at least a dozen rounds in his stomach, five in his leg, and another three in his chest.

Misha answered by raising the gun from his belt holster and firing.

The first bullet punctured Hendershot's right lung. The second one caught him lower, in the liver. The impacts knocked him back, but he spit blood and kept firing.

Misha dove forward, down the hole in the middle of the street, leftover from the previous night. He landed with a splash into the sewers below. He staggered off into the darkness, growling in pain.

Misha's only comfort was that he had killed the ninja, and Marco would be his slave, —if not tonight, then within 48 hours.

Marco was already starting to become one of his own. Misha could smell it.

Robert Catalano scrambled away from the werewolf as his son crashed into it. The werewolf thrashed and bucked under Marco, and he made certain that he was nowhere near the claws. It was bad enough that Marco had been infected, he didn't want to catch it as well.

Robert stared at his son, laughing over the slaughtered corpse of the creature that just attacked him.

It wasn't so much that Marco had killed it with his bare hands—Robert was used to that by now.

The insane laughter wasn't … *too* off-putting; Robert knew his son had a dark side to him.

However, the laughter went on for a full minute, and it became creepy after the first ten seconds.

The laughter died away, leaving Marco breathless. He bent over the body, catching himself on the floor as he steadied his breathing, forcing breaths to come slower.

Marco rose from the corpse and turned towards Robert. His eyes were a bright gold, and his hand dripped with blood. He dropped the vertebrae, then brought the hand up, like a surgeon ready for cleaning.

"This is infectious," he said absently. He stared at it, and looked around it, making sure that no blood splattered on the floor. He cocked his head to one side, as though listening to the wind.

It was at that point that Robert noticed that the sounds of gunfire had died off.

Marco nodded and looked to his father. "I'm going to wash this off. Wouldn't want to spread it around."

He left the room, and Robert let out a breath that he hadn't known he was holding. *Well*, he thought, *that was different.*

The sound of footsteps thudded in the hallway, and Robert held onto the steak knife as he strode towards it.

He wasn't expecting the two slabs of concrete rammed into the walls of his home. And he definitely hadn't imagined seeing four Vatican ninjas dragging in their commander, who looked like he'd been gut shot.

The faint sour smell coming from his body confirmed it.

"Lay him on the floor," Robert said immediately. He charged in and helped them place Hendershot in place. He looked up at Bram. "My medical bag, in the living room, next to my desk. Bring it."

Bram nodded and darted off. Robert gently moved Dougherty's hands away from the bullet hole and winced at the placement. "It hit his liver. We need an ambulance. Now. Call 911, tell them officer down. Give them Donald's badge number, I'll apologize later."

The redheaded ninja nodded and backed away, drawing his cell phone. Bram replaced him, bag in hand. Robert took it, placed it on the floor, and opened it up, ready to get to work.

"Hendershot?" Marco asked from the doorway.

Robert winced. The last thing he needed was Marco becoming feral on him.

Marco dropped to Hendershot's other side. His hands were clean of blood, but not for long. He ripped away the shirt from the wound. He winced at the damage. He looked at Robert, and his father met Marco's—now blue—eyes and gave a slight nod.

The odds of saving Hendershot would have been great, if they had him in a hospital at that instant.

Marco gave Hendershot a smile. It wasn't amused, it wasn't sardonic, and Robert could only presume that he had practiced a look meant to be reassuring. "Come on, man. You're going to be fine." He gripped Hendershot's hand and squeezed it. "Don't wimp out on me now, you pussy," he said softly. "Especially over a scratch. Your men are watching."

Hendershot rolled his eyes and scoffed.

Marco frowned, and his voice was serious. "I promise you, Hendershot, we're going to kill the little bastard."

Hendershot gave a tight, grim smile. "It's funny. I was born a Calvinist, but I didn't believe." He coughed violently, and Robert struggled to keep the pressure on the wound. His breathing started to speed up. "I had never known faith until I became Catholic. Now, to hear the angels call my name…"

"No," Marco growled. "No. God can't have you yet. You're with me. You're one of my people. You're a cold fish, icy bastard, Hendershot, but you're *my* bastard."

Hendershot actually, for the first time Marco could recall, laughed. "No, you egomaniac. I will go to my God like a soldier. You're not Him." Hendershot gasped in pain and grabbed Marco's arm. "Rodgers.

He should tell my family, I died … saving my men."
He pulled Marco closer. "I died saving *our* men."

Marco nodded firmly. "Our men."

The Ninja commander's breathing came fast and shallow. "No regrets, Marco. No fear. We're the light." His icy eyes locked on Marco's face. "Though the darkness surrounds us, remember who you are. Kill them, Marco. Kill them all." His ground his teeth, fighting against the pain, and Hendershot's teeth cracked. *"Deus vult! Deus … vult!"*

Marco nodded. "God wills it."

Hendershot's body tensed and spasmed once.

Vatican Ninja Captain Hendershot joined their God.

At his rectory, Monsignor Rodgers answered his cell phone … only to discover that it wasn't his usual phone for church business. It was the red phone that never rang. Not unless his day phone was turned off. Both were encrypted, but the red cell phone—blood red, of course—was the emergency phone.

Rodgers couldn't consider what emergency was so severe that the ninjas would go straight to the red phone without even trying his regular one.

He looked around the main office of the rectory, then answered. "Hello!" he boomed. "What seems to be the problem?"

"Hello, Monsignor," Bram said.

Rodgers paused and knew something significant had happened. Because Bram didn't call him. He would have gone through Hendershot, as per protocol.

In short, something had happened to Hendershot.

"How bad? Hospital or morgue?"

"The morgue," Bram whispered, as though worried someone might be listening in.

"Are you alone?" Rodgers asked.

"For the moment. Misha attacked us in open daylight."

Rodgers frowned. He had heard of several engagements during daylight hours. Even the assassin Nuala had been strong enough to leap from one building into another without igniting. "We've seen other vampires run in the open for a few seconds."

"This was several minutes," Bram corrected him. "Nothing even scratched him until the captain hit him with wooden bullets he'd sprayed down with holy water. All that did was drive him off."

Rodgers let out a deep breath, deflating. "Okay. Is there any way to contain the scene?"

"After a fashion. Officer Tolbert arrived a few minutes after the shooting stopped. But we have one live minion, two dead werewolves, and the street is ripped apart like somebody made potholes with heavy artillery. So situation normal."

Rodgers didn't need him to complete the acronym SNAFU. "I'll be there shortly. Make sure you're not seen by anyone other than our people. We don't want to drag in even more of the unwary."

"Already done. All of our equipment is off-site, and one of the EMTs is working with Tolbert and the cops."

"What about the werewolves?" the priest asked. "Any more bites or scratches?"

"No, but it was a near run thing. And … You know what, never mind, we'll talk about it when you get in."

"Copy that."

Rodgers hung up. He crossed himself, then crossed his arms, leaning against the wall, and prayed for the soul of Captain Hendershot.

# Chapter 21

# Cleanup

The black SUV pulled up to the Greenpoint street with caution. The entire street had been cordoned off, as though it was going to host a block party that evening. Only instead of just putting up blue wooden police barricades, it was joined by crime-scene tape. The sidewalk and the street were sealed off. The fire department evaluated and evacuated homes, in case gas lines had been ruptured.

The SUV parked in front of the barricade. The doors opened to reveal Police Commissioner Raymond Wilson. He wore his usual three-piece suit, dark shades, and an NYPD baseball cap. He strode down the sidewalk, quietly observing the level of damage. Three buildings were on the verge of collapse—one wall completely ripped out and thrown across the street, leaving a building's main support wall listing dangerously, two buildings with cracked foundations, and the front door and window of the third entirely destroyed. The street had two large holes like bombs had gone off, and two-lane wide strips had been pulled up and left like misshapen tiles across a different patch of street. The sidewalk was also torn up, some leaving holes that peeked into storm drains. Wilson couldn't figure out why until he stopped in front of the brownstone and observed where hunks of familiar gray concrete were driven into the walls.

The wreckage that used to be cars on the side of the road also demanded his attention. Three of them had been torn in half, both lengthwise and across the center. The jagged cuts and countless perforations he'd only seen once outside wartime. It had to be a minigun. It was usually a vehicle-mounted weapon, but the vehicle that had it was gone from the scene. It made Wilson wonder who had the minigun, and he wasn't certain who would worry him more. If the attackers had the minigun, that was a problem. If the defenders had the minigun and still couldn't stop the onslaught, that was a bigger problem.

Wilson walked up the steps of the residence and was apparently unnoticed by the cops and CSU people around him. He stopped at the threshold of the doorway, took off his sunglasses, and studied the wreckage. The bullet holes in the walls caught his eye, as did the AK on the stairs.

Wilson walked along the edge of the floor, careful to avoid the blood trails. He passed the front room, which had the window smashed in. Glass glittered on the floor as he walked. He stopped at the second door on the left; he peered inside and saw the gathering of officers and civilians. He could see into the third room, which was a dining room with a smashed table.

Wilson looked down and took a long step over and around the blood trail, walking into the living room. There were only three civilians, all on the same couch.

One was a tall, thin, older man, with salt-and-pepper hair. He wore glasses and had a tan that seemed more Italian in nature than a tanning bed or a beach. His features were sharp, but his deep brown eyes were sharper. His arm was around the younger, blond man next to him, but his eyes flicked to the newcomer. He was the first person who seemed to notice Wilson was even there.

The young man next to him wasn't exactly thin, but more of a dancer regarding build. Perhaps a martial artist. His head hung low, almost on his chest, and his shoulders were slumped as he sagged against the couch. His head tipped back a little as he caught sight of Wilson's shoes, and then his eyes flicked up to take in Wilson's presence. He arched a brow, and just sagged back, deflated.

However, on the other end of the couch was someone he knew. Her red-gold hair was flowing and distinctive. Her high cheekbones and profile were even easier to spot. It was hard to forget one of his first crushes, even though he had been 18, in the jungles of Vietnam.

But she didn't even notice him, all of her focus was on the young man in the middle, her arm around him.

"Everyone with a badge," Wilson stated simply, "I need the room."

Suddenly, five of the six officers in the room straightened up, saluted, and swept out, almost like they had evaporated.

One stayed. He was a tall black officer, bigger than even the PC. His posture was ramrod straight as he moved to the couch, next to Amanda. His hat was tucked under his arm, like a knight holding his helmet in the presence of a superior officer.

Wilson said nothing for a moment but sauntered over to the uniform. "Your name, officer?"

"Donald Tolbert, sir."

Wilson gave a small nod. "Are you not a police officer?"

"Not now, sir," Tolbert answered. "I'm a friend of the family."

"Ah. I understand." His eyes flicked from the couch to the officer. "I'm still going to need the room."

Amanda Colt put her hand on Tolbert's arm. "Donald. It is okay."

Tolbert glanced at her and nodded. He strode out of the room. Wilson's eyebrows moved up, paused, then down. "It seems you have more authority with my men than I do," he said casually. Wilson grabbed the large red leather armchair and pulled it over to face the three of them as he sat down. "Hi." He looked to all of them. "You know who I am, yes?"

The older man reached over, grabbed the newspaper from the side table, and flipped to the front page. It showed a photograph of PC Wilson. "You could say that," he drawled.

Wilson nodded. "Granted. You are Doctor Robert Catalano?"

"I am."

Wilson nodded to the redhead. "Miss Colt and I have met." He locked straight onto the man in the middle. "And I presume that this is Marco."

Marco barely lifted his hand from his lap and gave him a single wave to acknowledge his presence.

"Is there a Missus Catalano?" he asked.

"She's out of town," Robert answered. "At a medical conference."

The Commissioner nodded. He looked to each in turn for a moment, trying to assess everything. "So,"

Wilson began, "what exactly happened here? Miss Colt, would you like to begin?"

"A vampire attack," she said flatly. "He is strong enough to attack in broad daylight."

Wilson nodded slowly and thoughtfully, just taking in the information. "I didn't think such a thing was possible."

"It shouldn't be. But it is."

"Telekinetic shield," Marco muttered. "Blocked bullets with it. But he doesn't need it. He seems to be invulnerable to almost anything we throw at him." He actually looked at the commissioner, with dark blue eyes that were sad and tired. "Saw the cars outside?"

Wilson nodded. "I did. Minigun?"

Amanda stroked Marco's arm, still not looking at Wilson. "All of those bullets hit him."

Wilson flinched but tried to hide it. "I see." He looked over them and waited for someone to finish the rest of the story. "But you drove him off somehow."

Marco cleared his throat. "Hendershot did." He pointed towards the blood trail in the outer hallway. "Holy water on wooden bullets."

"Ah. I'm sorry about your friend."

Marco actually smiled a little and laughed. "I couldn't stand the bastard. He had all the charisma of a brick and just as charming." His eyes met Wilson's, and they narrowed. "But he was one of mine, Commissioner. You understand that, don't you?"

Wilson gave a single nod. "I do. I heard there were two gunmen?"

"Three," Amanda corrected. "One blew up."

The Commissioner gave no visible reaction. "Of course he did. And the two men in the dining room?"

"Werewolves," Robert Catalano answered. "We're going to need a lot of silver polish."

*Now* Wilson winced. Getting blood out of good silver would indeed be a pain. "One of them had part of his spine missing?"

"My fault," Marco answered. "I got excited."

The PC arched his brows. "Really? And what are you?"

"I'll let you know in the next day or two," he answered. "I was only bitten yesterday. I'm not entirely certain that our plan to keep me in check is going to work as well as I thought."

"Ah." He looked over the three of them. "Anything else?"

"Good luck filling out the police report," Marco said.

The Commissioner actually smiled at that. "Terrorists blew up your hospital back in September, for the anniversary of 9-11." He looked at Robert. "They tried to finish the job a few weeks ago, back in December. And today was another attempt to do just that. But like all terrorists, they have a tendency to be liberal with the explosives, but short on the aiming."

Marco actually smirked at that. "Okay. You win."

"I'm glad you approve." He looked to the vampire. "Miss Colt. May I talk to you for a moment outside?"

"I hope you mean in the hallway," Marco muttered. "It's a nice sunny day out there."

"Of course."

"Kitchen is probably better," Robert added. "No CSU guys in there."

Wilson nodded, and Amanda slowly followed suit, patting Marco on the arm as she moved away from him.

When they made it into the kitchen, Wilson leaned up against the island in the middle, keeping his hands in his pockets the entire time. "So, fifty years, and I don't even get a handshake?"

Amanda smiled sadly. "Apologies. This has been a bad day."

"Aw, I'll forgive that. Though it would have been nice to know you were in my city for the last two decades. I've had a good job or two since then."

Amanda gave a little chuckle. "I had noticed. I just wanted to be left alone. Until I met Marco, I had been doing a good job."

"Not so much lately, huh?"

"No."

Wilson took in a deep breath, and let out a hearty sigh. "So, what now? A vampire that can walk around in daylight? He can take anything but holy objects? If he can block bullets with his mind, should I guess that he threw those slabs of concrete the same way?" he asked, pointing to the front hallway. "The kind of creature that can do that is not one I want running around my city."

"I know, Ray. We will handle it. We must. He wants us dead."

"I gathered that. My question is how? With what forces? He has minions and werewolves, and he's his own one-man band. And since you're working with Merle Kraft—yes, we've met—I presume that there are also vampire underlings involved in this organization. What do you have? Some street thugs, a few SpecOps guys, and some of my cops. That's it. Do you have a plan, at least?"

"Not yet," she said, exasperated. "He only revealed himself last night."

"He really wants you dead," he stated. "I gather this is connected to the two other attacks I mentioned? On the hospital?"

Amanda nodded. "Yes. But we don't know what his full capabilities are."

Wilson sighed and humphed. "Okay. Listen, I have a few guys I can call in on the whole vampire thing. Let me know if and when you need help."

"I will. Thank you."

"That being said, where are you folks going to spend the night? You can't stay here. If it was this bad in daylight, nighttime won't fare any better."

Amanda smiled. "Do you think we can find one fortified position in all of New York that's religious in nature?"

The Commissioner gave a broad, tight smile. "I think we can manage that." He straightened, moving back towards the living room. "By the way, Jen sends her regards."

Amanda furrowed her brows and frowned prettily. "Jennifer Bosley?"

He nodded. "You know each other, don't you?"

"Yes. But how do you?" She pointed between the two of them. "You and I know each other from Vietnam. But *Bosley*?"

Another little smile. "Jen's been a good friend to me, and the department, since I was a uniform. She cleaned up some of the messes that had threatened to become high profile before they got away from her—mostly vampires who thought that they could rampage throughout our city without any backlash. She was the backlash. She said it was pragmatic."

Amanda frowned. Jennifer Bosley had never told her any of this. Though it made her even more curious about how Bosley had never interceded in the first appearance of the vampire menace arising in Brooklyn over a year ago.

*Except … Bosley already said that the Vampire Association was intimidated by whatever was behind Mikhail, Day and Nuala – i.e.: The Council. We know Misha is probably part of the Council. He could be what's left of the Council, for all we know. If this is a mess that not even Bosley wants to clean up—her and a few thousand vampires—then we might all be in trouble.*

# Chapter 22

# Hideaway

In Queens, New York, at the intersection of Wexford Terrace and Edgerton Boulevard, lies the end of the world in New York City environs. It is the Eastern end of the subway system, which for many Manhattanites is the same thing. It is six miles short of the border between Queens and Nassau County, referred to as "the Island" … the political entity that is Long Island.

Many people, even citizens, regularly remain oblivious that New York City is on multiple islands. Manhattan and Staten Islands are islands unto themselves, and Queens and Brooklyn are on The Isle of Long, which is different from the political entity of Long Island. "Long Island" consists of Nassau County, Suffolk County, and, thinking they are enclave all their own, the Hamptons.

At the End of the World, there are only two buildings. On one side, left as you go up the steep incline of Edgerton, are the stone walls and iron rail fence of The Mary Louis Academy. Yes, "The" is part of their title, in capital letters. There's a reason the location is referred to as "Snob Hill". "The" Academy in question is an all-girls high school. It was attached to a convent, designed in California mission-style. It held the Sisters of St. Joseph, the order of nuns who founded and taught at the school.

The other side of the street, directly across from the convent, was the Passionist monastery of the Immaculate Conception. Edgerton was one of the few places you could really see the monastery portion of the compound. Most of what the average pedestrian could see as they walked up the hill was the church and the driveway. If someone walked along Wexford Terrace, they could barely see over the low wall and iron rail fence—the view was obscured by the steep angle of the hill, as well as the flora. Coming up the other blocks provided few good sight lines—the monastery was hidden by trees or another Catholic school.

This made the area perfect for anyone looking to hide from determined, murderous vampires without leaving the city limits. It was practically the other end of the world from Greenpoint, Brooklyn. Geographically, it wouldn't be easy to guess where they were. The location itself would prevent psychic listening by Misha-- or anyone else for that matter.

Which was exactly what Police Commissioner Wilson and Amanda Colt had in mind.

The quarters weren't lavish. The best accommodation was a monk's cell, which wasn't much larger than a Tombs prison cell. In fact, the ACLU would complain if prisoners were treated like the average monk.

Marco didn't mind. He was busy being ill.

Marco's introduction to his temporary living quarters saw him staggering into the room and stumbling onto the thin, narrow bed.

Amanda walked in close behind him, trying to be polite to their host— who solicitously followed them in. The pastor had heard from Monsignor Rodgers and knew that Amanda and Marco needed to hide. Marco also had a "condition."

No one mentioned the condition was becoming a were-beastie.

Amanda closed the door behind her, watching Marco pull himself farther onto the mattress. His condition had devolved on the way. Since it was too easy to have eyes on the subways, they had taken the surface—just another black SUV on the road. Unfortunately, police procedure had taken hours—it was difficult to have a war in the middle of a city street and *not* have a few pounds of paperwork to fill out.

Between that and negotiating traffic in the late afternoon, it was already dark by the time they got to the monastery.

Despite biting Marco yet again, he already exhibited the effects of the bite. He shook, damp with cold sweats, and he held onto the bed sheets as though he'd fall off the world if he let go. He couldn't even sit up; the sweat-dampened pillows flattened under his wide shoulders and listless bulk. The bed creaked alarmingly every time he moved. It looked like going through withdrawal.

Amanda shook her head as she approached. She had to do something, perhaps bite him again—

Her train of thought interrupted by a knock on the door.

Amanda stopped, furrowed her brows, and eyed the door. She held herself very still. She took a breath, then caught a whiff of a familiar, stupid combination of scents. It was marijuana with a hint of meth. Her eyes glowed briefly, and she stifled them in frustration.

*Damn it, really?* She turned, pulling open the door just enough to slip out into the hall.

She wasn't entirely prepared for what awaited her.

There was the green-eyed redhead, Yana, who Amanda had expected. She had been thin, but hollow cheeks and jutting jaw bones lent harshness to her soft features, emphasized by her new severe butch haircut. Ribs were visible through her thin, form-fitting "So Mote It Be" tee shirt. There were dark circles under her eyes, hinting at last month's ordeal—between losing her girlfriend, and being forcibly controlled by a thousand-year-old evil, Yana had earned a few sleepless nights.

The next one was a brunette, who Amanda hadn't been able to smell over the scent of Yana's drug use. She was slender, healthier, and athletically built, with broader shoulders than Yana. Her complexion was either a dark Russian, or a light-complected Hispanic, with high cheekbones, and cocoa brown eyes. Amanda concluded that this was the one Marco described as "Jackie."

The last one nearly floored her in surprise, but she recognized his ugly mug faster than her hair-trigger reflexes. He was the short, male redhead, like a younger Barry Fitzgerald, with hair the bright red native to fire engines.

"Rory, how are you?" Amanda hugged him. He jumped in surprise and took a moment to return the hug.

"I'm good, lass," he said with his thick brogue. He patted her back, and she let go.

Amanda turned to the two women and held out her hand. Yana shook Amanda's hand. Jackie pulled Amanda into a hug, which became a little bit too casual. When Amanda felt Jackie's hand moving down her back, Amanda pulled away. She pushed off Jackie.

"I'm Jackie."

Amanda's eyes narrowed. "I could guess." She looked at Rory. "What brings you three to New York?"

"Merle, of course," Rory answered. "All hands on deck, and all that." He smiled. He unzipped his heavy, Kelly green winter coat, and pulled back a lapel, showing off the shiny new pistol at home in his shoulder holster. "Thankfully, George is a good lad, and provided me with a few of me own toys."

Amanda smiled. She didn't know how good bullets would be in this situation, but with Misha directing a pack of werewolves, she could understand having a gunslinger around. They needed all the help they could get.

Wait a second … *"You* saw George?"

"Aye," Rory said. "Who do you think picked us up from the airport? He and his men should be in position by now."

Amanda sagged a little in relief. With the ninjas *and* Merle's SpecOps forces outside, she felt a lot better.

The church would keep out vampires. And while prayer could keep Misha from tracking their thoughts, werewolves could technically pick up their scent. The odds of that were low but having a strike force outside made her relax.

She grinned at Rory. "Thank you for coming."

"Of course," Rory said. "I owe the little blighter."

Amanda furrowed her brows and cocked her head. "What do you mean? Which blighter?"

Rory shrugged. "I was dog-piled by a bunch of minions a few days ago. Marco pulled me out of it. It's a good thing he doesn't have a problem with getting his hands dirty. Otherwise, I'd be a pile of ash by now."

Amanda smiled. "Indeed." She looked at Jackie and Yana. "You two are here to help as well?"

Yana nodded. "Yup. We figured that some extra eyes couldn't hurt."

Jackie shrugged. "We wanted to see New York."

Amanda rolled her eyes. "Of course."

Yana looked around Amanda, towards the door. "Is Marco okay?"

"He was bitten by a werewolf. No."

Yana gasped. "But George is a good puppy."

Rory chuckled and pulled out a cigarette. He paused since he couldn't smoke in there. "Aye. Except that George's dark side isn't exactly *Marco's*, now is it?"

Yana winced as she thought it over. "Oh. Right. That could be … yikes. Do we know what he's going to turn into?"

"Whatever best reflects him," Rory answered. "It could be anything, really. But werewolves are the most common. Aggressive predators who will follow an Alpha?"

Yana frowned. "You make wolves sound like sheep of death."

He shrugged. "No comment." He held up the cigarette. "Pardon me, but I have to get a smoke."

"Where should we be?" Yana asked.

Amanda took a slow, deep breath. "I don't think we have anyone in the church. It is down the hallway."

Jackie nodded. "Deal." She punched Yana in the arm. "Come on, sexy. Let's go set up shop."

Amanda waited until they were out of *her* earshot before she sighed. She couldn't imagine a good reason why Merle had sent them over, short of really being worried.

*With what Misha did, aren't we all?*

Amanda opened the door and slid back into the room, quietly closing the door behind her. She turned back to Marco. He still lay on the bed, curled up into a ball. He had grown motionless, and no longer actively sweated. She moved towards him and was about to lay a hand on his shoulder when he turned.

Marco's eyes had turned a bright, unnatural gold. His chin had developed a sudden five o'clock shadow (PM, not AM), and his nails had lengthened. His teeth had already grown visibly sharper.

He looked at Amanda like she was lunch.

# Chapter 23

# Dark Passion Play

Marco lunged for Amanda. Before she could stop him, he had her pinned to the wall by her wrists.

Then he kissed her. Her head thumped against the drywall, but she didn't notice. The move was sudden and shocking, and she gasped as his tongue penetrated her mouth. Her stomach muscles clenched as he pressed against her.

Amanda's breaths came in gasps, straining with exertion that she didn't understand. A distant part of her brain told her that she should have seen this coming. He would have less impulse control as his dark side came closer to physical manifestation. And they had both known what his darker impulses wanted to do with her.

The more active part of her brain just didn't care why. Her body strained with a hunger born of a century without passion.

Marco pressed the full length of his body against hers. She groaned when she felt herself being poked in the stomach. He released Amanda's wrists, but the tips of his fingernails went to the pads of her fingers. Slowly, with control she wouldn't have credited Marco with on his *best* days, his claws slid down her fingers, almost like a caress. The sharp nails lightly scratched over her palms, down the inside of her wrists, and into the crook of her elbow.

All the while, his kiss became more intense and wouldn't let up. His arms slid down and around Amandas body, holding her against him. His hand moved up her spine, and his fingers pushed between her head and the drywall, burying into her hair. He held her prisoner in the kiss as he moved her from the wall and carried her to the bed.

Amanda grabbed Marco's head with both hands and pulled him away from the kiss. She looked into his eyes. They glowed so brightly, she was certain a human could read comfortably. His eyes were wild, but his teeth had pulled back, in response to Frenching her.

Amanda wrapped her legs around Marco and pinned him against her so he couldn't advance. She had to fight down the thrill it gave her to have him like that. She desperately wanted to fall into his madness.

"Marco," she whispered. Her eyes searched his for signs of awareness. "Talk to me."

His breaths came heavy, and each exhale sounded like a growl. His fingers tightened in her hair. His other hand slid down to her hip, gripping her flesh just enough to let her know it was there.

Amanda took several deep, slow breaths, calming herself. No matter how much she wanted Marco to continue where he wanted to, if he wasn't in his right mind, this wasn't going to happen. "I need to bite you now. I need—"

His eyes met hers, and she could see little in his mind, except for images of his intentions toward her. The only clear thought she could catch was more of a feeling, but it translated to *It's my turn to bite you.*

The mental overload caused Amanda's body to lurch. While that distracted her, Marco's head shot forward, and his mouth went to her neck. It started as a kiss, but turned to sucking, and nibbling, and licking. Her arms tightened around his body as he continued to work her neck, hoping to hold him just long enough for her to figure out what to do. His bones began to creak under pressure, but he didn't seem to notice.

Amanda tried to ignore the sensations flooding her mind and body and held on. The main thing keeping her in line was the knowledge that moonrise hadn't happened yet.

If Marco was half-transformed and out of control before the full moon had even come out, she didn't want to imagine what would happen in another hour or two. She had to stop this now, while he still wasn't a threat.

While he isn't a *physical* threat, anyway.

Amanda popped out her fangs and drove them down into Marco's shoulder.

Marco tensed a little, jaw and fingers gripping harder. She was actually worried for a moment that he would draw blood…

*Well, that's a thought.*

Amanda winced, and not from pain. Technically, she could speed up the process by having Marco drink her blood, but that could have had all sorts of nasty side effects, up to and including blood addiction, and becoming her puppet.

*Then again, there are other ways to feed him bodily fluids.*

That caused another wince, but for completely different reasons. There was so much to go wrong. If she went in that direction, there was no guarantee to prevent things from going too far. She couldn't be certain about *her* actions, to heck with Marco's.

Amanda sucked in some of Marco's blood. She could taste the difference. His blood was filling with the lycanthropy virus—which meant that the virus surged during the full moon. Worse, it meant that the vampire virus in her saliva wasn't suppressing it fast enough. She needed more virus in his system, as quick as possible.

*Well, damn.*

Amanda tightened her hug around Marco, reaching one hand towards another. She jabbed her left thumbnail into the web of flesh between her right thumb and index finger, using the nail the open the skin.

*I hope this doesn't make him a mindless minion.*

She grabbed him by the back of the head, pulled his mouth away from her neck, and shoved the bloody wound into his mouth.

And Marco willingly, gleefully, drank Amanda's blood. His throat visibly worked as he swallowed. He even bit down to squeeze out more blood.

After the fifth or sixth swallow, the reaction was immediate. His body racked, and he gasped. His hands went to the bed sheets, and gripped them so hard, they tore. He bit down harder and growled. But he drank deeper, despite the effect it had on him. His body thrashed, as though trying to escape, but his mouth stayed locked on her hand.

After a few more seconds, his entire body shook, like he was having an epileptic fit. His eyes rolled back in his head, and his body looked like it was about to shake apart. The bed clattered in response.

Amanda held onto Marco with her legs and held his head in place with both hands. He thrashed, and trembled, and couldn't escape her grasp.

With one firm lurch, Amanda rolled them over, putting Marco on his back, hoping the mattress would help. As the seizures grew more violent, Amanda started to worry that he would seize so hard he would break his spine.

Marco's back arched one more time and stayed still for a long moment before he fell back to the bed. Amanda removed her hand from his mouth, and she felt his pulse. It was like a trip hammer. She reached down to his eye and pulled at the eyelid. His eyes were no longer a glowing gold, but their usual deep blue.

Marco let out a breath, then coughed, and cleared his throat before looking back to Amanda. He gave her a weak smile. "Well … That was less than fun." He sagged against the mattress and let out another breath. Relaxing against the bed, he blinked slowly a few times. One hand patted her hip.

Then his smile returned, and he met her eyes. He squeezed her hip gently, and playfully flared his eyes. "Though I must admit, I could get used to this."

Amanda frowned at him a moment, then became deeply aware of their position. She demurely moved off of Marco and settled next to him on the bed. "I'm sorry about the blood, but—"

Marco gave a single short laugh. "Please. I'm just glad you did it before I did."

She raised a brow and looked at him. He was still flat on his back, but his left hand stroked her spine. "What?"

"There was a lot of noise in my head," he explained, "but I knew I had to bite you. Though in my condition, it might have been to rip your throat out. Your guess is as good as mine."

"I wouldn't want you to become my minion," she said.

He chuckled. It took him a minute, but he sat up. He caught himself before he tipped over. Once balanced, he gave her an amused look. "Too late."

Amanda's eyes widened, horrified as Marco turned around, and lowered himself to one knee before her. He bowed his head deeply. "Command me."

"No! Marco, I—"

His hand shot up, and the tips of his middle three fingers pressed against her lips. He looked at her, a smile on his lips. "To be your minion is to let you into my mind and do your bidding. Been there, done that.

I already proposed to you. As far as I'm concerned, I already belong to you. I would already do anything for you. Let you into my mind for any reason."

He slowly rose, leaning into her with a gentle, lingering kiss. He pulled back with a mischievous glint in his eyes. "Command me however you like," he whispered.

Amanda's jaw dropped, and she felt more affected by that than all of their rolling around together. She hesitated. Finally, she said, "Cuddle with me."

"I can manage that."

# Chapter 24

# Ceremonies Of The Damned

Yana sat on the floor of the church, behind the final pew in the back, and made little chalk circles in the four corners on the floor around her. Bundles of herbs and stones marked each circle. A pretty silver dagger sat on a black square of silk in front of her, ignored for now. She leaned forward and backwards and from side to side, making sure that she had all of the directions covered. She occasionally referred to the large book in her lap before making adjustments to her outlines.

Up against the wall, Jackie stood next to an open window. She had a lit cigarette that was only a cigarette. She watched her girlfriend work, blowing smoke out the window after each inhale, and flicking the ashes outside to join them. While she wasn't big on religion or faith, she at least had enough respect not to make a mess or leave the scent of tobacco lingering in the air.

As for what her girlfriend was doing? That was a different kettle of fish.

"It's not really nice to leave a mess on the floor, is it?" she asked Yana.

The redhead kept working and didn't even look in Jackie's direction. "It's just chalk and stones. We're not going to damage anything."

Jackie grimaced, looking around at the hovering statues of saints and angels in stained glass windows, then back to the markings. "But you're not exactly being very respectful here."

Yana gave a quick shrug. "It's all the same thing. Christians just worship the White God. We're just tapping into an aspect of it."

Jackie arched a brow. "What do you mean *we*, pale face?" she muttered. She sighed, and said louder, "What exactly are you going to do?"

"First, we're going to summon some nature spirits," Yana continued. "Bind them. You know, for support purposes. After that, I'm going to pray to Hecate for a bit."

"Who's that?"

"Mother of Underworld. Worshiped all over the world."

Jackie shook her head, then turned to stare out the side window. There wasn't a lot to see, just a parking lot. "At the very least, it strikes me as rude in someone else's church."

Yana laughed. "Oh, there is no someone else, it's all the same thing. Would you feel better if I summoned archangels?"

"It would at least be in the right wheelhouse."

"I'll see what I can do after I pray to Hecate."

The vampire known as Misha opened his eyes. At the moment, they were orbs of deepest, endless black, like the compound eyes of an insect. He smiled with razor sharp teeth and rose from his armchair.

Striding out onto the catwalk, above the main room of the old factory, he looked down into his den of werewolves.

"Tully!" he barked. "Karl! Take your packs, and prepare a raid for tomorrow morning!"

# Chapter 25
# The Daylight Raid

January 6<sup>th</sup>

Jackie woke as sunlight poured in through the church windows. She tried moving from the pew but had to take it slowly. Her back hurt from laying down on the hard wood all night. She would have considered another option, but the marble floor was worse. Between the two, she preferred being off the floor.

Jackie managed to get her legs over the side of the pew and sat up. She breathed a sigh of relief that she got that far. Stretching from side to side, she then leaned forward to stretch out her lower back. When she finally felt limber, she straightened up and rolled her shoulders.

*Damn, I need a cigarette.*

Jackie walked over to the side window, where she had taken up her position last night. She'd rather have all of her butts in one place, just to make things easier for when she went out to police them later.

Jackie opened and braced the window. She breathed in the nice fresh air of the morning, relatively cool. She was from San Francisco—a New York winter felt like a mild spring to her.

Jackie leaned up against the windowsill, tapped out a cigarette, then used a lighter. She took a nice, slow drag, and leaned over to blow out the smoke. She slid the lighter away and settled in for more boring watch duty.

A furry arm shot through the window, and a great claw clamped down on Jackie's shoulder. It ripped her through the open window and hurled her to the ground. A ravenous, howling wolf leaped on her.

Yana awoke to Jackie's blood-curdling screams of pain and terror.

Marco Catalano opened his eyes and looked into the lovely, sleeping face of Amanda. She looked so adorable, cuddled up against the crook of his arm. It was the second morning in a row he had woken up with her against him. He could get used to it.

*Granted, I have to become a night person. She can only stay awake for so long.*

The window crashed in, flooding the room with light.

Amanda leaped off the bed, and dove under the window, staying as much in the shadow as possible. Something had crashed through the window and landed in the corner. It looked like a big ball of black fur …

Until, of course, it unfurled itself into a seven-foot werewolf.

Marco rolled off the bed, onto his feet, and wished he had any silver on him. His toys had been taken the other night by the Vatican Ninjas, before the police showed up and confiscated things like his Desert Eagle or inquired too closely about how many sharpened stakes he had in the house.

He would have to settle for whatever he had.

Marco reached down, grabbed the bed frame, and pulled up. The mattress flipped over and covered Amanda, protecting her from the sunlight. Using both hands, he swung the metal frame like a club.

With a single swipe, the werewolf sliced the bed frame to pieces, leaving Marco with a single bar of metal, cut off at the end.

Marco narrowed his eyes and glared at the intruder. The creature didn't have much time. Merle's SpecOps team, lead by George, would be ready to come down on this sucker. And the Vatican Ninjas were also probably in the neighborhood by now. These guys were toast.

Then another werewolf crashed through the window and slammed right into him.

Rory had been just inside the door of the monastery since before the sun came up. He was content to hide within the door, protected from the sunlight. The sun was a mite troublesome since he was never that powerful—for good or ill. He could take the average human, but he wasn't certain he could take Marco. He wasn't going anywhere near the sun if he didn't have to.

He only had a few seconds, but he smelled the wolves coming. Being a former IRA gunman, he knew enough to hold his position regardless. Everyone had their area of responsibility, and by God, was he going to hold his.

He drew his gun and heard everything go to Hell a second later. He heard Jackie's screams behind him, and he heard the window crash in Marco's room. He was about to turn and defend his flank, —but several wolves burst through the tree line in front of him.

Rory grinned and proceeded to blast away. The gun fired and flared as fast as he could pull the trigger—since he was a vampire, it was as fast as a machine gun.

He laughed aloud as he sprayed them down with hollow-points stuffed with silver balls. He began to sing, "Oh come out ye Black and Tans! Come out and fight me like a man! Show your wife how you won medals down in Fla-a-anders! Tell her how the IRA, made ye run like Hell away, from the green and lovely lanes of Killeshandra!"

Werewolves were everywhere. They were starting to annoy the Hell out of George Berkeley.

He had been on one of the perches atop the convent across the street when he caught the first whiff. Numbers were hard to distinguish at this distance. It came from down the hill. He double-clicked his communication unit, alerting his people. He did it once more to identify the enemy type—though he probably didn't need to. It was already daylight. It was unlikely that run-of-the-mill humans would be a problem.

George leaped from his perch into a roll, bounded to his feet, running for the church. If Marco was the bait, then George was one of the jaws about to clamp shut.

George ran for the opening to the convent driveway. The exit had walls on either side. As he stepped past them, two other werewolves slammed into him. Each of them wore a ring of car air fresheners around their necks, making them smell like the pine trees behind them.

He didn't know if the werewolves had been alerted by his smell, if their vampire master had somehow detected him, or if Nuala had reported that Marco and Amanda had a shapeshifter of their own.

George knew he was in trouble. Both werewolves slammed him through the door of an SUV with a loud report of twisting metal. He slammed against the other door on the inside of the SUV, and the entire car rolled over, onto the roof. The force of the turn dumped him on his head.

George kneed one of the werewolves in the face. He reared back as far as he could, punching the second one in the nose. He used both hands to grab the wolf by the snout and the back of the neck, and slammed it through the roof, against the concrete.

George reached down to his holster, drew his gun, and blew the wolf's brains all over the car.

The other wolf scrambled out of the car. George tried to reach around the corpse in front of him, but it was already an awkward position.

*Screw it.* George reached down, unlocked the door and opened it, and bolted out into the street. He came up, pistol in hand, and swung around, intending to use the car as cover as he hunted the other werewolf.

The second werewolf already leapt at him from the top of the car.

Marco felt like he was hit by a one-ton piece of ravenous animal. The beast was closer to four hundred pounds, and slammed him right through the door, into the hallway. He slammed against the opposite wall, leaving a hole in the drywall.

Marco barely tracked the action. One moment he had an idea about skewering a wolf on the remains of a bed frame, the next he was concussed, dazed, and his world had become a blur. He shot out with an elbow, and he felt it hit something relatively soft. There was no reaction from the beast, and it flung him over its shoulder like a weightless sack of potatoes.

The creature took off, with Marco in a fireman's carry. Marco twisted, thrashed, and reached back, managing to get his arm around the wolf's throat. He pulled with all of his strength.

The resistance was insurmountable. The wolf didn't even notice.

Marco winced. To get through the full moon without becoming some sort of, furry abomination, he had dosed himself with enough of Amanda's blood to become a minion. Her Vampire blood suppressed the lycanthropy and the extra strength that came with it. He didn't even have minion-level strength because the vampire infection flooding his veins was busy with the shape-shifting virus.

In short, Marco was screwed, exhausted, and he couldn't do anything about it.

*Amanda now would be a good time to—*

Just as he thought it, a second werewolf exploded through the wall of his room and hurled a round black object into it.

The flash-bang went off as the werewolf carrying him charged from the hallway. Marco winced in sympathy. Merle had used a string of flash-bangs against a cave of vampires in Afghanistan last month, and the effects were painful—to vampires. Their enhanced hearing didn't react well with the over 200-decibel blast, or the brightness of a million candles.

Marco's heart sank.

The second werewolf charged past Marco.

Yana cowered on her knees, frightened out of her mind. The world exploded in screams and gunfire, and the loud staccato of detonations. She gripped the back of the last pew, frozen stiff. She heard Jackie scream, which wasn't nearly as bad as the tearing of flesh, and bones snapping like branches in a raging storm.

Yana wasn't even all there. No, she was back in the horrid den of a Vampire assassin last month. She'd *had* to drink blood, then forced to do … other things that she had spent all of her time trying not to think about. Acts even *she* considered unnatural. She had done her best to move on by replacing the girlfriend she lost and making sure to relax. By doing more recreational drugs.

Now, lost in a haze of unreality, her head whipped around to every sound, flinching or whimpering at the slightest stimulation.

Then the doors burst open as a werewolf crashed through. It was a big black beast the size of a bear. A glancing blow bowled her over. The wolf slid to a stop as claws skidded along marble floors and whirled to face her.

Another wolf came from the hallway that led from the monastery. It was a taller wolf that walked on two legs, carrying Marco over its shoulder. Marco's had his arm wrapped around the wolf's throat, as though trying to strangle it.

The wolf glared down at Yana. She whimpered, trying to scramble backwards on her rear. The bipedal wolf slammed a clawed foot down on her stomach, and the pinpoints of the claws dug into her skin. It looked down at her with its big gray eyes and gave her a grin that ran the length of its snout.

"Yes," it growled, in a voice like gravel. "You're the one. I thank you, little witch. Your prayers were not in vain. Reaching out to Hecate as you did pierced the cloak of holiness from the church, and enabled my master to sense my brother wolf here."

Yana's green eyes widened with the realization that everything happening here, from Jackie to this moment, was all her fault. Her and her stupid, drug-addled brain, and what Marco had once called her even dumber new-age neo-pagan gibberish, had opened the door for all of this.

The wolf dug its claws deeper into Yana's stomach, and raked down, spilling her guts all over the floor of the church.

George took one bounding sidestep as the werewolf dove for him. He swung the gun into position, and fired three rounds into the wolf's side, then once in its head.

"It's a different game when the other guy is armed and ready for you, isn't it?" George muttered over the corpse.

He looked back to the church as the sounds of gunfire broke out all over the neighborhood. His men were mixed in with the Vatican Ninjas, and they were scattered all over, mostly hiding in apartments with absent tenants, or scattered on rooftops. Some of the gunshots came from farther down the hill, or on the south side of the monastery, and even on the opposite end of the compound, beyond the tree line, on Midland Parkway.

But there were no gunshots over on the north side of the complex.

George clicked his transmitter. "Chavez, you there?"

"Confirm. What's up?"

"Tangos coming your way. It's why they're on every other side—they're feints. Any extraction will go right through you. You might be under attack any moment. I'm going to intercept the package."

George rushed for the church door, and ripped it off its hinges, splintering wood.

He saw a werewolf carrying Marco down the middle of the church, while another one brought up the rear.

George drew down, firing into the back of the nearest wolf. The wolf took the first round in the shoulder, and staggered, falling against the row of pews. It bounded back, pushing forward, and caught the next round in the back, near the spine. It lurched the other way, and George readjusted his aim for the lead wolf, carrying Marco. It had already turned so that the side with Marco faced George. George aimed low, and for the front, hoping to catch the wolf at the hip, without injuring Marco. The first two bullets went wide, and the third caught the front pew. The werewolf burst out the side door, and George was about to give chase when the sound of a car screeched to a stop outside.

Chavez's voice came from his radio, "Tangos have an armored car, and just came right past me."

George growled, and took two steps backwards through the door, aiming for the driveway that ran the length of the property. If the car gunned the engine, it would come to him. If it took a moment to turn, it would be going back towards Chavez and his team and caught between the two of them. Without hesitation, he ejected a magazine and refreshed it with a collection of armor-piercing bullets.

The armored car gunned the engine, and George was ready, firing four rounds into the front tire, six into the driver's side door, and then another four into the rear tire.

The car neither stopped, nor slowed, and hung a right turn, heading out of George's sight as he emptied the magazine into the other back wheel.

George swept up the discarded magazine and rammed it back in. He knew that he hit the damn thing several times, in several places.

*Which means they have run-flat tires.*

George decided to take off after the car—unlike the proverbial dog chasing the bus, George knew exactly what he would do if he caught it. But he finally noticed a putrid smell of carnage from inside the church. He hadn't even seen his friend Yana inside, where he had left her the night before.

George ran back inside the church. Yana was there, on the floor, holding her hands over her stomach. Tears ran down her face, and she whimpered through the pain.

And he saw that she was trying to hold her guts in.

He dropped to one knee at her side, and immediately radioed for a medic, even though he knew that there was no way she could be saved, even if he bit her. Amanda couldn't turning her either. Too much of Yana was already on the floor.

George put his hand over Yana's and smiled at her. "It's okay, Yana. You're going to be fine. I've got people coming."

Yana looked up at him imploringly. Her eyes were wide, and he couldn't tell if it was terror or pain. She opened her mouth, and nothing came out but a wail, filled with sorrow and pain. It turned into a sob. She whispered, "My fault, George. All my fault." She sobbed again, weaker this time. "Me and my stupid Hecate. Stupid. So stupid,"

George didn't know what to say to that. He always knew that Yana was a little flaky, with her Wicca and her hatred of guns (even though she'd used a crossbow against vampires in the past). But he had known her since she was six, in kindergarten, when she thought that *Charmed* was a documentary, and her Hippie parents made unfortunate brownies for PTA meetings.

All he could say was, "Don't worry. We can fix this. We'll get Marco back. He's tough."

Yana's pale green eyes met George's, and she tried to give him a weak smile.

Instead, she gave one last gasp. Her body relaxed, and she sagged in George's arms.

Good to the Last Drop

# Chapter 26

# Slow And The Furriest

Marco Catalano woke up in blinding pain and screaming. He growled, infuriated, and then thrashed, pulling against the bonds that chained him to the wall. They burned against his skin, telling Marco that they were silver, meant to contain him.

*In that case, they have another thing coming when I get out of here and kill every last one of them.*

The sizzle as Marco strained against the silver warned him that all of the blood Amanda had given him had already burned through his system.

*But this means that I should be as strong as a werewolf now. If I can get free, I can give them merry hell.*

Marco growled as he pulled and thrashed against the restraints. He knew he should have a plan, but between the rampant rage in his head, and the blinding pain shooting through his arms and legs, he couldn't even think.

"Oh, good," came a deep, smooth voice, tinged with a Russian accent. "You're awake. That will make things so much more delicious."

Marco's eyes narrowed, coming into focus. The first thing he was able to see was the vampire that had started this latest fresh Hell. It was probably the best view he'd had of the him since this entire mess started. Misha was good looking, downright handsome even—despite the scar in his face, left by Amanda's teeth. Like his brother, Mikhail the Bear, Misha was big, well over six feet tall, and wide.

Marco smiled. "Fine, then. Bite me, you blood sucking little twit. I hope you choke on me."

"Not that sort of tasty." Misha smirked but said nothing, his deep, dark eyes flicking to another side of the room. "John, if you would be so kind?"

Marco followed the gaze to another man in the room. He was long and lanky, nothing like Misha; his body type was something along the line of "wire brush" or "pipe cleaner." He had a thick black beard with matching ponytail. There was a shock of pink in his forelock. His outfit was meth user chic, sporting a dirty gray t-shirt and torn sweatpants.

John staggered a little in front of Marco, stopped, looked at him, and said, "Sit, stay."

Marco wondered if this trick was supposed to do anything. He looked at the vampire. "Really?" Marco said, incredulous. "Hipsters? A hipster werewolf pack? I would have thought they would have turned into sheep, not wolves." He chuckled darkly to himself. "Although in this case, they should be called *Yip*sters."

Misha shrugged. "A man's dark side can only manifest as a predator. Wolves are pack animals, so are people. It's why there are so many stories about werewolves. Other variants are outliers."

Marco glared at John in disgust. "Tell me that *this* pathetic worm isn't the one who took me. That would be embarrassing."

"No," Misha drawled, "that would be Tully. He led the raid." He smacked John on the arm, causing the werewolf to stagger into the wall next to Marco. "Now give him a *real* command."

John looked at Marco, pushed off the wall, and straightened. "Shut up and listen to the master. And stop thrashing about."

Marco gave him a look and an arched eyebrow, but he said nothing.

John nodded. "So *there*." He focused on Misha. "Let me know if you need anything else."

Misha grabbed him and shoved him onto the floor. The vampire's eyes still bored into Marco as he ordered the wolf, "Don't go anywhere. I'll need you to explain something."

Marco's dark blue eyes tracked Misha as he walked towards him. "You will be relieved to know," Misha continued, "that you will *not* be part of our dining tonight. In fact, you will not be part of anything, except our side."

Marco scoffed, then shook his head, saying nothing.

The vampire smiled. "Your lack of smart ass remarks, for example, is a result of John giving you an order to be quiet. You may think you're controlled and calm, but you're not, believe me on that."

Marco gave him a little smile that spoke volumes: somewhere between a comment about his control and calm, then rolled his eyes.

Misha's eyes narrowed, and he smiled evilly, a tight little smile that was a mirror to Marco's own. "Tonight, with the full moon out and shining, you will do anything you're told. There may be a little left of Amanda's blood in your system. The more it is burned out of your veins, you will lack even more control."

He reached forward and grabbed Marco's chin, slamming his head back against the wall. Marco ground his teeth and moved his head around … and felt that his head had created a divot in the wall. Misha's eyes both glowed with malice. They became even deeper and darker. Marco could see the vile carcass behind his handsome mask.

"And then," Misha said, "once the creature has its total and complete domination of you, any wolf, even a beta like John here, can give you an order. You will do *any*thing that *any*one tells you to do. You will serve us. Tonight, we will turn you loose on Alina Savinkova, and you will kill her. Then, we will keep you as our pet until you're no longer entertaining. Afterward, we feed you to the other dogs!"

The vampire smacked Marco, making the divot in the wall even deeper. Marco shook his head, clearing his head and his vision as best as possible. There was something wrong with Misha's voice—or perhaps he had been hit in the head too hard, and he heard things. It was almost as though the vampire's voice was echoing. The eyes seemed darker again. It was like during Misha's assault on Marco's home, there had been something so familiar about them. But he couldn't think about it at the time, and even now, it was so difficult to put a thought together. There was something wrong. He knew there was something he should be worried about with Misha. There was something familiar about all of this.

"Never happen," Marco said, coughing on plaster dust. "I'll kill myself first."

Misha waved it away, dismissively. "Win-win." He frowned, then kicked John aside like, well, a dog. "Worthless cur. Out of my sight, and tell me when Tully returns." John scurried away. "We'll obviously need an alpha to handle you on a long-term basis, even if John's orders work now. Doesn't matter. Either way, tonight you *will* kill Alina, and you *will* live with it. That we can guarantee you."

Marco shook his head. He was definitely hearing things. There's no way Misha's voice could echo in this… His eyes flicked around the room. It looked like some sort of factory storage room. He focused on Misha again. "All this so you and whatever may be left of the Council can take over the world?"

Misha blanched and cocked his head at Marco. "You're guessing."

Marco shrugged as best he could with his hands chained above his head. He didn't want to tip off Misha that the UN was bugged by Merle. But he needed more information. "Mister Day—Asmodeus, whatever—was seen walking into the UN. Your brother's right-hand creature, the one Merle Kraft killed? We called him Scarface. He was spotted after he ate an FBI agent. He destroyed the laser microphone the agent had pointed at the United Nations building. So the UN is crucial to your plans.

Or it was, until Merle hit it with all the holy water in their pipes."

Misha sneered. "The plan is alive as long as *I* am alive. I *am* the Council, boy."

*Gotcha, sucker*, Marco thought. "You're already dead," he countered.

"A technicality."

Marco rolled his eyes. "The UN is a building filled with dictators, and you're *already* giving vampire soldiers to terrorist groups. I don't have to make a great leap in logic to think about how many times you can pull that off throughout the world. I mean, hell, make Europe desperate enough, they're probably… what, months, weeks away from being talked into a vampire army?"

Misha narrowed his eyes, and he laughed, his laughter echoing throughout the room. "Close enough. We'll start with all the countries with political prisoners and go on from there."

Marco looked off to the side, thinking about it. Or trying to. But Misha's statement helped. That was easy enough of a list for him to consider: Cuba, North Korea, China, Vietnam, most of the Sandbox. The list of non-tyrannies was probably a shorter list. Then he chuckled. "What did you tell them? That you can *automatically* control any new vampires? Like new werewolves? Except it doesn't work like that. You turn them to vampires, and … what, sic them on their captors?" He furrowed his brow, thinking over how everything else would happen next.

"You forget," Misha said, "every group on the world who ever hated every other group? They will want to join the ranks of the vampires in self-defense. Your racial groups will join us so they can advance their agendas. Your abortion groups, who are already sacrificing millions of children to our cause, will want to join for *their* self-defense. It will spiral from there."

Marco nodded, as though he already knew that. "And you can probably pull this off as part of your function as The Council. But still, it's a basic take-over-the-world plan, isn't it? I mean, that's it? *That is* the whole plot? Thousands of years between you, Day, your brother, and Nuala, and you basically have the plot of a Saturday-morning cartoon show. And really, the Council? You couldn't have come up with a better name for the four of you?"

Misha shook his head. "No. This is Hell on Earth by the time we're done," he explained. "A paradise for vampire and demon alike. Chaos and wrath. An eternal night, where vampires reign and humans live in cages for our dining pleasure." He jabbed Marco in the chest with a finger. "And *your* leaders will hand it over to us. And *you* will hand it over to us."

Marco shook his head. "But why come after *me*? You blew major resources of the Council on… me. Mikhail I understand; I was killing off his people *en masse*. But Day? Sending *him* after me? That was a heck of a resource to burn."

Misha grinned. "True. But that was why we sent him after you, and later Nuala. You killed my brother. Day had nothing else to do for a few days, and he was *happy* to oblige. He is a demon of wrath and lust. He would kill you, and rape Alina to death."

Marco's eyes went dark at the sound of Amanda's real name in this creature's mouth. Marco grimaced. He grabbed the chains with his bare hands. His skin sizzled, and he held onto them and pulled at the chains, despite the silver. "I'll freaking kill you. I will rip your head off and use it for a soccer ball before it turns to dust."

Misha laughed and slapped him on the chest. "After you dispatched Day, we knew that you were a threat to us *and* to the plan. That was Nuala's job."

The vampire swiped his finger at the tip of Marco's nose, slashing it with a fingernail. It healed in seconds. Misha nodded, sure the lycanthropy was entirely in charge of Marco's system. "We knew you were dangerous, a threat we *needed* to eliminate. Nuala just took her time assembling her forces." Misha rolled his eyes at that. "Obviously, it didn't work. But tonight, we have the ultimate weapon against the forces of God." He jabbed Marco in the chest, cracking the sternum. It healed immediately, but it still hurt. "You. You will be at *our* beck and call, whether you like it or not, beyond your control. Alina would not dare harm you."

Marco squinted at him, then looked around the room. The werewolf called John was gone, and there was only Misha and Marco. "Who the Hell is this *we*, anyway? Your brother is dead. Day is vanquished. Nuala is *really* dead. Far as I can tell, it's just you. You can't possibly be counting those lousy wolves. You're not the type that shares power."

Misha grinned and stared at Marco. The pupils of his eyes grew. First, they covered the iris, and then the whites of Misha's eyes. They were the bottomless black compound eyes of a fly.

Misha spoke again, but it wasn't *just* Misha this time. Beneath the easy, mellow Russian voice was a second one, a smooth, cultured thing Marco had heard once before, and occasionally in his nightmares. It was possibly the only monster Marco had ever faced that had scared him into actively praying for his own sake during a battle. It had taken him in its great black hands and nearly smashed him. Only a miracle had saved Marco's hide.

And now, it was back from the abyss.

"Demons never die, Marco," came the voice of Misha and Asmodeus. "We just go back to Hell. And we always come back."

# Chapter 27

## After Action Report

**M**erle Kraft looked at George Berkeley through the bleary eyes of a man who desperately needed coffee.

He'd had a rough twenty hours, and an even rougher seventy-two hours. He hadn't had much in the way of sleep since his arrival in New York City.

After the assault, Merle had spent hours being yelled at by about everybody who knew he existed. They yelled about the sovereignty of nations. They yelled about treaties. They yelled about neutrality, and bargains, and diplomatic immunity, and assassination—at least one of the ambassadors, and multiple aides, had been vampires. At least one person brought up *parking tickets*.

After a while, Merle became fed up and told off the politicos, in painstaking and explicit detail.

Merle explained to them that vampires affected by holy water weren't just "people with fangs," or an "endangered species," or "people we can bargain with"; but that they had once been human beings who traded anything that resembled their humanity for power.

Merle told them of every vampire he had ever seen, and every vampire he had ever killed, and exactly how much they had cost him, personally, and the cities of San Francisco and New York.

Merle told them of "Mister Day," who had turned into a dragon and nearly burned down the Wharf, who *also* made deals and bargains with the United Nations. Who had been sent, quite literally, screaming back to Hell by a guardian angel who had peeled himself out of stone and concrete.

After a few minutes of doing just that, the calls finally stopped, and he was allowed to at least *look* at his bed.

But, then, George had come in to tell Merle about the attack on Marco's home in Greenpoint. That led to an interesting conference call between Police Commissioner Wilson, Enrico the Mobster, Jennifer Bosley the Vampire Queen of New York, Monsignor William Rodgers, as well as the head of at least one street gang.

At long last, after being awake and on the move for well over forty-eight hours, Merle Kraft was finally allowed to sleep.

He woke up to *this*.

"What do you mean, Marco was taken?" He looked at George as though the commando had grown another head. "You had the Vatican Ninjas, you had your own guys, and you had Rory and Amanda. How is it even *possible* they made it through?"

"They had a platoon of wolves," George said simply. "It took everyone we have to even hold back the ones we saw. They had an armor-plated vehicle with run-flat tires, so we couldn't stop them with the spike strips we had laid down. We thought RPGs would have been too much for a residential neighborhood."

Merle sighed and grabbed the nearest cup of coffee. He couldn't remember if it was his or George's, but he needed the caffeine so much, he didn't care.

His midnight blue eyes studied George for a long moment. George was very stiff and very formal. His eyes had locked onto a point just above Merle's head and didn't flicker away from it. This wasn't exactly in George's wheelhouse. George had been a civilian less than a year ago and was only allowed on the SpecOps team because he was both a werewolf and had enough discipline to follow orders. He became *de facto* team leader after a few months, due to a knowledge of vampires, and his willingness to take even more risks than anyone else. The first team leader Merle was assigned had died. Even though George didn't have the rank, he had enough skills in front-line combat with the undead that no one was going to ignore his thoughts during an engagement. The men took to calling him "Sarge," since he wasn't an officer, but everyone followed him anyway.

George's quiet stoicism now worried him.

"What have you left out, George?"

George cleared his throat. His eyes didn't move from the point on the wall. "Yana and Jackie didn't make it. The werewolves took Jackie by surprise, and Yana got in their way during their exfil."

Merle winced. When he first started the little anti-vampire crusade back in San Francisco, Yana had actually approached *him* about putting together a team. She had brought Rory on board, and her friend Sarah.

Then Sarah had been ripped apart. Now Yana. She had been the trusting one. The one who had seen Marco beat a human being to a pulp before she realized he was more than just someone who killed vampires for a hobby.

Merle sighed. Mourning was a luxury he didn't have time for. "Did we take any of the attackers alive?"

George shook his head. "None of the wolves would stop until we killed them or were so damaged they couldn't survive their injuries."

Damn it, Dalf was right, he thought. I have boots on the ground, and I need more firepower. Just when I thought I could do something as breathtakingly odd as sleeping for a few hours.

Merle frowned. "Of course. Just our luck. Okay. I need to know where the hell everyone is, and right now."

In the Church of Saint Anthony-Saint Alphonsus, Doctor Robert Catalano held his face in his hand and tried not to slam his forehead into the rectory's coffee table.

The sniper, Bram, stood across the table from him, standing at attention. His rifle was against the wall, and his Uzi sidearm was slung over one shoulder. His soft brown eyes studied the older man, struggling for some bit of good news.

Next to Robert was Monsignor Rodgers, his hand on the doctor's back in an attempt to be reassuring. But the old priest didn't look too great himself. He had already lost Hendershot, and he had baptized Marco as an infant. The Catalanos were not just parishioners, but friends from way back.

"Here's the good news," Bram said, trying to get their attention. "They took Marco. They want him alive."

"Or torture him to death," Robert corrected. He lowered his hands and raised his eyes. "They are demonic creatures from blackest Hell, after all—and if they're not, they worked with them. Wasn't there this Mister Day creature you folks talked about? Some sort of demon?"

"Yes. But it's hard to torture Marco," Bram replied. He gave a little smile. "Please remember, he tried going a few rounds *with* Hendershot, and didn't do *too* badly. He has enough mental control to look into a vampire's eyes and read *their* mind. Torture? Won't work. The longer he goes without Amanda's bite or blood, the stronger he'll become, and harder it is to hurt him."

Robert met Bram's eyes with a cynical look. "Or they use silver."

The Vatican ninja-sniper sighed, frustrated. Sometimes talking with civilians, even *rational* civilians, strained his patience. "Yes, but Marco has been shown to be more trouble than he's worth. And they're on the run. Despite our losses, we've been winning. The vampires are flooded out of the UN. Their leader can't make deals when the carpets and the floors are soaked with holy water. Merle has FBI agents watching the top brass of the UN, so they're covered. They lost a lot of wolves last night. They tried to directly engage us because they're desperate. In the case of Marco, torture would be counter-productive."

Robert's look turned sharp. "What do you mean?" He looked to Rodgers. "What does he mean? Why *wouldn't* they want to hurt Marco?"

The priest gave a heavy sigh, then looked to Bram, more sad than anything else. It would be little comfort for Robert to know what was most likely in store for his son.

"Remember when we said that any werewolf could give a new lycanthrope a command during the first few full moons?" Bram asked. "This makes Marco the best weapon they have against Amanda. After Marco, she has to be the biggest threat to them. They've been trying to kill both of them since this started. So…"

Robert narrowed his eyes. "So you thought you'd gloss over *Your Son Won't Be Tortured to Death* with *He'll Be Used as a Weapon to Murder His Girlfriend*? This, by you, is comforting?" He shook his head. "Speaking of which, where is Amanda? How is she taking all of this?"

"According to George, she had him get her a specific piece of clothing, then took off like a bat out of Hell."

Robert arched an eyebrow and looked out the window. The sky had gotten darker, which meant, in perfect New York City fashion, that the weather had actually gotten warmer out there. The gray cloud cover was probably enough that Amanda could survive if she took proper precautions and kept an eye on the skies. But that just left one question.

"Where the heck would she go?"

# Chapter 28

# There Will Be Blood

The vampire known only as Kalsey had an ornate office designed to intimidate. The upper runner of the room was lined with swords of various and sundry types, all sharp and functional. The rugs and wall tapestries were Indian. The desk was mahogany, and older than most of the buildings in New York City.

All of the ornate decorations covered a very practical room. Beneath the tapestries and the wood overlay was solid concrete, for the floors, walls, and ceilings. The door was armored, with bars like a bank vault, locking it into the door frame.

Kalsey himself was tall, dark, Sikh, and dressed in Joss Whedon chic: long black leather duster, and everything else solid black. Armani from top to bottom. The only exception to all of this was his gold, top of the line Rolex *Le President*. He was somewhat handsome; his looks were aristocratic, with a sharp nose, smooth features, and proper posture, even when he was seated behind his desk.

When the door to his office exploded, he barely flinched, moving just enough to avoid being decapitated by the steel door as it went flying off its hinges. The door sheared off the back of his desk chair and clipped off several hairs from his head. It embedded firmly in the wall behind him—through the wood, and deep into the concrete below.

A red-cloaked figure followed hotly behind the door, leaping atop of Kalsey's desk. It grabbed Kalsey by the lapels of his jacket and lifted him straight out of his chair, cracking his head against the ceiling. The only source of light illuminating the face within the hood was two points of amber glowing where the eyes should have been.

The figured slammed Kalsey's head against the ceiling with each punctuation mark. "Where. Is. Marco?"

Kalsey shook his head. He was being abused by a woman, that much he could tell from the voice. But– "What? I haven't seen him—"

She hopped back, off the desk, and slammed Kalsey face-first onto the blotter. Her right hand came down on the back of his head, as her left drove the front of a crucifix into his cheek. "*Where is he?* You're one of the few evil bastards in the city who would make a move on him. And if you don't know where he is, you know where he might be."

"I don't know," he answered. "That is the truth, Miss Colt."

Amanda waited for Kalsey's skin to start sizzling and smoking from the touch of the crucifix. Three seconds were usually enough to leave a mark.

She waited.

And waited.

The part of Kalsey's face that wasn't embedded in his desk was blasé, even tolerant of being manhandled. "If you're waiting for the cross to hurt me, it won't anymore."

Amanda unhanded him and stepped back, her eyes no longer enraged, but confused. She pushed the hood back, revealing the rest of her face. Her hair spilled out, over her shoulders and down her front.

Kalsey slid off the desk and straightened his jacket. He looked at the damage done to the door frame. "I hope you haven't killed too many of my men."

"Nail guns don't kill vampires," she replied.

Kalsey leaned to one side, looking around Amanda. Two of his bodyguards were up against the wall, with railroad spikes pinning them to the wall like butterflies, three feet off the ground. He straightened and shrugged. "I hate to break it to you, but we have all turned over a new leaf."

Amanda raised an eyebrow. "I am skeptical."

Kalsey gave her a smirk. "I do try to be practical about such things, Miss Colt. Once you and the entire Vatican Ninja squad became a difficulty, it became obvious that virtue was going to be easier than vice. Especially in my case." His eyes narrowed at her. "Do you know what I had to endure just to confess?" His voice dropped to a deadly whisper. "It. Hurt."

Her mouth twisted into a smile. "I can imagine."

Kalsey nodded. "You've apparently had a slight power upgrade. Nice to see that virtue agrees with you."

"I confess weekly," she answered. "It helps." Her eyes narrowed. "Right now, I am trying to save the man I love. Who is an innocent victim."

Kalsey gave a humorless chuckle. "I would hardly call him innocent, but I understand. Your motives are pure." He slid out a pack of Turkish cigarettes and popped one into his mouth. "But, really, I don't have anything for you. I have stopped being associated with that crowd for months now." He picked up a lighter from his desk that looked so heavy, it doubled as a paperweight. He took a few puffs and placed it down.

"After all, wouldn't want to endanger my immortal soul, now would I?"

Amanda's eyes narrowed at him. He laughed. "Yes, I know, I was stringing up humans for lunch only last year, but it was business. I didn't care as long as it didn't hurt me." He shrugged. "Then it hurt when you and your lousy ninjas got involved." He smiled at the wreckage. "How many of them did you need to get through my men this time?"

"None."

He studied Amanda for a long moment, looking her up and down. Yes, the red cloak covered her from head to toe, but still, moving like that with her level of strength during the daytime was still a feat. "Impressive. Are you trying for sainthood?"

"No. I have no such pretensions. I just want Marco back before tonight."

He gestured at her outfit with his cigarette. "That explains the Little Red Riding Hood outfit." He took a long, drawn-out drag on the cigarette, and let it out slowly. "What's the rush, exactly? If he's not dead already—and I'm surprised he's not, he's not the sort of person I'd keep around—then why will tonight spell his doom?"

"He's been bitten by a werewolf."

Kalsey winced and tried to imagine what creature that Marco would turn into. Even by the standards of the general viciousness of the human race, Marco wasn't someone Kalsey wanted to deal with. He and the human had never actually come into contact, but every employee who had gone near Amanda's human had not survived the encounter.

Kalsey didn't know what was worse: an out-of-control Marco as a shapeshifter, or an *in*-control, shape-shifting Marco.

"I presume you've already talked to Bosley?"

Amanda nodded. "I sent her a text message. I have yet to hear back from her."

Kalsey snuffed the cigarette in an ashtray. "I'll put out some feelers. See if we can get to him before tonight. I have some people in the minion community."

"*They* have a community?"

Kalsey smiled as he pulled out a cell phone and started tapping out text messages. "Not everyone wants mindless slaves to do their bidding. Some vampires merely want capable employees who won't be easily killed in the crossfire."

Amanda nodded. It made a certain level of sense, after all. "Why are you doing this?"

Kalsey chuckled and didn't even look up from the phone. "It's my good deed for the day." He paused and spared her a glance. "Believe it or not, when running a business, being a mediocre good is better for a vampire than being a mediocre evil. Good comes with fewer drawbacks, and evil doesn't have enough positives when there are people like you crawling around out there." He went back to tapping out messages. "Like Bosley says, sometimes being good is just being pragmatic."

# Chapter 29

# Heart Of Marco

Marco growled in frustration as he hung from the silver chains in the back room. His wrists hurt, his ankle hurt, and he desperately wanted to rip his restraints out of the wall and use them to beat one of these furry little bastards to death. In fact, beating any of them to death would be a good change at this point.

Marco glanced at the wall. It was noon, and he could feel his control slipping—over both body and mind. It had been hard to focus before, and he was even having trouble remembering parts of the conversation he'd only just had with Misha.

Except for Misha being possessed by Asmodeus. That part would stay with him forever.

*God, thank you for not letting me try to hack into his brain like I did with his brother. I don't want to see exactly what's in this guy's head right now.*

"I hope you don't mind an observation," came a friendly voice with a mild Southern accent, "but it's going to go badly for you if you didn't change last night."

Marco snapped in front of him, his eyes clapping onto a tall, fit fellow. He had slightly graying, neatly slicked back hair. His chin was covered with an equally gray beard. His eyes were a bright gray …

Just like the wolf that killed Yana. "Tully, right?" Marco drawled.

He smiled and nodded. "Yessir." He pointed up and down Marco. "You didn't shift last night, did you?" He clucked his tongue and shook his head. "Sorry to see that. It's going to be so much worse for you tonight."

Marco ground his teeth together as his eyes narrowed. "Better to suffer this than have one of you bitches order me outside to play fetch with hand grenades."

Tully blinked, then laughed, amused and a little surprised. "Wow. You can still make jokes. Congratulations. You should feel fortunate that you can even speak."

Marco's amused little smile came back. "Oh, I'll show you how I feel. Just let me out of these, and we'll have a conversation."

Tully sighed, and shook his head, trying hard to be patient. "Pity you don't know what's happening here.

Once the moon is up, you'll do anything we say. And I mean anything. You're barely even in control now. There's nothing for you to do. No one resists an Alpha's orders for their first full moons—even if they themselves *are* Alphas."

Marco raised a brow. "So I heard. Why is that?"

Tully shrugged. "All manner of reasons. Some have never handled their dark side before. Some have never felt the need to restrain their darkness. And sometimes, it's just a simple matter of becoming a feral quadruped. Some people can't take it. But don't worry. Nothing untoward is going to happen to you. We'll just have you murder some people. No biggie."

Usually, on a day-to-day basis, when he wasn't being assaulted by a demonic dragon, shot at by minions, or batted around by a vampire assassin, the worst thing Marco Catalano had to endure was being bored. With a mind like his, he bored easily. It's why he went for being a Physician Assistant instead of becoming a doctor—it was the same work in half the time. Even then, he read and understood the textbooks, and eagerly awaited clinical cycles of his education—the data was easy, the day-to-day was hard. His greatest challenge would be dealing with patients. It's why Marco considered becoming a surgical PA—next to surgeons, who believed that "MD" stood for Medical Divinity, he would seem downright personable.

And then, Marco had been bitten by a werewolf.

On the one hand, Marco felt like he alternated between withdrawal and DTs. His innards twisted, as though knives were trying to work their way through his intestines. Were he more functional, he would have pondered how much of it was the lycanthropy fighting off the virus from Amanda's blood, and how much it worked through his digestive tract. Or he would have considered that his body really was shifting and changing, and that included his insides as well. He hadn't made the change during the full moon last night, and perhaps it was going to become even worse than the night before. But he could barely remember that Tully had already told him just that.

After hours of struggling, Marco had decided on an entirely different plan. One that he hoped he would still remember come nightfall.

Once he settled down, two of the lesser Alphas came in and plugged IV bags of nutrients into Marco's arms. No one was going to get close enough to his teeth to try and feed him, but he would need plenty of energy and calories to go through another full moon. The only solution was intravenous feeding. Tully was the only one who seemed able to control him.

When that time finally came, Tully approached him. He smiled and nodded at Marco, respectful, even polite. "Evening, son," he drawled.

Marco barely had the energy to give him a look.

Tully nodded, understanding. "Don't worry. You'll feel better after you have a nice meal. We'll lengthen those chains, leave you alone in here with a pile of food. In about fifteen minutes, after you're done with it, we're going to take you for a test run."

Marco's eyes narrowed at him. "What test run?"

The convoy of werewolves pulled to a stop in the middle of Brooklyn. As much as they could have wandered the streets and no one would have noticed, at some point, somebody would have made mention of Marco being led through the streets on chains. Unless they were in Greenwich Village. So a collection of vans to carry the pack was best.

The lead van pulled in front of a dumpy little place off Manhattan Avenue, where all of the apartment building ran together as one massive wall with metal doors in the front.

Tully got out first and opened the back. Five of his associates held the chains binding Marco. The chains themselves weren't silver. The silver around Marco's neck, wrists and ankles was what kept him at bay.

Tully looked at Marco himself and smiled. The new lycan thrashed wildly, pissed off. That was good. If Marco had lost control of himself, it was easier for Tully to control him.

Tully pointed to Marco, then waved him out with one finger. "Come out."

Marco led the way, the other members of the pack following him out of the van. Tully pointed at the bonds. "Remove the chains, leave cuffs on him, we want him to stay human. He doesn't need to go full furry for a few humans."

The thin one named John smacked Marco in the face. "Yeah. We'll save that for your girlfriend." He grabbed himself and smirked. "Pity there won't be anything left of her when you're done. Otherwise, we'd get to play with her."

Marco's jaw snapped at John, and the shifter jerked back. Tully cuffed John upside the head. "Down, boy.

That's just rude. And you never taunt a new guy like that. He's going to have enough trouble. And you'll have the trouble if he remembers later on."

John rolled his eyes. "He ain't gonna live that long."

Tully sighed and shook his head. Sometimes, they didn't listen to anything but force.

Tully grabbed John by the scruff of the neck and hurled him aside. "Idiot." He looked back. The chains were removed from Marco, his form restrained by the silver collar and cuffs. "Marco. Go through the door, attack everyone inside. Bring me their cell phones."

Marco lunged for the door, crashing into the metal plate. He dented it and burst through it.

In the dilapidated apartment, the men turned around—Hector Vega and Donald Tolbert were in the front room, taken aback by the assault. Officer Tolbert had his hand in his holster flap but hesitated when he saw Marco.

Marco didn't hesitate.

Marco sent Tolbert flying across the room, through a doorway, deeper into the apartment. Marco whirled on Hector. Hector held up his hands, backing away. "Hey, man, sorry about hitting on Amanda, okay?"

Marco only growled, jumping for Hector. He smashed his fist into Hector's ribcage, then hurled him aside.

He grabbed the cell phones from both of them and left the two men behind.

Tully took a cell phone from Marco, and promptly restrained him again. The Alpha looked through the cell phone and found the one phone number Misha wanted him to text. Tully tapped out the message, which provided GPS location on Marco.

The label was "Amanda Colt."

Amanda checked the GPS on her borrowed phone. As much as she didn't like using expensive toys like this, the text message from Officer Tolbert had come with very specific instructions, including a GPS tag. So when the message came in, she had to use someone else's phone to do it.

I just hope I don't break this phone as well, she thought. *Bosley may not like it.*

The two text messages were particular, and she followed her instructions to the letter.

Amanda readjusted the large duffel bag over her shoulder as she looked around.

The location brought her to an alley. Which made a certain level of sense.

That the alley was in Maspeth also made a certain amount of sense.

She walked in and stopped.

The growl from behind her told her all that she needed to know.

Amanda turned as Marco charged into the alley. She looked into his eyes, and they gleamed a bright, shining gold. He sprouted dark red fur, his hands already claws.

Then the screaming started.

Tully smiled as he listened to the screams. He and his pack sauntered towards the alley. He hadn't wanted Amanda to get spooked by the smell of werewolf pack, so they had stayed far away until she had been spotted.

When she entered the alley, the wolves removed the silver restraints from Marco, and his transformation started as soon as the final silver cuff came off.

Tully pointed, and Marco charged.

The screaming started shortly after that.

Tully smiled and waved for his men to stay. He jogged towards the alley to check on Marco's progress. He stepped in front of the alley.

The dumpster came at him with the speed of a freight train. It slammed into Tully and carried him to the other side of the street, crushing him into the side of a building.

The werewolf named John blinked as his Alpha went flying out of the alley in short order. John loped forward, peeking his head around the corner. He saw exactly what he had hoped to see.

There was Marco Catalano, on the floor of the alley, curled up into a ball, crying his eyes out.

John smiled.

Amanda Colt was dead.

# Chapter 30

# Blow Your House Down

The werewolf named John looked around. It was thoroughly trashed. There had been pulverized brick from the impact of fists, body, and probably even somebody's head. The trash cans had been, well, trashed—the metal ones had been flattened, and the plastic ones were just splinters and scattered trash. There were smashed wooden boards, and chunks of bricks ripped out and embedded in a few places.

It looked like a war had happened between a vampire and a werewolf, all right.

John frowned. There was one problem with the condition of the crime scene—one that he could not put his finger on it.

"Okay," he muttered to himself. "Blood would blow away with the death of the vampire." He sniffed the air as he walked closer to Marco, still weeping on the ground. He didn't mind the lack of ashes, because it was an alley filled with garbage, not even his eyes or nose could detect the remains of a fireplace.

He discovered the problem. "Where are the clothes?" he asked, partially to himself, and partially to Marco.

There wasn't a scrap of fabric around the alley, anywhere. No shredded clothing from Marco's transformation, no clothing left behind by Amanda dissolving to dust after being ravaged by Marco's claws. It was almost as though someone had trashed the alley some more, stripped Marco naked, and let Amanda get away.

But that was utterly and completely impossible.

Marco's tears stopped. "Oh well, so much for that idea," he said, clearly and concisely. His hands shot up and grabbed John by the genitals. He squeezed. John felt the sharp points of nails driving into his flesh.

Marco's eyes locked onto John's. His eyes were cool, and clear, and a deep, dark blue. But the amused, entertained smile on his lips didn't reach his eyes. They were alive with rage.

Marco rose from the alley floor, naked as the day he was born. He didn't seem to notice as he came eye-to-eye with John. "You bastards wanted to see my dark side?"

Marco's claws lengthened, ripping through flesh.

John's screams could be heard clearly from the alley, and three streets down.

Marco stepped out to meet the other werewolves, still in the street. He moved with controlled grace, like a dancer, and stood square against the pack. "Hi, guys."

The dumpster moved, shifted, and rolled aside. Tully emerged, damaged but otherwise okay. He stared at Marco. "How? No one can control their dark side that well. Not during their first change."

Marco gave him a smile. "You made two mistakes, Tully. So did Misha."

One of the thinner werewolves leaped at Marco, and he leaned to one side, letting the were pass him. Marco grabbed the wolf's ankle in passing, and jerked him out of the air, slamming him down against the pavement. His eyes never left Tully's as he proceeded to slam the were against the asphalt as a form of punctuation.

"Never." Slam. "Send." Slam. "A wolf. After. His. Mate!" He grinned as he hurled the wolf away into the alley like he was no heavier than a garbage bag. "I mate for life. Like wolves. Or Catholics."

Tully looked at Marco, pointed to another were, named Ben, and gave a "Get him" gesture at Marco.

Ben growled and turned furry as he charged Marco. Marco calmly remained in place until Ben leaped for him. Marco followed the arc of his flight path, then jumped back, slamming his foot down on a manhole cover, flipping it up into his hands. Ben fell into the hole headfirst, and Marco slammed the cover back down onto him. There was a resounding *crack* from Ben's spine as vertebrae and ribs shattered upon impact.

"Your second problem?" He shrugged. "You said it yourself. Going furry is just the physical manifestation of one's dark side."

Tully charged him, coming to a stop just out of arm's length. Marco swept down, picking up the manhole cover, and threw it, bottom first, into Tully's face. Tully easily batted it away, but it covered Marco's drop-kick into Tully's knees. Tully roared in pain as Marco bounded to his feet and shot in. His nails extended like claws and jabbed into Tully's skin around the collarbone. He drove in with his fingers, pushing into his flesh. Grabbing the collarbone like a handle, he yanked down hard and shattering the bone. It rendered Tully's right shoulder totally useless.

Just because it wasn't permanent damage caused by silver, didn't mean it didn't hurt.

Marco grinned and stared deep into Tully's eyes. His own had a hint of gold in them now. "Because, Tully, Asmodeus should have told you: I *am* my dark side."

Marco hurled Tully to the ground and looked to the rest of the wolf pack. "As of right now, I claim my place as your new Alpha. Are there any objections?"

One of the larger weres shot from the pack, right for Marco.

Marco grabbed the manhole cover and hurled it like Captain America's shield. It crashed into the large wolf's chest, caving it in.

"Anyone else?" Marco asked, darkly.

The wolf pack shrank back. One or two of them literally rolled over on their backs, showing their bellies.

"Great." Marco looked up at the roof of one of the two buildings that formed the alley. He said casually, "Amanda, my love, you can come down now."

Amanda fell from the top of the building, landing easily on her feet. She slung the duffel from her back and said, "I think you'll need these."

Marco nodded and smiled. "Thank you." He looked to the wolf pack. "You guys. Stay."

Marco walked back into the alley, Amanda right behind him.

"Do you have to get dressed?" Amanda joked. "I don't mind you like this."

Marco chuckled. The first thing he did was get underwear on. "Sorry. But I really need support. It's a guy thing. I don't quite think bras have the same issues." He grabbed the rosaries inside the pack and started applying them as needed. "I'm glad you got the text I sent you from Hector's phone. I worried that Tully was smart enough to wonder why I only gave him one phone."

Amanda smiled. Before she had gotten the text with the GPS coordinates for the alley, she had received one a moment before that read: *The next text is a trap. Prep accordingly: Marco.*

"How did you know that you would be able to do that?" she asked.

"I didn't," he answered. "I was relatively certain that I wouldn't go after you, but that was all I knew until they sicced me on Hector and Tolbert."

Marco stepped out of the alley. He now wore a white winter coat, jeans, and boots. "I guess you figured out that I'd need clothes?"

"Yes," she admitted. "But I thought you might need them in the morning."

"Good call."

She smiled at him. "How did you know that you wouldn't go after me?" she asked.

Marco moved in close to her. He took her in his arms, brought her close, and kissed her lightly on the lips. "As I said. You're my mate. Wolves mate for life.

And so do I." He shrugged. "You think that I proposed on a whim?"

Amanda flinched. "Yes. I think you did."

His omnipresent smile widened just a tad, and he tapped her on the tip of her nose. "Hey. If your power is connected towards your ability to love, just say yes, the sky's the limit," he said jocularly.

"Marco, I—" Amanda stopped dead and glanced around. "I think we're in trouble."

Marco blinked. "Why? What's the—"

The wolves started to whimper. Marco looked down the street and saw the problem coming around the corner.

Misha.

*Oh darn.* "We're in trouble." Marco took a step forward and looked at his wolves. *Pity, I wanted to hang on to them.* "Okay, men," Marco barked. He pointed at the coming vampire. "Kill him!"

The wolves charged the vampire.

Marco grabbed Amanda's hand and ran in the other direction.

Good to the Last Drop

# Chapter 31

# Revenge Of The Mount Olivet Incident

Marco and Amanda ran until they ran into a very familiar death trap: one of their own. It was Mount Olivet Cemetery.

Marco's eyes narrowed. "Son of a…"

Amanda saw it as well. *I wonder if Misha wanted us here.*

*I'm certain of it,* Marco thought back at her as they continued to run.

*You can hear me?* She asked.

*Yup.* Marco ran up Eliot Avenue, and Amanda followed. The stretch of road ran right between two cemeteries: Mount Olivet and All Faiths. *You have to stop being surprised that you've got boiler-plate telepathy. We've barely figured out how powerful you can be at your current level.*

Amanda reached forward, picked up Marco, and ran at full speed, shooting them both to the top of the hill in a matter of seconds. *Powerful enough for you?*

"I think so," he muttered. He looked around. *Yeah, he wanted us here,* Marco thought at her. *Right at the cemetery where we defeated most of his brother's forces. He wanted to kill at least one of us here—me. If I failed to kill you, or you, if something went wrong with his plan.* Marco paused a second and decided to leap over the fence. *At the very least, he knew how to escape from the cemetery if he needed to.*

As Amanda vaulted over the fence, Marco caught her and stopped. His eyes were locked on the darkness, in the distance. He had only just realized that he heard the howls and growling of the pack whimper and die off. "Run," he told her, loudly and firmly. "Run away, and don't look back."

Amanda looked at Marco, but he avoided eye contact. And she didn't hear anything from his mind. All she felt was his determination. "We can't stop him," he said. "Not by ourselves. And you're more likely to stop him than I am."

He turned to her, wrapped her up in her arms, and kissed her deeply. He poured as much love into his kiss as he could. He knew exactly one thing: if she followed his advice and ran, he was going to die.

And if she stayed with him, they were both going to die.

Marco pulled back and gave her a sad smile. "I only wish you'd said yes."

He turned away and ran into the cemetery.

Amanda watched him run away from her, and whispered, "So do I."

Marco stood in the middle of the cemetery all by himself. He would enjoy the calm, cool, quiet night for just a few more minutes.

He took a deep breath of cold air, letting it fill him and wake him up.

And then he started singing.

"I was born on a Brooklyn street where the vamp're drums did beat, and those bloodstained demon feet they walked all o'er us. And each and every night, when my girl would come home light, she'd invite the suckers outside with this choooo-rus:, Oh come out ye God-darn vamps, come out and fight me like a man, show your girl how you would mow us down in Hellll-A—"

"Don't you *ever* shut up?"

Marco stopped and smiled down the empty night. "Hi, Igor, how are you?"

There was a motion from one side. A black blur swept down as the vampire landed on the soft earth of the cemetery in a crouch, growling. He straightened, unfurling like a great cloud of smoke. "Don't you have anything better to do than sing variations on 'Come out Ye Black and Tans'?"

Marco smiled. "No." He looked around. As far as he could tell, he was the only living thing around there for blocks. The vampire seemed to be the only unliving thing around for blocks, so they were about even.

Marco narrowed his eyes and gave Misha his patented smile. He would go down snarking, if not fighting. "Ever see *Casablanca*?" he asked casually, even lightly. "Bogart told the Major how 'there are certain sections of New York, that I wouldn't advise you to try to invade.' You just found one."

"We shall see."

Marco only smiled, raised his hands, and beckoned Misha come forward with his fingers in a classic *Come and get me* gesture.

Even with the enhanced speed and reflexes of a werewolf at Marco's disposal, Misha was a blur. Marco had only seen just enough of the vampire's body to see that an uppercut was heading straight for him. He barely twisted out of the way. The vampire's punch scraped along Marco's chest. It was a glancing, fleeting blow. Had it been done in slow motion, it would have almost been a light feather drawn along his skin.

The impact shattered Marco's rib cage, and hurled him across the cemetery, slamming him into a tree.

The tree shuddered under the impact. Marco felt the wood pulp against his body. He coughed and something that was decidedly not spit come out of his mouth. The copper taste confirmed it: he was aspirating blood.

*He did all this, even though I'm a freaking were-something. Oh … kay. I'm screwed.*

Marco straightened his body, forcing himself to stand. With a sound like Rice Krispies being ground underfoot, his ribcage snapped back into place.

He had to keep himself from screaming in utter agony. Breaking the bones had taken less than a second. Fixing them took longer, and it hurt more.

Marco caught sight of Misha up the hill from him, standing on the ridge, hands on his hips. Just waiting.

Marco winced again, but not in pain this time. At the realization that Misha wasn't interested in just killing him. Marco already knew that he needed fuel to keep up the powers from his werewolf bite, it's why they fed him so well before sending him out to kill Amanda. It only figured that he could run out of fuel, supernatural beastie or not.

Marco realized that Misha's plan was simple: he was going to beat Marco to death. After a while, his body would fail to heal, and he would just die.

*Lovely.*

Marco rolled his shoulders, set his jaw, and muttered, "Is that all you got, Igor?"

Misha blurred again.

The vampire came in at Marco so fast, most people couldn't have seen it, including most vampires. Misha threw himself at Marco, spinning like a buzzsaw. The vampire swung with a left-backhand, a right hook, followed it up with a right roundhouse kick.

Marco dropped and rolled to the side, avoiding all of the strikes. He swept up a splintered piece of tree from where he'd struck it and rolled back at Misha. He rammed the stake behind Misha's left kneecap, and twisted, popping the kneecap right off of the bone.

That part hurt.

Misha stumbled, putting his right leg down on the ground to steady himself before he fell over. Marco rammed one of his turpentine knives—courtesy of Amanda—directly between Misha's legs before rolling away and to his feet. The firecracker attached to the stake hit his skin and the turpentine ignited.

Misha stood there for a moment, grabbing the tree to balance himself. The vampire ground his teeth in pain but did nothing. The fire went out, as though covered with a glass bowl to suffocate the flames. He quickly extracted the pieces with a bit of telekinesis and whirled on Marco, hurling it at him.

But Marco was already a moving target, bounding around the ground and rolling, even as Misha launched his projectiles. He came up, drawing out two wooden knives from his jacket, holding them as though ready for combat.

"That's one thing I learned from Day," Marco said. "You can still feel pain."

Misha stopped and contemplated his adversary. "It's been a while since I've had someone who thinks like me."

"By the way, how many of you did Nuala train?"

Marco thought about Misha's next move, expecting a different attack pattern, probably a simple left-right hook combination, or a left-feint and right hook combo, just to test how much force he needed.

"Only me and my brother."

"Why the two?"

"She killed the rest on the first day of training." He smiled. "They were weak."

Marco tested the point of the wooden blade and glanced at it out of the corner of his eye.

He could just about see the moisture in the wood.

And he grinned.

Marco flung one of the knives at Misha. The vampire didn't even flinch—why should he? Being possessed by Asmodeus, he was impervious to daylight. Wood was barely an issue.

The wood jammed into Misha's knee, and this time, it hurt for real, punching through the kneecap, and coming out the back of the knee.

Misha screamed in surprise and agony. He growled in pain as his eyes briefly turned "Mister Day" black. Misha pulled the knife away and broke it in one hand. He blinked his eyes clear again. The wood had been treated with holy water. The damage would be permanent, and not even the demonic power of Asmodeus would heal the wound.

Despite having only one functioning leg, he rose and launched himself at Marco. He was already slowing down, the holy damage to his knee sapping some of his demonic strength.

But for Marco, slowing Misha down was more important than making him weaker.

This time, when the vampire came in with a right feint and a left hook, Marco could actually see Misha as he charged. Marco had expected a different move, but it didn't matter. He used the time of the feint to judge where he should move next. Marco ducked and weaved under the left hook and rammed one knife into Misha's left tricep and the other into his gut before throwing himself to one side.

Marco rolled to his feet, two more knives in hand.

Misha roared, ignoring both hurts. He threw himself at the tree next to him, pushing off and flying at Marco. The human dropped and rolled forward, under Misha, and came to his feet as the vampire whirled at him. Marco didn't move as he observed the vampire's body—totally unhurt. Both of the stakes had disappeared, and only the vampire's clothing was damaged.

Most importantly, the pants leg was missing over Misha's left knee, but the knee was completely healed.

It only took a quick second for Marco to figure out what the problem was. When he had fought Mister Day, Day would remove the parts of his body that had been "infected" with holy water or damaged with chemicals. Up to and including digging in and removing the affected sections. Misha moved fast enough to remove all of the damaged parts from his body without Marco even seeing it.

*Yup. I'm in trouble.*

Misha lunged, and Marco dropped to one knee, ramming the left-hand knife into the left side of Misha's chest. Misha's left hand clipped Marco on the back of the head. Marco rolled, feeling a mild concussion coming on.

Marco jumped to his feet, his legs unsteady. He caught his fall against a mausoleum. *Good God, I hope the werewolf healing handles this.*

He dug his hands in his pockets, knowing that he was going to need better weaponry. The fingers of his left hand reached through a string of beads, and his right hand grasped another piece of wood.

His vision still blurred, Misha charged him again. Marco whipped up his hand, hoping to catch Misha in the face.

The vampire figured that nothing could come from being smacked, once, by anything that Marco had on him.

Except that Marco's next blow was the flat side of a crucifix.

Misha's face sizzled as Marco rammed his kidneys with the rosary-clad left jab and torqued for a right-hook with the cross before leaping back.

Unfortunately, Misha struggled through the pain and grabbed Marco's right wrist, avoiding the cross, and twisted, hurling him through the air and into the side of the mausoleum. Marco spun in midair to distribute the force of the blow, but that only contained the damage to the left side of his body, cracking three ribs.

Marco dropped to the ground hard, hitting his head on a rock. He was sure he'd have a concussion by the end of the evening, lycanthropy or no lycanthropy. Assuming he wasn't dead.

Misha kicked Marco in the stomach, breaking something organ-related inside him. Marco coughed up blood.

*And that was just from a stomach blow. If he had kicked my chest, it would have just collapsed. God only knows what shape it's in now.*

Marco stabbed Misha in the foot with the sharpened end of the cross, then again in the thigh. Misha ignored it and stomped on his calf.

"I will break you slowly, over time, for your arrogance."

Misha stepped away, laughing. Marco knew what was going to happen this time. Once again, Misha would wait for him to heal.

*You can wait, I'm not going to.*

Marco reached inside his jacket and came out with two vials, driving the nail through the cork in the top of each, shook them, and acted like he was about to throw them.

Misha heard this, turned, and cocked a brow. "And?"

Marco groaned. "Never mind. Keep the holy water, Igor," and tossed them *to* the vampire.

Even though Misha's mouth didn't open, Marco heard another voice, the voice of "Mister Day," screaming *NNNNOOOOOO* as the vampire caught the test tubes.

The tubes exploded. The flash of nitroglycerin blinded Misha briefly, long enough for Marco to attack. He threw knife after knife from inside his coat, from the neck sheathes, from up his arm, and from his pockets.

When Amanda packed for him, she was as thorough as he was.

*God, I love that woman.*

Misha had flames all over his body, and he whirled, putting out each flame in turn. His speed made the stakes fly in all directions. He roared with pain and rage. Lunging for Marco, the vampire scooped him up in one hand by the front of his shirt. Misha's eyes shifted to solid black, and his face became deformed. His mouth had plenty of sharp teeth.

Marco stared into the vampire's eyes and growled at him…and then the vampire's eyes started to change. Something within the blackness of his eyes, something cold and angry, shifted. It had the look of Asmodeus, but different.

Suddenly it started to pour out of his eyes in a rolling black flame. It came out of his pores and his orifices, curling around him like a cloak.

This, Marco Catalano realized, was Soul Fire.

And like the condition of his skin matched the condition of his soul, the Soul Fire also mirrored Misha's mind. The fire was a perversion of real flame—black and ice cold.

The flames covered the vampire like a second skin, reaching down over his boots. The grass at his feet withered.

"Now," Asmodeus and Misha, their voices intertwining and blending together so that they came out three octaves lower than usual. The words dripped with so much malice Marco's head hurt. "You will suffer. And then, you will die."

The black flame curled up his arm, moving for Marco's chest.

Marco grabbed his arm and the Soul Fire stopped. The flames retreated.

Misha's arm burned. Marco slipped from his fingers… or more precisely, Misha's fingers slipped off of his hand.

The demon-vampire roared and backed away. The entire arm disintegrated from Misha's body.

Marco had a crucifix under his shirt in the exact place where Misha had grabbed him.

In a move that Marco had seen Mister Day use, Misha reached over and grabbed his right shoulder with his left hand, and ripped off his own arm, hurling it to one side. The arm disintegrated in mid-air. A spurt of black Soul Fire flared from his body from the ruined stump…making an entirely new arm.

Marco blinked. "Crud."

Misha/Asmodeus stared at Marco. Black fire still covered his body. The eyes staring back at him were black and insectoid.

He knew he was going to die.

# Chapter 32

# Black Fire

**M**arco tried to move, and his internal organs objected. The lycanthropy was healing him, but it still hurt like hell. He used the mausoleum to pull himself up, despite the agony he was in. Misha must have delivered multiple killing blows to his body for it to take so long to heal.

"You think your crucifix can spare you?" the demon-vampire asked. The black Soul Fire swelled in Misha's hands.

Marco tottered on his feet and gave the demon a feral smile. "The power of God versus the power of a freaking, imbecilic *demon*," he spat. "And his *pathetic, moronic* lackey?" he gasped. "I think I like those odds."

The vampire smiled, and so did the eyes of the demon within. "Think again," they said and threw forth their hands. Black fire poured forward in an endless stream.

Marco stepped forward, into a kneeling position, and crossed his wrists in front of them. One of the multiple things that Amanda had given him was a collection of rosaries. He had wrapped them around each of his wrists.

And now he was glad he had.

The stream of fire struck just at the point where Marco's wrists crossed. It stopped at an impact point three inches in the air in front of him, held back by the power of God.

And that was enough for Marco.

Except the darkness didn't stop there. The darkness inched towards him, spreading out around Marco and his rosaries. The fire and the flames covered his entire body. As though the grace of God formed a shield around him, the fire flowed around him, creating a bubble. It protected him from the darkness.

The darkness still wanted in.

It fell all around him. Marco felt the darkness push against him, a physical and metaphysical force. It wanted him. It wanted *in*.

And the darkness began to whisper to him. The darkness knew him. It spoke of his lust for death. His murderous impulses. It spoke to every thrill he had ever had when deliberately hurting someone. Every time he had his hands on someone's throat. Every time he broke bone and felt a rush go through his body. It knew that Amanda wouldn't marry him because he was evil. Without vampires, he would just be another serial killer, roaming the streets for prey. He *was* the darkness, so why not let it in? Marco knew it to be true, didn't he? The darkness was his life. He played with it routinely, and always came back unharmed. That was his sin. It was his life.

It was as though every doubt, anxiety, and fear he had ever had in his entire life came for him. They would devour him whole because they were all him. He couldn't really defeat himself. If he could overcome his own weaknesses, why hadn't he yet?

He leaned into the spiritual attack. Still it pressed him backwards. Despite starting forward, like a football player with his arms crossed before him, his back was almost straight. The next step would be a full retreat. And he had no place to go. His left foot touched the mausoleum, his knees in the dirt.

Though the darkness moved around him like an endless tide, it didn't mean that anything else was safe. The ground beneath him stayed stable, but the cemetery itself burned and corroded. The Soul Fire cascaded over him in waves, and ate away at the headstones, the grass, consuming the trees as they disintegrated.

There was no way for him to win.

In the small, still roar of Soul Fire, in the white noise (perhaps "black noise") that consumed Marco's world, he heard one tiny voice in the back of his head. A sardonic voice that sounded much like Marco himself. It was something that was as integral to Marco as Marco was himself.

It was a voice that he had only heard once, on a San Francisco pier, after it had first defeated "Mister Day."

The voice belonged to someone named Da'ni'el, and it was Marco's guardian angel.

It simply said, "Remember who you are."

Only four words. But the phrase triggered other memories for Marco, from another conversation: Have you ever considered that you're just a soldier who merely enjoys his job? … You both choose to stand between the darkness and everyone else on the planet. Sometimes, you die. Welcome to being a soldier … a soldier in a war where evil cannot be stopped without lethal force. You were prepared early for a war that would come with or without you.

No. God wanted him like this. Maybe not exactly like this, but enough. He was a soldier. He was a killer. He was the slayer of God's enemies. He was the destroyer of evil. He was going to mutilate, slash, burn, and destroy anything that got in the way.

Perhaps that was what Hendershot had tried to tell him with his dying breath: *Deus vult.*

God wills it.

Perhaps this was what his entire life was building to. He didn't like destiny, as a concept or as a video game. But if this was something God had in mind, then it was time for him to embrace it.

In the end, all that mattered was he remembered who he was. He was a monster to other monsters. He was the terror the darkness had feared. He had persevered against demons direct from Hell.

Amanda loved him, and he was a soldier for God.

He held onto that thought, onto this moment, and would never let it slip away. His was a good life. Amanda loved him. As long as she did, his life was a gift, filled with infinite possibilities. He was going to fight for it, and everything he loved. Even if he died for it.

One more line he remembered from Da'ni'el: You spend half of your time either angry or in prayer. You think that doesn't make a difference? There is holiness in you. Mikhail could not have savaged your mind any more than Asmodeus could possess you.

Which meant that Marco already knew what to do. It was what he always did in the still of the night when the anger reached out for him and drove him to distraction.

"Saint Michael the Archangel, defend us in battle," Marco intoned as he leaned forward into the black

Soul Fire that threatened to consume him. "Be our protection against the wickedness and snares of the Devil." Marco stood and took a single step forward. "May God rebuke him, we humbly pray." Another step. "And do Thou, O Prince of the Heavenly Host—" Step. "By the Divine Power of God." Another step. "Cast into Hell, Satan and all the evil spirits, who roam throughout the world seeking the ruin of souls. Amen."

The eyes of Misha and Asmodeus grew wide as Marco proceeded to walk towards him, arms crossed at the rosaries at his wrist.

"Angels and ministers of grace defend us," Marco intoned, and then started with the Our Father.

The vampire-demon roared. He stopped pointing one hand at Marco, and swiped the fire along the ground, creating a trench between him and Marco.

Then the onslaught of black fire stopped. Misha drew it back into his body like breath.

Misha smiled. He looked around the graveyard and shook his head, sighing. "I have been giving you too much credit. Why bother striking you with supernatural power …"

Stone broke a little further down the cemetery, to Marco's right.

"…when I can throw the cemetery at you?"

A slab of marble the size of Misha slammed Marco into the side of another mausoleum, pancaking him. It wasn't full-bore Wyle E Coyote, but it smashed in his body, crushing him into the rock.

Misha's resulting laughter cut off as someone grabbed his ankle, and twisted, hurling him like a discus. He smacked face first into a headstone. A sword rammed through his body.

The vampire ripped himself from the stone and turned on his assailant.

Merle smiled and gave a little finger wave. "Hi there."

He raised a brow. "*You* did that?"

Merle shrugged. "Eh. You'll find my fingerprints on the sword hilt."

"You're not a threat, you're a snack. But Marco first."

The vampire-demon turned back to face Marco and had an encounter with a headstone across his face, knocking him off his feet.

Misha felt his teeth and found his canines missing. He looked up at Amanda in front of him.

"If you touch him, I will kill you."

Misha's eyes narrowed. "Alina...I have the army here, child."

"Oh?" Amanda said, amused. "Where would they be?"

His eyes flared with Soul Fire. He gestured around the cemetery.

Marco looked up from the ground, slowly letting the world come back into focus. Even though marble didn't hurt him like silver, his body still needed fuel to power through an impact like a wrecking ball.

Marco's eyes narrowed, but his vision wouldn't clear. It was still foggy. He refocused to the ground, and slowly looked out and away from him … and he saw that it wasn't his eyes. A heavy mist covered the area. It stayed outside the bounds of the cemetery, as though the fog itself had been a spectator to his battle royale with Misha.

"Come!" they said, in a voice as deep and as forbidding as death.

The mist flowed into the cemetery and solidified. Solid figures materialized. One by one, vampires appeared from the mist, surrounding Misha, Marco, Merle, and Amanda.

Merle backed towards Marco, and Amanda came with him, keeping an eye on the vampires as they emerged from the fog.

Amanda whispered one word, "Smoke-eater."

Marco looked over at Merle and Amanda and made certain to turn back to the encroaching legions of the damned. They didn't look particularly happy to see him. "Hey, love."

"Hello," Amanda said. "Good fight?"

"It's been interesting," Marco drawled, still not looking at the others. Amanda bumped into his left side, and Merle his right. "I don't have to tell you that Misha's possessed, do I?"

Merle scoffed. "Even I saw the eyes. I hope it's not anyone we know."

"It's Day. He's back."

Amanda frowned, and pieces fell into place. "If he has the same powers as before, that explains why Misha could be out in daylight."

Marco nodded, even though she wasn't looking at him. "Day was healing him so fast, it only looked like the sun didn't damage him."

The three of them watched as the others closed in. "I hope someone sent in a memo for a MOAB," Marco said.

"That worked *so* well on Nuala," Merle muttered.

Marco nodded. That was true. He frowned as he eyed the legions. "Should I ask what 'smoke-eater' means? Some obscure Russian swear word that only sounds like English?"

Marco was so focused on the threat in front of him that he didn't notice the steady beat of propellers in the air until they were already well within range of standard human hearing. The regular beating grew closer and louder as they closed in.

Helicopters.

Misha ignored the threat. Both the vampire and the demon within listened to the helicopters. They were not gunships. They were not troops carriers. They were nothing but regular helicopters.

Marco, however, laughed.

Misha rolled his eyes and stalked towards the trio. He stepped within six feet of Marco. "And what do you think is so funny?"

Marco merely grinned. "I got the joke."

"About?"

"Smoke-eaters."

Misha looked up. The helicopters came to a stop overhead and hovered in a formation over the cemetery. They had encircled it…

They floated directly over his vampires. He only realized the threat as doors in the bellies of all the helicopters opened and released their cargo.

Misha threw himself against the wall of a mausoleum, seeking protection from the death from the sky.

The helicopters weren't anything particularly hazardous. They weren't gunships. They hadn't carried men, or weapons, or guns.

They were firefighting helicopters, only this time, they carried holy water. With the ten helicopters, several hundreds of gallons of water poured onto the cemetery.

Every vampire melted away faster than Nazis in front of the Ark of the Covenant.

# Chapter 33
# All The Forces Of Hell

The possessed vampire watched from safety as all of his vampire legions were wiped out. The holy water rained down from the sky like a waterfall. The flood swept away hundreds of men. In some places, only body parts remained. Even those began to dissolve as the holy water seeped into the ground.

Misha and the demon felt the holy water wash in like the tide. It swept over the ground, and Misha stood there, looking at the trio of heroes as they turned to face the combined threat.

Marco smirked. "Oh, look who we've caught on holy ground. Your powers are suppressed by holy water. I'd like to see just how well Asmodeus heals you when we push you face-first into ground soaked with holy water."

Marco stepped forward. Amanda caught his arm and shook her head.

And then, the vampire-demon laughed. Misha spread his arms out, roaring with laughter. He sounded like thunder ripped from the Heavens.

"Come to me, my minions!" they roared. The twin voices sounded more like they came from Godzilla a puny human being. "Come, every foul thing and creature. Come unto your master!" The black, insectoid eyes looked at the three of them, alight with unholy mirth and damnation. "And now, you face me, Alina, and all the forces of Hell!"

Marco raised a hand. "Excuse me?" He looked around the cemetery. "Your minions are now only so much dust. Where exactly do you think they're going to come from?"

The world shook, catching Marco off-guard. Years of riding the subway had taught him how to adjust for when the ground gave out beneath his feet, and his head whipped around, looking for the next threat.

They came up from the sewers for miles around. They marched in military-straight lines with coordinated footwork to put *Riverdance* to shame. And they *marched*. They marched like the Roman days of old, down the alleys and the side streets, as many as five abreast, each line never longer than the width of the street. And they marched onto the cemetery, their lines crossing and merging. When the lines each hit the end opposite from which they came, and they stopped, as one, and turned on their heel in a right turn so perfectly timed that engineers at NASA would marvel.

Their faces were clearly demonic, their teeth straight, their postures erect. They looked like the Teutonic Knights ready for battle against Alexander Nevsky. There had to be at least two thousand of them, fangs bared, all ready to drink blood. Their faces made for nightmares.

More vampires came to Misha. Black tactical vests and hats made them hard to see against the dark of the night. And they wore boots. High-laced, military boots, perfectly waterproof. Treading over the holy water-soaked ground caused no issues.

"Did you think we didn't remember?" Misha and Asmodeus asked. "You laid in wait for my brother, a trap in this very cemetery. Marco was bait in San Francisco—*twice*. You can have all the tricks in the world. But you've sprung your trap. You've shot your bolt. It's time for *my* trap."

Amanda nodded her appreciation.

Kraft did as well. "How Mordor-esque."

Misha gave him a toothy grin. "Yes, and now we're going to play a little Helm's Deep."

Merle frowned. "Aww, and I wanted to play a little *Apocalypse Now*."

Swooping in from under the 59th Street Bridge from upper Manhattan, down the East River, came the two scariest notes outside of *O Fortuna*—the opening notes to *Flight of the Valkyries*.

Misha barely heard it at first, but as the notes chewed up airspace, the picture in his mind formed with crystal clarity. His eyes widened in surprise.

It was too late.

The gunship fired its napalm.

The rockets hit the ground with devastating effect, vaporizing rows of vampires in one flash of light apiece. The rocket impacts drew closer to Misha, but he didn't care. He grabbed a lamp post, bellowing, "Disperse!"

He disappeared into a ball of fire.

The anti-tank Gatling gun mounted on the military gunship quickly picked off the stragglers. Each burst was enough to blow apart a jeep.

As the flames subsided a little, Amanda could see Misha, standing in the glow of the fire as the heat bent around him and his own personal telekinetic shield. The iron pole still in hand, he hefted it and hurled it. The metal rod pierced the helicopter's bulletproof cockpit glass, through the pilot, his chair, and the roof of the helicopter, damaging the engine. It floated off, the copilot taking control.

Amanda flinched at the helicopter going down. But it disturbed her even more that Misha already had his power back.

But as the napalm burned the ground, she realized why. The flames that scorched the vampires down to their boots also evaporated the holy water.

Misha whirled on them. He laughed as his men from other sections of the cemetery closed in on the trio.

"You think you can stop us!" Misha roared. "I have endless resources. I have *thousands* of my brother's men!"

Marco winced as the vampires closed in. He focused on his hands, and felt them shift, twist and change into claws. "We always knew Mikhail had nests all over the world. I guess Misha brought them all here, just for us."

Amanda whispered. "Fight until you die or drop."

Marco blinked and looked at her. It was a line from one of his favorite songs, *March of Cambreadth*.

He eyed the ground around him. They seemed to be waiting on the order. The demonic vampire was probably considering whether he wanted to murder the three of them himself or if it was too much trouble for personal indulgence.

"How many of them can kill?" he asked.

"Not yet," Amanda whispered harshly, but not to Marco.

This time, the vampire army reached back over the hill of Mount Olivet, flooding out into the street. More of them even came over the fence from the houses on the other side.

Marco saw something else, though. A wave of dark green started interweaving throughout the black. There were so many vampires that the ones in black hadn't noticed. For everyone in black, there was at least one other in green. Marco couldn't tell if these were two different units, or if there were just so many vampires from all over the world, they just didn't know each other. After all, it would be impossible, unless there was some sort of FangBook or Flitter, or some sort of social media for vampires.

Misha stepped through the waves of vampires, coming for the three of them.

"I think he's decided to kill us himself," Marco said.

Misha waded through the ranks of his men when another vampire stepped in front of him. Misha blinked, confused for a moment. She wasn't wearing tactical black but tactical green camouflage. She at least had the combat boots. But her head was uncovered, and her gold blonde hair stood out in the barren night.

She had two men on either side of her. One was either an Irish cop or an Irish bartender—Misha had met both and could never tell the difference. The other was a taller, slender, Indian chap with a cane. He also wore digital camouflage, but his looked as though it had been supplied by Armani. In the back of Misha's head, even Asmodeus, who had been a bit of a clothes horse when alive, had never seen such a thing.

"Hello," she said in a proper British accent. "How are you this evening?"

Misha glared down at her. "In the middle of something, thank you," he growled. "Who are you? A telemarketer?"

She shook her head gently. "No. We're from the New York City Vampires Association, and we'd like to register a complaint."

Misha's eyes narrowed. *Bosley!* He raised his right hand, his fingers shifting into claws…

And it finally registered that these three were not the only ones in this horde that were dressed in green.

Jennifer Bosley, bartender Patrick Lynch, and Kalsey punched him as one. The triple impact lifted Misha off his feet and sent him flying back into his own men. Kalsey whipped out the sword from his cane and severed the head off three vampires around him. Patrick Lynch pulled out a pump-action, magazine-fed shotgun, and blew off the faces of the two nearest vampires. Bosley grabbed the nearest vampire and ripped his head clean off his shoulders.

That was the signal for the entire New York City Vampires Association to attack.

Vampires in green set upon vampires in black, and the screaming commenced in earnest. Even the vampires near Marco and Amanda turned to engage the latest threat. And that was a mistake. As Marco and Amanda ripped into them from behind. Merle pulled out his stakes and also went to work.

The ranks of black were cut through in short order. They had been matched in manpower, and NYC-VA had caught them by surprise, turning Misha's easy victory into a rout.

And then the top of the hill exploded into a great big ball of black Soul Fire. Misha emerged from the center. It had grown bigger, and his skin changed to black, taking on a sheen like armor. His eyes glowed green, and his hands looked more like claws.

Marco had a bad feeling he knew where this was going.

"Everyone, fall back," he whispered.

Amanda didn't hesitate. "Phase two," she called.

The wave of green vampires moved as one, up the hill, moving deeper into the cemetery, moving parallel to the streets, away from the houses.

Misha jumped forward, landing in front of Marco and the others in a single bound. "Marco. Come. Embrace your death!"

Marco unzipped his jacket, and his smile grew sharper. He threw off his coat, and his eyes took on a sheen of gold.

Amanda put her hand on his arm. "Marco, now is not the time."

"Get them back," he said calmly. His voice didn't sound like Marco's usual deep voice, but something from the barrel of a drum. It was the voice that belonged to a Disney villain … or a monster.

Marco's grin grew feral, his teeth elongating, and his eyes bright with excitement. "I've got something inside me that's wanted to play for two days."

Marco darted right for Misha. He was only halfway there when he leaped for him.

The two crashed in midair. Marco slammed the vampire to the ground and rolled off of him. Marco came to his feet, but no longer looked human. Red fur sprouted all over his skin. He grew larger, his shirt ripping to briefly expose a surprising amount of muscle before his chest, too, was covered in fur. The rosaries and the cross stayed on, even though they grew taut over his body at the wrists and neck.

Marco's final form was about the size of a horse. It was big and red, and vaguely wolf-like, with a narrower face, and ears like a coyote. He reared back on his hind legs, and then came down with a crash. His golden eyes locked onto Misha, finding his prey.

"Red wolf," Merle muttered. "Figures."

As the vampire she hated most in the world clashed with the love of her afterlife, Amanda flinched and looked at Merle briefly. "What?"

Merle shrugged. "It's part wolf, part coyote. He's a bit of a pack leader, and like coyote, the trickster, he cheats."

Marco leaped on Misha, digging his forepaws into Misha's chest, and the rear ones into his stomach while biting down on his beck.

Misha whirled, hurling Marco through an intact mausoleum, pulverizing it entirely.

The vampire roared with laughter. "I am fueled with the power of a *demon*. What did you think you were going to do, *dog*? Huh? Hurt me?"

A streak of red shot out from the marble wreckage, running straight for the vampire's ankles. The red wolf's jaws clamped down over the joint and the tendon. Yanking back with his powerful jaws, he ripped Misha off of the ground and hurled him across the graveyard. Misha crashed through a tree a hundred feet away.

The vampire bounced back and returned as a blur. When Misha stopped again, he had the wolf by the neck, lifting it up over his head.

The wolf thrashed for a moment, paws kicking at the air.

Amanda bull-rushed Misha, slamming into his side so hard, she knocked all three of them against a massive cross. Misha howled in pain. He used Marco as a club to swat Amanda away.

"Hey, schmuck," came a sardonic voice, "put down the puppy."

Misha barely had time to catch a glimpse of dark blue windbreaker before the government spy emptied two magazines into his head.

Misha shook it off and laughed. "You think that will stop me? Bullets? Ask your precious Vatican ninjas."

"I did. I'm just a distraction."

Misha grunted, then looked around. The red wolf shifted from a purely animal quadruped into a bipedal form. The forepaws turned into massive, furry hands with long, razor-sharp claws.

Marco's were-form was anthropomorphic enough to have the same sardonic smile he always wore. His golden eyes gleamed evilly, and with a feral snarl, he grabbed Misha's arm with both hands. The rosaries on his wrists burned the vampire and kept him from healing. Marco extended his claws and ripped Misha's arm right off at the elbow.

Misha growled as though it was all an annoyance. With his one hand he grabbed Marco by the pelt. Misha pivoted his upper body, throwing him at Merle, but the spy had already disappeared.

Marco went flying and crashed through three mausoleums this time – smashing through six solid marble walls without slowing down, pulverizing each wall into a fine powder cloud. He only stopped when he hit the incline of the hill in the middle of the cemetery, leaving an impact crater that knocked over two dozen headstones all around him.

"Strike!" Misha crowed.

Amanda dashed over to Marco's landing point. His body was twisted, obviously broken. Any human being would have been dead in a dozen different ways, and it wasn't looking too good for Marco as a werewolf either. His body twisted, and his mouth opened in a silent scream as he shifted back into a human being.

He looked up at Amanda, his eyes returning to blue, and gave her a weak smile. "I think I screwed that one up."

Misha stomped on the ground as he took his next step. Black fire poured out of his open wound and solidified. It reformed his arm in a matter of seconds.

Another step made the ground shake. His head became more reptilian, his skin still armored and black. More of his vampires flooded in, squaring off against the NYC-VA.

Amanda started to think that Marco was right. They were in serious trouble. Some of the vampires in green still rallied, with little skirmishes breaking out with the incoming replacement. She also didn't like what form Misha was changing into. It looked too familiar.

At which point, an enormous, furry creature the size of a bear bowled into Misha, knocking him over. The two tumbled for a bit before the furball came to its feet, a straightforward wolf with gray eyes.

Within the blink of an eye, it had turned into a slightly graying human. "You killed my men!" Tully roared at the vampire.

Misha shrugged, the shifting of armor plate grating like metal on metal. "They attacked me."

Tully pointed at Marco. "Because he beat me in combat. Had you just killed him, we would have bowed down at your feet, damn it!"

Misha rolled his head, as though rolling his eyes. "Begone, you."

"Screw you. And your plans. And your army." Tully growled, shifted, and charged.

Misha caught Tully in the middle of his next leap and shook him like a rag doll. He opened his mouth, reared back his head, and breathed out pure black Soul Fire right into Tully's face. The werewolf roared and screamed in pain. Thrashing, the fire literally burned off Tully's face, and then his entire head.

Misha tossed the headless body to one side and turned to Amanda and Marco on the ground. Marco tried to get up. Misha laughed.

Amanda touched her earpiece, and said, "Send these bastards back to Hell."

"Present arms!" bellowed a voice from atop of a roof. Misha looked behind him and his men.

Behind the fence were residential houses that ran the length of the cemetery. Every window opened up. Men came out of the homes with belt-fed machine-guns. There were teenagers and kids barely in their twenties, mostly Hispanic and Asian, with gang logos of tigers and dragons. There were men in NYPD windbreakers and body armor. There were men in jeans and sweaters, with slicked-back hair, who would take the terms "Guido" and "Goomba" as compliments. There were men in full tactical kit, wearing enough weapons for war. There were the dark green and royal blue stripes of the Vatican Ninjas.

The source of the voice came from the top of a roof in the middle of a row of houses. It was a shorter vampire, whose entire face crinkled with laugh and smile lines. His hair was an unearthly, chemical shade of red, and he spoke with a brogue as he said, "Fire!"

Misha's eyes opened wide. Amanda's vampires had the high ground on one side, and soldiers had flanked his him.

He and his men were caught in the middle.

Flaming crossbow bolts launched from the house behind the vampire army. Occasionally, they caught an overcharged minion, which exploded into great balls of white fire. Machine-guns fired wooden rounds sprayed with holy water, mowing down vampires by the lots. Other windows fired paintball guns with holy water in the splat balls. And finally, there was a new weapon, also wielded by Kraft's military unit: variable kinetic rounds. VK rounds were typically small razor-discs that sliced through anything in their path. In this case, the VK rounds were small, razor-sharp Stars of David.

Some of Misha's legions scattered. Only at the bottom of the hill, out at the street, a van pulled up, and the back opened, revealing a Vatican Ninja with a mini-gun. The gun opened up, blowing through vampires left and right, cutting some in half, setting others on fire.

There was only one way to avoid the jaws of the trap, and that was through Amanda, Marco, Merle, and the entire New York City Vampires Association.

Misha looked at the madness around him and felt himself undone. He summoned all his power and trained it on the houses, ready to level them at a thought.

A star bit into his chest, punching into his scaly black armor. He blinked and fell back, looking down at his chest as his body twisted and reshaped into his more human form. The armor fell away. He groaned and ripped out the ruined flesh with his bare hand, using the hunks to prevent direct contact with the star.

Misha threw away the hunks of flesh around the Star of David. Black fire leaked from the wound like blood. The fire surged, reforming the parts he had just thrown away.

Misha turned away from the kill zone towards the man who shot him. Merle Kraft kept firing, nonstop. Misha didn't even bother dodging the rounds. He stared at the headstones between him and Kraft and mentally yanked them out of the ground. Using their momentum, he knocked the stars out of the air before they ever got him.

Amanda wondered how he could have survived a Star of David into the heart—even Asmodeus couldn't heal a wound caused by a holy object.

Amanda recalled a rare medical condition where the organs of the human body were mirrored, opposite from the side of the chest they should actually be on…

Marco had stabbed him in the heart, where it should be, on the left, and it hadn't slowed him down…

*His heart was on the right side of this chest.*

Amanda smiled.

Merle cursed and reloaded the gun. A torrent of rocks shot at him, forcing him to dodge. He needed to get through the bricks to get to Misha, but that would take too long.

Misha allowed the bricks do their work on Merle and lunged for the vampire he had sired. Amanda let him come. She twisted, turning into a spin-kick that snapped Misha's head back with a resounding crack.

He blinked. He hadn't been kicked that hard since he first trained with Nuala. "Let's see how well you play against my *skill*."

The vampire whirled, going for a left roundhouse backhand. Instead of blocking it, Amanda noted that he pivoted on the right foot, leaving the left foot in the air. If she blocked the backhand, the kick would be unchecked.

Amanda neatly stepped back two paces, and when he kicked out, she caught the ankle a good two feet in front of her. She pulled back, yanking him off his feet. She spun around and threw him at one of the broken tree branches.

The branch came out his back, on his right side. Where his mirrored heart was.

Marco was dying, and he knew it. His body wouldn't react to his commands. That was that. No more Marco. While the rest took on the vampire army, he would simply fade away into the night.

*Well, after all, I'm not needed by anyone. Amanda's faring well, everyone's alive, except for me, and all will be well, except for the bother of a funeral.*

Amanda had aimed just right.

Misha went flying, right into the business end of a broken tree branch. The limb staked Misha's heart. Marco smiled, content to die in peace, knowing that his love had won.

Until he saw Misha pushing off of the tree and landing on the ground. He rose, unsteady on his feet, and glared at Amanda.

"No…" Marco groaned. *Asmodeus can heal even a stake to the heart.*

He coughed up some blood. *Amanda could not win against something that would not die. He had faith in her ability to kill all the vampires in the world, but not if they couldn't actually die. Eventually, Misha would kill her—she would become tired, make a slip, and that would be the end.*

Marco forced his left arm to move, praying for the ability to turn himself over.

And that was the last of his strength. He couldn't move again.

*Darn, and what was it they were all worried about? "A saint in training…you don't believe in your own limits, so they don't apply. You make your own reality; only it's a scary reality because you enforce it on the rest of us. You say that you are whatever you need to be, and you are." Pul-leaze.*

One thought occurred to him. He *was* always what he needed to be. He needed to be in control as a werewolf. He needed to be a thug to talk to thugs. He willed himself to be what he needed to be.

He needed to be alive.

Misha slowly moved for her, at first, and then lunged with a right uppercut. Amanda guessed that he would know that she could dodge any first blow, and so the payoff would be the second shot. She weaved to her left, around the fist, and dove, expecting him to sweep the right foot in anticipation of her ducking a kick.

Amanda leaped over the sweeping kick and rolled away. She twirled and launched a stake from her belt like a spear into his chest before he was even finished with his uppercut.

The stake went through him.

"Enough," he snapped. Misha drew the sources of his powers together to himself. His body surged with energy, and his hands and feet burst into white-hot flames. "I can set myself on fire, and–!"

Suddenly, Misha froze, his body numb. In his peripheral vision, he saw something sticking out of his neck as he fell to his knees—it was a foot-long wooden throwing knife that had slipped between the cartilage of his spine and severed it at the C4 vertebrae, making him an instant quadriplegic. He concentrated his powers on moving his limbs independently of the central nervous system, but nothing happened.

His eyes flicked to Amanda, closing in on him, and he focused his power into a fireball from his eyes. A second later, a knife entered his occipital lobe—the part of the brain that processes vision—and his eyes went dark.

"No," he croaked.

Marco Catalano, prone on the ground, sighed after the exertion of throwing the last two knives.

Misha growled as his body suddenly moved, floating away from Amanda. Both wooden blades flew in opposite directions out of his neck. Soul Fire created an aura around him while he healed himself. In the blink of an eye, he stood upright, both of his eyes solid black.

Misha spared Marco a passing glance. Amanda held Marco's cavalry sword. He'd had enough of playing with these people.

A cannon-like weapon boomed, and his chest burst into flames. He turned, and saw Marco, still flat on his back, holding a fifty-caliber Desert Eagle.

Amanda felt for her belt. She knew she had forgotten something. Marco must have lifted it from her.

"Wooden bullets," Marco explained. "You should have kept your telekinetic shield up."

Two more bullets entered his chest before Misha could move. He growled. He had to withdraw his Soul Fire and only use it to keep himself alive. His body was reaching its limit, the strain of the Soul Fire wearing on him. The fire burned inside his chest, searing away the dead flesh and regrowing useful tissue.

Amanda advanced on him. He jumped back, away from both of them and scooped up a rock from the ground. Misha whirled, hurling the stone at Marco's chest. The impact shattered several of his ribs and dropped him back.

Misha eyed Marco's sword in Amanda's hand. He spun, grabbing a lamp post and intending to beat her to death with it. Swinging the pole through the air, Amanda suddenly appeared directly in front of him. She was only inches away, and her sword sliced through the air. It cut his arm from his body.

Misha reached forward to break her neck, but Amanda swung the sword back around, slicing through his neck.

Amanda turned away from Misha. The embers of the dying vampire army burned in front of her eyes. They still fought hard, but the battle was lost. In another five or ten minutes, they would all be dead.

She ran to Marco's side. He laid on his back, one side of his ribcage caved in. The injury wasn't healing. Blood stained his teeth and his skin.

"Hi, honey," he muttered. "I forgot to duck." He turned his head and coughed. Blood aspirated onto his chest. He paused a moment, and swallowed, trying to clear his mouth.

Marco turned back to her and smiled weakly. "Wouldn't want to suffer from blood breath…" He grinned. "You got the bastard."

"*We* got him," she corrected.

He shook his head almost imperceptibly. "Your kill, fair and square. I only softened him up a little for you… or more accurately, he softened up my ribcage. I screwed up, and now…"

Amanda took his hand and leaned in close. "You're not going anywhere. You're going to stay here, with me…"

Marco reached up with his other hand, ignoring the flare of pain that racked his body. He gently caressed her cheek. "I love you. I've loved you since nearly the start. I loved you so much, I ran to San Francisco because I was afraid of it. I didn't want to let you get hurt by me. I wanted you safe and away from me— trouble follows me, you may have noticed."

Amanda smiled. She kissed him on the lips, lingering for a long moment before pulling back. "I don't care. I love you, and I'll wait two years. I'll wait five. I'd follow you into Hell. You're mine, Catalano, and you're not getting away from me. I'm going to marry you. Do you hear me? I do. I accept your proposal," she whispered.

Marco smiled, pleasantly surprised.

Then his eyes rolled back into his head, and he slumped over. His hand fell away from her face.

Amanda felt for Marco's pulse. It was there but fading. She couldn't even save him by making him drink from her—his lycanthropy would get in the way of that. It might even kill him faster.

Marco was going to die. Nothing short of a miracle could save him.

"Do not worry, little Alina, you will follow him shortly."

# Chapter 34

## Dance Of Death

Amanda turned, looking at Misha as he loomed over her like a fogbank. His neck wound had already healed, without even a scar.

Misha's Soul Fire blazed colder than ever. His skin turned black and armored again. The vampire-demon's face changed, becoming reptilian once more.

And he grew, quickly and easily. He unfurled himself into what Amanda feared.

Now an enormous black dragon loomed in front of her, standing five stories tall. Huge claws spread out across the cemetery ground. The full moon back-lit his dragon form

Misha became the physical manifestation of Asmodeus, Prince of Hell. It looked exactly as it had back in September on the pier of San Francisco.

She was screwed.

Amanda had a fleeting hope that this would be when a guardian angel came out. But Marco had told her why the angel had waited during the first fight with "Mister Day."

*"Until Asmodeus slipped his human suit, he was just a possessed human being…It still counted under human-on-human violence…When Asmodeus tried to use direct action against you as a demon, that's when I could intervene."*

This was another reason that Day possessed Misha—as a vampire, Misha's form was already malleable, from everything from mist to bats. He didn't need any extra demonic powers to shift bodies. As it was, Misha was just a vampire who had turned into something bigger than usual.

This "something bigger" was just fueled by the power of Hell itself.

Amanda's head tilted back farther and farther to see the top of the dragon's massive form. She was witnessing the death of everything she had ever known. It was the beginning of Hell on Earth.

Amanda looked at Marco, smiled sadly, and then turned back towards Misha, eyes narrowed and raging.

If she was going to die, she was going to take him with her.

Her hands flattened into blades in the manner of *penjakt silat*, and she started to briefly mutter a prayer…

And something inside her snapped into place, like the final piece of a jigsaw puzzle.

*…Marco ducked, and her fist had cracked the pedestal of the Lion at the Library.*

*…Her priest joked that if she became any more spiritual, she would become a mystic…*

*"…you don't have a power level commensurate with your level of virtue," Merle had told her. "You've been scared out of your mind by the level of power you might have….you're in love with him…urges like that can bring out the worst in us, certainly, but then again, they could also bring out the best…"*

*…I'm not a telepath, Amanda had told Marco—with her mind.*

Mystics and saints become so through any number of different ways. St. Thomas Aquinas became one by being a philosophical genius. Francis of Assisi threw himself into nature and the exuberance of life. St. Therese of the Little Flower found it through love…

At that point, so did Amanda.

Merle had been right, she had been holding back her love for Marco. Only Merle didn't know that one had been the result of the other. By cutting herself off from her love for Marco, she had cut herself off from the full power she possessed. But her power had been growing more and more steadily. Her strength had increased, her speed had heightened, and she had even been able to garner stray thought from Marco. Even after the impromptu wedding vows in Marco's room, there was still the slightest bit of reluctance in her.

But she meant what she said. She would marry Marco in a heartbeat if she could.

That reluctance broke with a tangible *snap* inside her. Holding back her love and restraining herself from Marco had held back her power.

A power that now consumed her with fire. Her eyes glowed with a bright, phosphorous white light. A light so bright it hurt to look at. It spread out from her body from her eyes.

The light moved and flickered like flame.

White Soul Fire.

The dragon hesitated. He opened his mouth and breathed black fire straight for Marco and Amanda.

Amanda growled and rose right into it, meeting the fire, and the flames. The tide of black fire poured over her.

The dragon fell a step backwards.

Amanda's hands raised before her, white flame meeting black. The dragon that was Misha and Asmodeus intensified his attack. Black fire poured over the cemetery like a blanket.

It never hit the ground. White Soul Fire spread out and met it, inch for inch. Light for darkness.

*"Exorcizo te,"* Amanda intoned, *"omnis spiritus immunde, in nomine Dei Patris omnipotentis, et in noimine Jesu Christi Filii ejus, Domini et Judicis nostri, et in virtute Spiritus."*

"I exorcise thee, every unclean spirit, in the name of God the Father Almighty, and in the name of Jesus Christ, His Son, our Lord and Judge, and in the power of the Holy Spirit, that thou depart from this creature of God."

The dragon shrank back as his fire came back at him, repulsed by the power of the white Soul Fire. Amanda's flame grew stronger with every word. Asmodeus knew the words. He knew Latin.

It was an exorcism.

The fire pushed on, driven by prayer.

*"Per eumdem Christum Dominum nostrum,"* she continued, *"qui venturus est judicare vivos et mortuos, et saeculum per ignem.*

*Through the same Christ our Lord, who shall come to judge the living and the dead, and the world by fire.*

The dragon shrank as its power clashed with the power Amanda drew on. But it wasn't Amanda's power, drawn from her soul. Not any more than Misha's power was from his own blackened and shriveled thing of a soul. Misha's had come from blackest Hell.

Amanda's, not so much.

*"Tu autem effugare, diabole,"* she cried. And for you, devil, begone! *"Appropinquabit enim judicium Dei."* For the judgment of God is at hand.

Amanda stepped forward, pressing towards the dragon, her body alight with divine fire. She continued, "I cast you out, unclean spirit, along with every Satanic power of the enemy, every specter from hell, and all your fell companions, in the name of our Lord Jesus Christ."

Her eyes burned from the tears streaming down her face, untouched by the flames that consumed her.

She thought of Marco, dead on the ground behind her. Beaten to death by this monster…this demon from Hell.

*"Begone and stay far from this creature of God,"* she screamed, thinking more of Marco than of Misha. "For it is *He* who commands you, *He* who flung you headlong from the heights of heaven into the depths of Hell,"

Amanda no longer approached a dragon from the depths of Hell, but Misha, his body naked, and burned, and covered in the darkness of his own soul. His onslaught buckled under hers as she grew closer.

"And it is He who demands you go back there!" she ad-libbed. "He who once stilled the sea and the wind and the storm."

Now she was only steps away from him. Her fire overtook him. "Tremble in fear, you enemy of the faith," she stepped forward, "you foe of the human race," and again, "you begetter of death," and again, "robber of life, corrupter of justice, root of all evil and vice." She got within arm's length of Misha, reared back, and punched him in the face. "Seducer of men." She backhanded him with a slap that left his face burning and steaming. "Betrayer of the nations."

Amanda grabbed Misha by the throat with both hands. He bellowed in pain and terror. The blackness receded from his eyes and his skin crackled and burned from the flames covering Amanda's hands. His skin burned away as he screamed and thrashed against her grip. But he couldn't break it.

"*He* drives you back into the everlasting fire. An unquenchable fire stands ready for you and your minions," Amanda shook Misha like a rag doll. "You prince of accursed murderers, father of lechery, instigator of sacrileges, model of vileness, promoter of heresies, inventor of every obscenity!"

Misha screamed as he burned away, leaving the face beneath. It was a plain, ordinary face, belonging to a smaller, slighter man.

A face that Amanda would occasionally see in her nightmares.

It was the face of "Mister Day."

The Prince of Hell roared and thrashed at her, punching at Amanda. She took his blows. They weren't weak blows either, but blows that would shatter concrete, fell buildings, and battle angels. They were blows that were the ruin of worlds.

Amanda didn't even slow down or stop for breath. He could kill her for all she cared. But he was going to go back to Hell if she had to escort him there herself. "Depart! Impious one! Depart, accursed one! Depart with all your deceits, for God has willed it. Give honor to God the Father Almighty! Give place to the Lord Jesus Christ! Give place to the Holy Spirit!"

Mister Day's deep black eyes widened, as he, too, began to scream in pain and terror. Amanda's fingers tightened on his neck, choking him, depriving him of even one final breath with which to bellow his damnation.

Amanda's temper flared. The white flame surrounding her did not so much flare as explode in a supernova of white phosphorus that flooded the entire street. The wall of fire expanded in a circle, emanating out from her in all directions.

The rest of Misha's vampires barely had time to brace for it. Many of them had raised their hands, even forming defensive walls with shattered marble. It didn't matter. Every one of Misha's vampires burned away as though drowned in a river of holy water. They didn't even take the time to disintegrate. One moment they were there, the next they weren't. There wasn't even time for them to scream. The shields fell over, their holders dead and departed.

Day was the last to give in. Day, who had held up against every onslaught and assault on his person, finally felt his body disintegrate under the attack. He tried, one final time, to hit Amanda, and his arm burned away.

With one final, definitive roar, she pronounced, "The power of Christ compels you, *you son of a bitch*!"

At long last, Mister Day, Asmodeus, prince of Hell, became dust in the wind.

After the small supernova, the fire winked out.

Amanda Colt, savior of the world from this latest invasion of the powers of Hell, fell to her knees and cried.

Marco was dead.

# Chapter 35

# Fire And Shadow Both Defied

"White Soul Fire," came a voice brittle with academia, "is the primary weapon for a good vampire who has not only talent and power, but incredible strength of will."

Amanda's tears stopped with the first three words. She turned her head before standing and saw an unscratched Marco Catalano striding towards her. He was still covered in blood, and naked, but otherwise perfectly fine. In fact, better than fine. He seemed … bigger. He had a swagger in his step, fully confident that he was perfectly fine, even in the cold.

"Its general physical effects," he continued wryly, "are a light warmth like the summer sun, and a bright white light that is exceedingly comforting and heartwarming. Mental effects include a feeling not unlike that of a Christmas morning with a light snow and every conceivable present that your heart ever desired." He bent down, courteously raising Amanda to her feet. "And uses attributed to white Soul Fire *happen* to be the vanquishing of evil *and* the ability to heal." He kissed her on the forehead. "You told me this, remember?" He paused, then shrugged. "Okay, you told me about the healing and evil bit. I added the rest from personal experience."

Amanda's eyes glistened, and she looked all over his body. *All* over. "You seem bigger somehow."

Marco shrugged. "I think I've gained ten pounds in muscle mass and lost maybe a few years' worth of aging. Besides, you remember how my vision is twenty-twenty?"

"Da?"

"I can see better now. Even better now than when I was a werewolf."

Merle Kraft jogged up to them. He skidded to a stop in the muddy ground and looked Marco up and down.

Marco nodded. "I'm not dead, yet."

"You and *Monty Python and the Holy Grail*," Merle smiled. "Besides, we can change that." He looked to the side. "You're really too good for him, you know that, right?"

Marco's eyes followed his to Amanda. "He's right, you know," he agreed.

Amanda squeezed his hand. "I'll settle." She hugged Marco close to her, and breathed him in … and started, pulling back from him. "You're human."

Marco's lips bunched up, and his brow furrowed. "Um … You're pretty cute, too? I guess?" His eyes searched hers, as though looking for an answer. "What am I missing?"

"You're not a furry anymore."

He blinked, and then looked off, as though feeling for something inside him. "Huh. You're right. I guess your Soul Fire treated it like a disease and cured me." He shrugged. "I'll take it."

Merle arched a brow. "That's a little bit too *deus ex machina* for me."

Amanda laughed. "Considering what it is, more like a simple *deus ex.*"

Marco smiled and pulled her in for a kiss.

"Hmmm," someone hummed appreciatively. "I can see why you're fond of him," came a classy, upper-class British accent.

Amanda sighed and turned her head towards Jennifer Bosley. Marco kept kissing her cheek, and her jaw, and down her neck. "Not now?"

Marco sighed, patted her on the back, and straightened. He turned to Bosley, dancer straight, unashamed of his condition. "Hello, Madam President. Sorry for my current state. But you saw what happened."

Bosley looked him up and down and gave him a cheeky little smile. "Not a problem." Her eyes flared comically. "Any time."

"Thank you for the help, though," he continued. He furrowed his brows and looked from her to Amanda and back. "How did you folks get all of this set up so fast?"

Bosley gestured to Amanda. "Ask her."

Amanda shrugged. She looked at Marco and sighed. She'd rather not be explaining herself. "When you disappeared, I knew that we were going to have to marshal our forces. After I stopped trying to beat your location out of the local vampires, I sat down with… everyone."

Bosley nodded. "I've had my people go to confession ever since they tried to blow me up." She gestured to the muddy ground, some of it still sodden with holy water. "That way, we wouldn't be caught in any crossfire. When Amanda met with me, your priest, Mister Kraft, Enrico, the Commissioner, and your… gangs," she sniffed snobbishly, "we got our act together."

Amanda nodded again. "When you sent me the text, warning that there would be a trap, I made arrangements with, well, everyone, to gather nearby. When you decided to make a stand here, we had the barest semblance of a plan. You bought us time to get people in position."

Marco nodded slowly. "And your multiple-layered plans?"

Amanda shrugged. "Why blow everything on the first attack? That's why there were helicopters first. Although, perhaps we should have saved the napalm for later. Burning a patch of holy water away wasn't my best idea."

Marco looked over his shoulder at Merle. "The gunships and such were your idea?"

Merle shrugged. "I arranged for it after the Nuala thing. My brother, of all people, warned me to bring in heavy artillery." He held up a hand. "Just give me a moment, I'm starting to get a headache." He rubbed his temples. "Amanda, do you think your white fire trick can burn out any demon you come against?"

The vampire blinked. "Maybe, why?"

He smiled. "How would you like to have your old security clearance back?" He looked at Marco. "You can come along if you want."

"Are you inviting me into government service?" Marco asked.

"No, I'm asking you to blow up vampires in *other* people's countries. I think you've done your fair share here."

Marco slid his hand down to squeeze Amanda's. "Amanda, if you're going, I am. I don't care what we do, as long as it's together. I'm not losing you. Period."

Amanda sighed and leaned against Marco. "Perhaps later." She rubbed her cheek against his arm. "We're going to get married first."

Marco put his arm around Amanda and held her against him. "If you want," Marco said, "I could finish my PA education, *then* we can get married. I won't object if you want to wait."

Amanda looked up at him, curious. "Really?"

Marco smiled as he met her eye. "Of course, my love. Because now, with the Council dead, we have time. All the time in the world."

Merle shrugged. "Here's hoping. Let me know your decision. I'm going to spend lord knows how long hunting down the humans the Council was connected to."

Marco chuckled. "Good luck with that." He pressed his side against Amanda. "If no one minds, I'd like to get indoors. It's starting to get cold out here."

Amanda took his arm in hers. "Come. I'll see what I can do to warm you up."

As they walked away, Merle muttered, "And for God's sake, someone get this guy some clothes."

# Epilogue

At a safe distance down the street, Dalf Kraft smiled at the progress. Yes, Merle had succeeded in thwarting a plot straight from Hell….

As had been expected.

As Dalf had said to his brother, he was an enforcer for the Army of Darkness, and could only do so much before being fired with extreme prejudice on the basis of mutiny.

"It's over, now, tell me what the Hell this was about?"

Dalf sighed, looking at his brother over his shoulder. Merle was getting better about being subtle—he hadn't even heard the man sneak up from down the street. "Merle, what do you want me to say? I am an archbishop of Hell, surely you don't think that I would have anything to do with those demon wanna-bes called vampires, do you?"

Merle narrowed his eyes. "Dalf, when all of this started, you *sent* Amanda to *me*."

Dalf nodded. "Yes, I did." He shrugged. "Perhaps I did not want Amanda or Marco to live." He grinned.

"Perhaps I am simply taking the other side's money as a double agent…" His eyes darkened, cold and angry. "Or perhaps…just perhaps…*they* decided to overstep their boundaries. The original mutiny, the First One, was over humans. Lucifer thought they weren't worth saving—how could his Lord and Master think about sacrificing Himself for those petulant things? Ever since it has become a matter of proving God wrong." Dalf's eyes grew colder and harder now, even angry.

"Yes, the human race can destroy itself; yes, it can be tempted out of existence. *That* is our *job*. *Not* that idiotic James Bond plot the Council devised. We have no interest in taking over the world."

Merle frowned, looking his brother up and down. "Why not? Hell on Earth sounds like what you'd be shooting for, isn't it?"

Dalf shook his head as he slid a cigarette into his mouth. The end glowed without any visible flame. "Don't you understand, Merle? Our job is to draw in the stupid and the weak-willed. To break the strong and sucker the smart. What does a world of Shadow bring? The strong become heroes, the smart become leaders, the weak flee to their God." Dalf shook his head. "No, things are better for me and my kind *this* way. We prefer to subvert. To twist. Tell the academics there is no right or wrong, no objective reality. We teach pride to the holy and the smart, wrath to the strong, and teach everyone that freedom means being slaves to your own whims and desires."

"But they were allowed to run loose for how many years?" Merle asked. "Centuries? I would have thought someone would have yanked their leash quite some time ago."

Dalf waved it away, scoffing. "Please, Merle, haven't you studied history at all? This isn't about the short term. It's about the long term. People are stupid, and they will give power to any random idiot who they think will give them what they want. The concept of Freedom centers around human beings. In America, the people decided that God granted Freedoms to human beings. They got around that by deciding that what made a human being was flexible—first with slaves, then with abortion. In Europe, they skipped over that step when they decided that freedom came to people from the state, and anyone the state decided was a non-person had no freedom.

*"That's* what the Council did. And they did so much to encourage them. They've resurrected Moloch with the abortion industry, fed Day with the free love of the West and the wrath of the entire Middle East. With their nudges, they've laid the groundwork for a true Hell on Earth: not physical power, but a world of

demons where you pitiful, shallow things do not cower before my master, but where you welcome him with open arms and invite him to rule."

Dalf shrugged and pulled on his cigarette. "Then they stopped being useful."

"And Day himself?"

Dalf rolled his eyes. "Always a hothead. He really wanted to kill you and didn't think farther ahead." He flicked some ashes off of his cigarette. "You seem to forget Merle, the Bible itself says that my master is the Prince of this World. We've already won."

Merle blinked. "On one hand, you talk like this, but on the other, you've destroyed a major force for evil, and set up a white vampire so powerful she can wipe out city blocks' worth of vampires. Exactly whose side are you on?"

"My own, of course. Aren't we all?"

Merle's eyes narrowed. "Who exactly do you mean when you say 'we'?"

Gandalf Kraft merely smiled.

With a solid *whump*, Dalf blinked, and took a step forward before he crumpled. Behind him, holding a rock, was Rory. He smiled and tossed the rock on Dalf's back.

"Don't you just hate it when they monologue?" Rory laughed.

Rory slid a cigarette into his mouth, lit it, and turned, walking off into the night.

## Author's Note

Hi. You've finished the series. Thanks for that. If you'd kindly review the novel over at Amazon.com, that would be amazingly helpful. And maybe a little review for the previous books, if you wouldn't mind.

Now that the series is over, I have to admit that I didn't see it coming. What had started as an experiment in a new genre for me became a lot more epic than I thought it would be.

I would like to thank all of you for reading the book. For nominating *Honor at Stake* and *Live and Let Bite* for the Dragon Awards. And for giving me some vague hope that this job has not been in vain.

Speaking of the Dragon Awards, they take place every year over at awards.dragoncon.org – if you could remember *Good to the Last Drop* when the time comes in 2018, that would be appreciated.

I'd like to thank the Superversive SF crew, Silver Empire publishing, Russell Newquist, as well as my CLFA people.

Specific thanks go to Jason Sarten for "Yipsters," Dawn (DawnWitzke.com) for the covers, Tully for being Tuckerized, Alfred Genneson (the Injustice Gamer) for all his support, and the beta reading. JD Cowan for his reviews. Lori Bird for *her* reviews. Matt Bowman for letting me ramble on The Catholic Geeks. Greg Stern for being a fan.

And Vanessa.

## About The Author

Declan Finn lives in a part of New York City unreachable by bus or subway. Who's Who has no record of him, his family, or his education. He has been trained in hand to hand combat and weapons at the most elite schools in Long Island, and figured out nine ways to kill with a pen when he was only fifteen. He escaped a free man from Fordham University's PhD program and has been on the run ever since. There was a brief incident where he was branded a terrorist, but only a court order can unseal those records, and really, why would you want to know?

He can be contacted at DeclanFinnInc@aol.com

Read his personal blog:
http://apiusmannovel.blogspot.com

Listen to his podcast, The Catholic Geek, on Blog Talk Radio, Sunday evenings at 7:00 pm EST.

# More From Declan Finn

## Love At First Bite
Honor At Stake
Demons Are Forever
Live and Let Bite
Good to the Last Drop

## The Pius Trilogy
A Pius Man
A Pius Legacy
A Pius Stand
Pius Tales
Pius History

## The Convention Killings
It Was Only On Stun
Set To Kill

If you've enjoyed this title, please check out the rest of the books in this Dragon award nominated series at https://threeravenspublishing.com/love-at-first-bite/.

Or check out some of our other Urban Fantasy titles at https://threeravenspublishing.com/urban-fantasy/
Such as the Lady of Death, Nightshade Series, or Paranormal City

Stephen Oliver
PARANORMAL CITY
J.F. Posthumus
THE FAE'S AMULET
A LADY OF DEATH NOVEL

Or take a look at some of our other award winning series at https://threeravenspublishing.com/series-universes/

Visit us at

Https://www.threeravenspublishing.com and sign up for our newsletter for the latest and greatest news on upcoming titles and events.

Good to the Last Drop

Also, check out our Affiliates and Sponsors
https://threeravenspublishing.com/affiliates-sponsors/

Declan Finn

www.ingramcontent.com/pod-product-compliance
Lightning Source LLC
Chambersburg PA
CBHW061613210726
48287CB00001B/119